Frequencies of Existence

Frequencies of Existence

Stories by Andrew Hook

NewCon Press
England

First edition, published in the UK October 2020
by NewCon Press

NCP245 (hardback)
NCP246 (softback)

10 9 8 7 6 5 4 3 2 1

Contents

Author's Acknowledgements

Many thanks to the following editors who previously published some of these stories:

Michael Bailey, Andy Cox, Peter Crowther, Trevor Denyer, Nick Gevers, James Hodgson, Ian Hunter, Des Lewis, Daniel Marchant, Justin Park, Rosalie Parker, Tim Shearer, Ian Whates, and the editors at Shirley Magazine.

Your Golden Hands

We went searching for gold.

The city was vast, spiralled, ten dozen stupas twisted skywards like mermaids' braids. Built on rock, edged by the sea, we approached in boats as white as clouds. From the beginning, you welcomed us.

Without speaking your language we invaded your homes. Your alcohol refreshed us. Bread, meat, replenished us. We told jokes you didn't understand. We said things whose truth you couldn't hear. Some of us were shamed.

A grinning fool, my face fatter than in my younger days, I thought I knew it all.

When you brought us sticky sweets on a silver tray I looked at you far longer than was necessary. In our years you would have been too young. Yet here I wouldn't contemplate your age.

Even before you smiled I had made my decision.

If the rumours were true we would take a long time finding it. The sun burnt high in the sky as we worked. Lorenzo died on the second day. The weight of the machinery shredded the rope. You showed us metal chains. After then, there were no more accidents. When I rubbed my stubbled chin and looked into the future I could see prostitutes in every corner of my room, all the latest electronic equipment, money tessellating the floor like fallen leaves in an autumn forest. Riches, heroism, fame. My cock, my soul, harder than ever before.

We were of the understanding that you didn't really know what we were looking for. Tradition told us that material things held no meaning for you. Metals, gems, other natural resources were not there to be exploited, just to be used as and when you saw fit. Like a hermit camped in a battered tent in the desert with an unknown oil well hundreds of feet beneath him, you had no urge to seek what you didn't know was there. Still, we kept the nature of our quest secret.

We exchanged our knowledge in return for your permission, although in reality we didn't need your permission. And you didn't need the knowledge that we gave you.

Your streets connected without sense. Myriad mazes confused us after nights imbibing alcohol. This way, that way! By the time I found your door I was exhausted, exhilarated. You took my large hand in your small one and led me into the darkness, assisted me upstairs. There was strength in you even then. I fell asleep with the roof spinning, inside a cone corkscrewing towards the stars, pitted with time.

In the morning, your family treated me with respect, though I felt I had broken some unspoken rule. It was too hard to know how aware your people were. You operated on levels different, those not inspired by greed, romance, desire. When I watched you lead your animals along the uneven pavements, grass beckoning in the distance, the sun backlit you like a halo. You glowed.

Even then I didn't really see it.

"Here."

"No, here."

Our machines dug into the earth. Wrenched soil spilled insects, fertility, minerals poured into our panniers. We shifted, shook the soil until there was nothing left. We had no idea how big our find was likely to be. But we knew it was here. Like the El Dorado of yore, there were enough legends to sustain a truth. Despite the complete lack of gold amongst your jewellery, utensils, building adornments, customs. Someone had seen it once.

When we turned our backs we knew you were watching. Puzzling over our activities. In the evenings, the knowledge we gave you also puzzled. It was as though you too were unaware of the worth of this mission. Still you carried on, drinking in our world view as we drank in your alcohol, getting drunk in symbolism. Spiritually, you were way ahead of us.

One night I touched the side of your face. Your wide, brown eyes widened further. Something pulled inside me. I tried to remember my family, then shook them out of my head. We ascended to my room as though taking the steps of a helter-skelter, each one more difficult than the last. The muscles in my ankles respired anaerobically. I undressed as you stood in the corner, uncomprehending.

My fingers were shaking as I undid the buttons of your dress, as I slid you out of your underwear. Pinned beneath me I raped you just as we raped the soil. My penis entered earth, digging inside you, searching for what I could only find within myself. With my hand over your mouth I felt your teeth against my palm. I wanted you to struggle, but none came even within your eyes. Just like everything in this city, I met with no resistance.

My semen coursed within you, unaware of its destination.

Within the hour you brought me more sticky sweets on that little silver tray. If I looked closely, I could see that it was tarnished.

We went deeper. One hundred metres, two hundred metres. We began examining the caves in the cliffs. Descending on ropes, the azure sea sparkling beneath us, cushioning the occasional fall, we swung into openings the size of small children. Guano soiled our boots, bat-like animals flitted around our heads. Our torches fought against the gloom, yet the caves weren't man-made. We had yet to find the secret of your resources, of your wealth.

In the evenings I drank less. My time was spent with you and not with my comrades, who, in their own way, also distanced themselves. I spoke words that I knew you couldn't understand. When I tried to teach you, gibberish came back. You showed me books woven from leaves and vines. As you turned the pages your soft voice was an incantation. I recalled fairy tales from my youth, stories which I'd heard but only understood as I grew older. Without meaning, I imparted my own meaning.

Each time I used you I tried to create that meaning, although for you it was different. I could see that it meant less and less. Your eyes transformed into slits.

So we continued. Sometimes at night I left you and went wandering. The houses with their wooden doors gave the illusion of being boarded up. I tried turning left at each junction, then retraced my steps by turning right. Either way, with your moon above illuminating, I was lost.

Each time I reached the edge of the city I was met with cliffs, the sea. Like a tiered cake there was a pinnacle. The rocks were the base, the sea the table. The houses were layers, the mountain a peak. Ever decreasing circles. The conical shape drew me upwards. I climbed in the night air, remembered Billy Meier's Wedding Cake UFO's. The base of the UFO had been very distinctive, four circular bands with three well-defined ridges between each. I wondered if you had the technology to build it.

By the time I reached the top of the mountain dawn was breaking through clouds that resembled white boats. Looking downwards I realised I wasn't standing on a cone, but a pyramid. Even then, the meaning was lost to me.

If your family knew I was raping you they showed no sign. Your hands lay by your sides. I no longer had course to pin them down.

Our anchored boats rocked on the sea, fibreglass gulls riding the waves. I took you there. It was clear you had never been on the ocean. When you retched over the side my semen salted the water in fishy trails. I laughed and your brow momentarily creased. Taking this as inspiration, we shifted our search to the ocean. Diving into its depths with tools and lifelines. Hacking away at the sea bed which clouded our vision, floated detritus around us. We built platforms. Bored beneath the sediment into rock and coral. Each time we surfaced empty-handed.

Now we kept our distance. We returned to our beds on the boats, drank our own alcohol, and regained some semblance of our culture and heritage. Played cards, won and lost matches, struck up conversations about what you were hiding.

Though it was taboo our talk gravitated towards sex. An all-male exploration could do little else. One by one we opened ourselves, found the same brittle substance inside.

Sometimes, when the others were working, I sought you out again. I named you Nula and it became the only word you understood. I realised that you couldn't help us because you didn't know what we were seeking. Despite the knowledge we had given you, there was no understanding. You had grasped that one plus one equalled two, although the actual meaning of 'plus' was lost on you. Whilst you had been cooperating on the surface, underneath there was no insight. I resolved to spend more time with you, to break the barriers between us that initially we hadn't realised were there.

The others thought you were hiding something, I just thought you were hiding.

Since we arrived, your tiny body, your soft brown skin, had become increasingly mottled with bruises. Yellowish tints seared the surface like jaundice. I had left my mark on you but you were no more mine than the gold that we sought. I had made an impression on you but only with your physicality. Your mind was something else.

I wasn't sure whether I wanted to hurt you or make you love me.

The longer we stayed, the less distinct the distinction became.

"Nula," I would say, and your head would turn and I knew that you had heard me, despite the variances in my intonation. If a word in the ancient Thai language could have five different meanings depending on nuance, then in your language there was not a single meaning. I concentrated when you talked between yourselves, but there were no words, just sighs, like the sound of wind caressing leaves, or the soughing of waves.

We began to fantasise about picking each of you off one by one. Pulling apart metaphorical wings to see if you could fly. Whether this spirituality you seemed to possess could survive the cruelty of our capabilities. Whether, through torture, your secrets would be revealed.

In retrospect, we had no understanding of a society that didn't operate by cold manufactured money coiling at its heart.

We became overt. Realising you had no use of gold, we bought our own trinkets out of hiding. I showed you my wedding ring, a 24-carat band which had no beginning just as it had no end. At last, there was some comprehension.

For the first time you laughed, but it was a mimicry of our laughter. It was an obvious concealment of fear.

I gripped your wrists knowing violence wasn't the answer.

Violence hadn't created your dread.

I reached for your hand, pulled your fingers towards me. When I slipped the ring onto you it disappeared. I dragged you from the bed, towards the window where morning light was bursting out of your sun.

Holding your hand up to the glass your skin became translucent. You glowed. You were hiding it all along. Your golden hands.

I sat back on the bed. Pulled the ring from you and turned it in my fingers. Pocketed it. I lit a cigarette, watched the smoke pool sideways like my semen in the sea. Out of the corner of my eye I saw you touch your belly.

Mumbling words of reassurance, I returned to the boat.

Andrew Hook

We spent two days making plans. A quiet intensity ran through us. No more the early bravado of the expedition. I recalled my family waving from the shoreline at our departing boats. My son held a wooden cross in his hand. I had promised to replace it with a gold one. As I remembered my promise, beads of sweat bobbled my forehead, ran down my face, and found the corners of my eyes. I took them to be the tears that I knew I wouldn't shed.

We understood what we had to do.

During the night we boarded up houses, sneaking through the streets, silently screwing entrances closed just as we had screwed your children. We didn't know if you had the capacity to dream, we shook premonition from our minds. It was the only way to exist.

Come morning, in the golden glow, we fashioned a metal vat from our supplies. We collected wood from the forest, working in silence. Only the grunts of our labours populating the air. Words between us had become as meaningless as when spoken to you.

Our hearts were in our mouths when we opened the doors.

You didn't come willingly. But once you were in the fire the steady stream of gold justified our actions. By mid-afternoon we no longer heard the sound of your screaming.

They left you, Nula, for last. I considered saving you, showcasing you in our world. But I knew that wasn't your life. You belonged here with your family. And when I melted you and you pooled at my feet, I saw a tiny part of me had been inside you.

I picked it up with tongs.

It was stone.

❀

I've never written story notes to accompany a collection before, but my publisher was eager for these to be part of the book and as it happens I do post a blog whenever a story has been published where I examine the gestalt behind a piece. Some of these notes have therefore been cribbed from those blog posts (without the pictures which might have accompanied them online), and some are new to this collection. I hope they provide an insight into how these pieces evolved.

Frequently I find myself with a title which then forms a story around it. Here I felt *Your Golden Hands* lent itself to a conquistador style of tale and a search for gold. I didn't want a standard South American-type tale, so the story is set on what is probably a far-future world. Nevertheless, base human desire is to the fore, and I'm very proud of the result. It has proven to be one of my favourites.

The Universe At Gun Point

Do not play around with the unknown amulets of your ephemeral understanding:
sanctify your beloved and verbal phials. God will pardon you if he sees fit from the
honourable centre of the united Eternity, where everything becomes known with solemnity
and conviction. The Determined One cannot freeze; the Passionate One obliterates
himself; the Irascible One has no reason to exist.

– Erik Satie

Once, when I was speaking to C – the one woman who never understood
me – the only one I wanted to – I explained how we begin from the
ephemeral and move towards the technical. She sat with one leg hung
languorously over the arm of my sofa. I wanted to complain, yet didn't.
Her toenails were alternately painted purple and green – a representation
of night and day. Shades of understanding.

She blew smoke from the corner of her mouth, her roll-up spilling
tobacco despite being shroud-tight; discolouring my ceiling without care.

"Hit me with it."

I disliked her rough dialogue, but her physical being, lovely eyes,
gentle hands and tiny feet entranced me. She knew it. Which was why she
kept her distance as I toyed with the piano.

"Everything is repetition," I said. "Like a form of self-perpetuating
evolution, reaching out for the numinous with each full turn, yet
technology has made this too easy. We spin too fast. There is no time for
contemplation."

I closed the piano lid and rested my hands atop. "Today music is an
electronic file, you can't even see it. If you want to hear something again,
it's just a button click away. Not too long ago it was a series of binary
codes burnt on a compact disc, the re-selection of a track only slightly
more complicated. Before that, the cassette tape. Music was remembered
by the tape through the creation of a magnetic field and to replay
something you had to physically rewind it. And before that, the vinyl
record; sound waves cut as grooves. To locate a track involved lifting the
record arm, dropping it on the clear groove immediately before the
chosen track. Another piece of physicality. And further back, the only way

to hear something again would be to request it from the musician, the orchestra. In those days, we started with the technical, the mechanical process of creating the music; and the method of listening to it was the ephemeral. Yet now, it is pure ephemera to create it and the technical has simply become a means with which to listen."

C blew an imperfect O.

"That argument is shot through with holes, Gunn."

I smiled, despite her disagreement. I adored it when she used my stage name.

"What I'm saying," I said, "is that everything nowadays is too easy. We're fighting evolution on a losing curve. I want to make it complicated again. It's only within the truly complicated that something can be appreciated."

C coughed. When she spoke there was an edge to her tone, as though sandpaper lined her throat. "We both know that isn't true."

She was right. Even in my compositions I had found that I was trying more than ever to get back to the basics. I wanted something simple, like the early works of Erik Satie. A piano without adornment; all circumstance, no pomp. As my eyes drifted again to the curvature of the little toe on her right foot my focus pulled all my realities in around my head like a blanket closed tight with a drawstring. Or like a kitten in a sack, suddenly immersed in the unknowing terror of the river.

Satie's 4th *Gnossienne* is perhaps the most meditative. The piece begins in the lower range, with simple D minor arpeggios that hypnotically ascend and descend. The entire work only uses five chords, and as the piece moves from one to the other the arpeggios are a constant, a simple repetition that takes the listener through the work as though it is already familiar to them. Familiar, yet otherworldly; haunting, perhaps. Ultimately, manic. On a loop a form of torture because of that expectation of the familiar: like a tap dripping on a saucepan in an otherwise empty sink.

I had played and studied Satie's piano pieces since leaving college: the *Gnossiennes*, the *Gymnopédies*, being my focus. So C had been right when she accused me of suggesting the complicated held more depth. What she hadn't considered was that the simple can only be found after dissecting the complicated. It was only after everything else was cut away that the simple could be located and it couldn't be created from scratch.

It had to be unearthed, and finding it was a challenge.

The circumstances had to be right.

London wasn't Paris. I dreamt of alternate architecture, the vocabulary of foreign sounds, the quiet chill of a morning air unencumbered by smog, the clatter of plastic carriers on fresh fruit market stalls; my idealism of Paris as a state of mind rather than the stinking city that it surely was: the disingenuous cousin of a London which had long since bored me but which I knew in reality I couldn't escape.

Despite my disparagement of the electronic file, I wandered London with Satie in my ears. A soulful accompaniment to the everyday. I watched escalators ascend and descend with the surety of his arpeggios, the spaces between the musical notes echoing the gaps between Underground trains and platforms, the quiet behind the music obfuscating the hustle and bustle of the twenty-first century: the hard rolling thunder of skateboards in concrete jungles, the incessant babble of mobile phone conversations, the stream of traffic like abandoned shopping trolleys being swept over waterfalls. With Satie in my ears the world was written anew. Yet it was also a challenge. My compositions were clumsy, from their inspiration through to their achievement, echoed through their titling. With a desire to find fame by association I created the ridiculous out of the sublime. When my piece, "A Man Named Ray Impersonates Man Ray Dressed as a Manta Ray in Monterey", accumulated both zeroes and derision throughout the music press I knew I had to find an alternative to my current path. This change of view was augmented by C, who decided to take me under her wing for her own amusement, if nothing else.

"Ray?"

"Hmmm?"

C wore the flimsiest of clothing; green antiquarian flapper material sourced from Camden Market. As she stood, legs apart, pyramidal from toes to crotch, the sun backlit her dress and almost blinded me in the process.

"Your music is too self-referential. You want your fifteen minutes of fame without having to work for it. You're lazy, incompetent. Perhaps worst of all, you're boring."

I felt her words deep in my heart. Was this some kind of pep talk? A stir to arms through breaking my soul?

The ebony of the piano lid was smooth under my fingers, just as I imagined her body might feel beneath mine. Yet even this was a fallacy.

She was slight, bony. Should we couple, her ribs would respond like depressed keys, I would force music out of her that shouldn't be heard by the human ear.

"Not only that," she continued, "but I don't think you have that hidden core of genius that those who are permanently successful require. Not that I'm measuring success in the commercial sense of the word, but longevity." She folded her arms across her chest. "Who will remember you, Ray, in five years, in ten years, in a hundred? Or if not you, who will remember your work? No one, I wager. Certainly not me."

She turned and left, the elongated sleeve of her costume catching the half-drunk cup of tea that had rested on the arm of my sofa. I watched it fall to the floor in slow-motion – or in slow-motion I watched it fall to the floor. C didn't notice as liquid emerged as a light brown tear, arced around the rim of the cup like a motorcycle rider on the wheel of death, slipped the tangent with unexpected velocity to land on my biography of Satie that lay open-leaved on the floor.

I closed my eyes, rested my cheek against the coolness of the piano lid, felt the bone hard against the wood, imagined all the ideas for compositions that I had falling out of my ear and seeping onto the keys, listened to them play as I fumbled for untroubled sleep.

The next morning I was awoken by the buzz of my mobile phone's vibration.

The display indicated C.

"Hello?" My voice was thick in my mouth, as though my tongue had swollen in dream.

"I'm hoping that following my words you wrote like a demon all night."

"Of course." The reflex was defensive. I swallowed.

"I'll be along later to hear it. Ciao."

She hung up, left me wondering who else other than Italians said *ciao* any more.

I lifted my head. The music stand atop the piano held a sheaf of papers which were blank other than my stage name written by my left hand in red ink: Ray Gunn. If I were to impress her I would have to fill the remainder of the page by evening when she'd visit.

I stood. My legs shaky, achy from the position in which I had slept, sat against my mode of creation. Passing the open biography of Satie on my way to the toilet, I saw that yesterday's tea stain had illuminated a portion of text like a brown highlighter pen. Making a mental note to return to it, I followed a further trail of brown's – from the toilet to my clothing to my breakfast – before retrieving the cup and saucer from the floor and resting on the sofa. The biography was heavy in my hands, my pianist fingers gripping the binding like an elderly statesman might clench a safety rail having been charged with the job of opening a new rollercoaster.

The book had been opened at a chapter listing Satie's frequent *hoaxes*. From the announcement of the premiere of *Le bâtard de Tristan*, an anti-Wagnerian opera he probably never composed through to his imaginary buildings, Satie appeared to have been as much a lover of the hoax as Luis Buñuel, whom he had briefly come to know.

The tea stain, however, covered only one paragraph on the right hand open page:

In a filing cabinet he maintained a collection of imaginary buildings, most of them described as being made out of some kind of metal, which he drew on little cards. Occasionally, extending the game, he would publish anonymous small announcements in local journals, offering some of these buildings, e.g. a 'castle in lead', for sale or rent.

Immediately I became charged, as though through the influx of electrical particles. Many a true word was spoken in jest. I reached for my phone and called C.

The line rang and rang and ended up as voicemail.

I heard my own voice record a message before I realised I was speaking.

"Don't look for me," I said. "I'm lost in music."

I took to the streets of London with Satie in my ears and a longing in my heart. The day was sicky yellow, a pallid haze hung over the city like a film of bile in an invalid's plastic bowl. The tinkering of *Gymnopédies Part 1* resonated within my skull, accentuating each pedestrian action: the raising of a shoe, the descent of a foot, the wind-whipped trouser leg, the melancholy of movement, the absurdist pursuit of happiness, the assimilation of importance within each and every step.

I watched three young female tourists attempt to cross the road. Stepping backwards and forwards into traffic, their squeals masked by the music – the hidden soundtrack to their lives – as double-decker buses obliterated then revealed them to me, as though by a magician's sleight of hand. From one corner of a black pram I observed a baby's fingertips wrapped around a colourful teether, shaking it at the periphery of my vision, at a speed faster than the music I heard yet somehow in time with it.

I saw all of this and I wanted it all. I wanted the universe at gun point. I wanted to believe what Kafka knew. That the world could offer itself freely to be unmasked, without choice. I wanted it to roll in ecstasy at my feet.

As the *Gymnopédies* concluded in my media player the *Ogives* took over. And as it did so, the veneer of London became replaced by the veneer of Paris: like the over-laid acetates of a movie poster prototype adorned with Letraset. I saw both simultaneously, walked two streets at once without losing my balance, found new corners and hidden corners and felt around walls for the places in between.

As the *Ogives* ran into the *Gnossiennes* my melancholia deepened. It was not only the streets which presented themselves to me, but the pedestrians. Each face a double negative, the face behind the face, the Parisian behind the Londoner. I was moved by the music into a different sphere of existence, and when I reached the place I recognised as Arcueil where Satie had lived for twenty-seven years before his death I understood that I was almost home.

The façade's architecture reverberated with the trace of the London building that concealed it, yet I was as sure of my destination as I would have been had I stood at the door to my apartment. I stepped up, an arm extended to push on the glass entrance, when my wrist was caught by a man who appeared from shadow.

"You know this is impossible."

I tried not to look at him, but when I did I saw that his face was unlike the others. It was clear – one-dimensional – he either existed in only one of the worlds or none of them.

"Do you know your arpeggios from your archipelagos?" His voice cut through the music which still held me by my ears.

I nodded.

"Then come inside."

I stepped into the building. Whilst all around me the scenery was fluid I detected my own passing created no ripples.

"You're not the first," the man said. "Although in all his time here no one ever visited his room."

"I was looking for *Le bâtard de Tristan*."

"I know. You want to impress the one with the lovely eyes, gentle hands and tiny feet. Satie would have understood."

We ascended floor after floor after floor, as though the apartment block were built by Escher. As we rose we went down, as we descended we ascended. I was reminded of a cartoon corridor with many doors: of a dog chasing a cat chasing a canary. Satie's music continued in my ears, embedded. Finally we reached his door.

My ethereal estate agent pulled out a solitary key. Inserted it into the lock and turned.

The room was as Satie had left it. I knew others had been here before, finding orchestral scores behind the piano, in the pockets of Satie's velvet suits, stuffed down the back of the sofa, hidden behind blown sheets of wallpaper. It was here that the score to *Parade* had been found, believed by a living Satie to have been left on a bus. Within this room had been located the *Vexations*, *The Dreamy Fish*, the *Schola Cantorum* exercises, and a previously unseen set of 'canine' piano pieces. I wouldn't find those here, no matter what time or place I inhabited. I was looking for something more complicated than that. I was looking for something that couldn't be found.

"You know this is impossible," the man repeated.

I said nothing until I located the filing cabinet.

I stuffed my pockets with drawings of imaginary buildings inscribed on rectangular cards. The ethereal estate agent looked on. His face expressionless.

Before I left the apartment, I reached out and picked up a bowler hat and umbrella. With the former on my head and the latter under my arm I crossed the threshold back into the corridor and allowed the man to lock the apartment behind me.

"Which one will it be, sir?" His tone was deferential. I believed this meant I was on the right track. That I had scored.

I held a finger to my lips.

We descended the stairway, my vision hazy as a double set of steps – some leading one way, some another – swam before my eyes. For a moment my concentration lacked and I realised my media player had reached the end of its sequence. Quickly I re-pressed *play*, thankful that contrary to my own preference I didn't have to instruct an entire orchestra to begin again, and the two worlds re-asserted themselves, the overlapping complete without seam.

"Hurry," a voice ventured into my ear. "We have little time."

On the street pedestrians avoided me as water circumvents a boulder in a stream. I pulled out the cards, regarded the drawings. Each depicted various buildings, each held annotations as to the types of metal used in their construction: lead, steel, bronze, gold. The choice was limited only by imagination. I became aware of the rushing of time – hurried along by the man's voice in my ear. It was relative, naturally. What was it Einstein had said? *Put your hand on a hot stove for a minute, and it seems like an hour. Sit with a pretty girl for an hour, and it seems like a minute. That's relativity.* I imagined sitting beside C, showing her my opera. Then I fanned out the buildings and held them before the man.

"Pick a card," I said. "Any card."

His fingers passed through four of them before a fifth could be gripped.

"That's the one, sir," he said. Perhaps it was my imagination but I detected a regretful edge to his final word.

I flipped the card over and revealed my destination.

"You know this is impossible."

C sat beside me on the sofa, her thin legs pressed against the material of my trousers. She was wearing them.

Outside, a heavy thunderstorm shook my windows in their frames, lightning silhouetted day against night.

C had become soaked on her journey to my apartment. It was the least I could do to offer her my clothes.

I repeated the story.

"So," she said, "What have you taken?"

For a moment I misunderstood her. I was about to reveal the opera, before I realised she meant illicit drugs. My laugh fell truncated, half-crazy. For a moment I doubted myself.

"Nothing," I said. "I took nothing. Yet I gained everything. I found the simple by means of the complicated. Just as I said I would."

Not for the first time I wondered what she was doing here. Why she entertained me.

I held the point of her chin between my thumb and forefinger, bent my head towards hers but at the last moment she turned and my lips only brushed her cheek.

I could still hear Satie's *Gymnopédies* playing even though I had removed my earphones hours before.

"Not yet," she said. It was enough for me to continue.

"I've written something," I said. "Something that came out of my reverie." I decided against telling her the truth.

Leaving her side, I sat by the piano. Played the opening to *Le bâtard de Tristan*.

C rested her chin on her knees. For a moment, I had her. She was mine and always would be. Yet, as I continued to play I realised there were two of her. One overlapping the other. Neither were distinct, both faint; as though my vision were blurred. Eventually, as I continued to play, both C's melted away and instead lay my clothes, stretched out on a sofa that contained the indentation of her presence before even that too regained shape, losing hers in the process.

After some time I reached the end of the score, closed the lid of the piano, and walked across to the window. Condensation had formed on the glass. I looked through it but nothing substantial was discernible. Whether it be London or Paris; or a simulacrum of both worlds depicted by Satie through his drawings, writings or music.

Either way, it didn't matter. I had the universe at last. The full unbridled madness of it. All I needed was an audience.

❁

This story was originally published in "The First Book of Classical Horror Stories" edited by DF Lewis. The remit for submissions was that the stories had to reference classical music or a specific composer, and whilst classical music isn't my first listening preference I thought I'd give it a go. Considering my punk sensibilities, however, who did I know well enough to select? Almost unbidden, Erik Satie popped into my head. I remembered that Dave Greenfield, the keyboard player from The Stranglers (sadly now deceased), had referenced Erik Satie in a piece of music on a solo outing called "Fire and Water", and I'd always been intrigued about the composer without knowing anything about him. Yet, to show how fallible memory is, googling indicated the song wasn't about Satie at all (it's titled "Trois Pedophiles Pour Erik Sabyr", although I do believe the keyboard style gives a nod to Satie). Nevertheless, with the connection already in my head I decided to go for Erik Satie regardless.

Researching Satie I quickly realised I was familiar with his music. Wikipedia also threw up some facts that I knew would be perfect for the story (he maintained a collection of 'imaginary buildings', enjoyed elaborate hoaxes, had contact with both Dadaists and Surrealists, and had become fixated by a woman with 'gentle hands and tiny feet'). I already had a title I'd been meaning to use for some time, "The Universe At Gun Point", which I had read as a line in the novel Mystery In Spiderville by James Hartley Williams. From these things, the story developed naturally. As stories tend to do.

Kodokushi

Ai sat upright on the Karasuma line heading towards Kyoto. On her lap, the plastic box containing freshly made *oyaku don* warmed her knees. She looked out of the window at the approaching industrial landscape. It felt good to be coming home. It had been far too long.

Oyaku don, a simple meal of chicken, egg and onions, was her father's favourite food. The younger of two children, Ai was born late in her father's life. Three weeks ago she had turned thirty-nine. Today, her father would be one hundred. He had married a second time, to a woman twenty years his junior. She admired him for that. For bucking the trend, as she had heard her American colleagues say. She was the daughter from .the second marriage, and her half-sister, Keiko, from the first.

Living and working in Hokkaido, she rarely returned home. Over recent months – years – she had let telephone calls slide. Letters she felt happier with. But her father didn't respond to letters, and it seemed her mother and half-sister kept him increasingly distant.

She knew this was her fault as much as theirs. It was easy to let things go, pretend they didn't affect her. She knew Keiko and her mother would look after him well, and she knew that the distance between her and her father pained him. She didn't want him to be reminded of that through infrequent contact, so she slipped into the shadows, knowing in her heart that it probably pained him all the more.

Modern life was different to the past. He needed to realise that society had changed. Ai was a successful chemist. She travelled all over the world for conventions and had spoken at several universities. Of course, he was proud of her. How couldn't he be? But she also knew that he was happier having her mother and Keiko caring for him. Again, a reason for distance. A need to keep things *just so*.

Her mother, Wami, was in her eighties, and in poor health. Whenever Ai spoke to her on the phone she sounded distant, more than a number of kilometres. Keiko was the one Ai usually spoke to. She would run on about matters that Ai had no interest in; local gossip regarding people she had long forgotten. For the past three years, whenever she had asked to speak to her father, she had been told he was too ill, too weak. She hadn't argued. Had, in fact, counted her blessings that she could keep him at arm's length.

Keiko was fifty-three. She had returned to look after Wami and their father, Makato, when her marriage had broken down. She had found solace here. There had been no recriminations. After all, her father's marriage had also broken down and when he met Wami she had been told that Keiko was pleased to have a second mother. Ai knew that divorce wasn't a shame in her family. What had been more contentious was that *she* had never married. Had, in fact, several live-in lovers over the past fifteen years. She had not conducted herself with the etiquette that her parents desired.

Still, this was of no consequence today. A little surprise. A family reunion. Bowls of *oyaku don* shared between them. Ai felt a little guilty at not having made the dish herself, yet her father had always said the best *oyaku don* came from railway station restaurants. It would remind him of the good times, of the holidays he had spent with them, and of his regular commute into work. A normal salaryman occupation which he had cultivated and made his own without any expectations other than to provide for his family.

Outside the window, Ai watched her reflection undulate across the scenery. It flashed over garish billboards for washing powder, noodles; the red and white of their hoardings with yellow lettering impinging on her subconscious. The adverts for the latest technology were monochromatic. All sleek. Her reflection dipped and sucked into them, like a seal playing beneath the waves. Sometimes her view was obliterated by the close proliferation of greenery: trees and bushes almost battering the windows of the train, extended branches reaching for her hair. When they changed lines and another train charged by in the opposite direction she saw a hundred faces imprinted over her own. A composite diagram of matching eyes, eyebrows, cheekbones, lips, ears, noses. She was something of everyone for a fraction of a second. And then gone: back to the scenery. Back to the ever decreasing landscape as they neared the station and the glass and metal structures of the city held sway.

She left the train at Karasuma Oike station. She hadn't brought much with her. A small backpack containing a few days' change of clothing, three tiny gifts, and the food which she clutched in her hand. She also carried a selection of photographs, polaroids she had taken on her journeys overseas and of her house and her cats and her new lover, Naoharu. She suspected her father would want to play catch up.

She preferred polaroids for their instantaneous quality. Whilst digital cameras had superseded their abilities, the tangible product of a square picture entranced her. She would take some family photos during her stay. It might be the last time she saw her father – perhaps even her mother.

Outside the station she caught a taxi to the apartment. Along the way she glimpsed the ugly façade of the *Kyōto Kokusai Manga Myūjiamu*. She had wanted to visit the Manga museum for some years. Maybe she would do so on this visit.

Her parents' apartment was simple. She often wondered why they had never moved, but suspected Keiko's mother had made certain financial demands which meant her father couldn't provide them with the life they deserved. Of course, he never spoke of such things. They had been happy there, to her knowledge. And there was space for all of them.

As the taxi parked and she paid the driver she looked upwards at the seven storey structure. Memories flooded back: Keiko laughing as she locked her in the utility cupboard, wedging a broom under the handle so she couldn't turn it.

Her mother, Wami, combing Keiko's hair in long soft strokes. Whilst Ai's own hair, a tangled tomboy mess, had caught in the comb's teeth, jerked her head back causing tears.

Her father, Makato, sitting beside her bed watching her fall asleep, reading a night time story of demons, backlit by the light from the hallway, casting him in an unearthly glow.

Ai shook her head, dislodged the false memories. Replaced them with real ones.

She approached the entranceway. When she lived here, an old man by the name of Haruki had sat on a wooden chair reading newspapers and grunting, occasionally wiping his nose on a miraculously clean handkerchief. Now the reception area was manned by a young woman flicking through a magazine. A bowl of ramen noodles steamed on the counter, next to an open bottle of pink nail varnish. The complex mixture of smells caught in Ai's throat and she coughed, as though she were trying to attract attention.

The woman looked up.

"Can I help you?"

"I'm here to see my family. Keiko is my half-sister." She didn't give the name of her parents; she knew they hardly left the building.

"Go straight up. I'm sure you know the way."

Ai nodded. In the olden days Haruki would have telephoned ahead, informed the residents that a visitor was present. Everything was the same, but different. It had been a long while since she was last here.

The elevator creaked during its ascent to the fifth floor. Another memory. She found her heart beating wildly. How could she have left it so long? And the trepidation of this surprise visit hit her. She had cocooned herself. Was it the right thing? If not, too late.

She watched as the elevator doors opened, watched her steps as she walked towards the familiar apartment, as her hand reached out, lightly knocked on the white door that needed a fresh coat of paint.

She watched as she waited.

Footsteps approached. The space darkened behind the fish-eye lens. There was a gasp. Then the footsteps retreated. Words she couldn't make out. Two female voices. Silence. She knocked again. A little more insistent. The footsteps returned. There was a pause. Then, as though a decision had been made, the door slowly opened.

"Surprise!"

The intensity of the word was false but she needed something to break the tension. Keiko stood still. Looked her up and down. Keiko herself was dressed in a ratty pink kimono, the edges frayed.

"Ai! Come in, come in."

She had exclaimed but there was no emotion, no sense of joy. As they embraced, Ai saw her mother at the end of the corridor. Again, her face showed no happiness. In fact, the expression... the expression was fearful.

Ai's heart slowed. "Mother?"

She watched as her mother slumped against the jamb of the open door. In resignation. What was this? She pulled herself away from Keiko and ran, the corners of her eyes bursting with tears, her throat swollen as though something were stuck there. And there was. An indigestible ball of love.

"I can't believe this." Ai looked at the two women sat at the kitchen table. The *oyaku don* coagulating in its container. Tears streaked her make-up, freshly applied on the train as she had contemplated their meeting.

Keiko's head was down. "We didn't know what else to do. This apartment isn't much, but it is expensive. We didn't want to leave here. Look at Wami, look at your mother, she's too ill to move. What else were we supposed to do?"

Keiko continued talking but Ai was no longer listening. She couldn't burn from her mind the image of her father. Lying in bed. His skin cracked, dried like a pupa from which no butterfly would emerge. Dead three years and left unburied. His pension payments accruing, keeping those two witches in a comfortable existence. If only they had told her, she had more than enough money to pay for this apartment and would willingly have done so. Yet her anger at this was nothing compared to the anger of loss. And this anger was nothing compared to the sadness, the impenetrable despair that racked her body because she had come too late. And in essence, because she had known she would come too late.

Her mother's withered hand gripped her wrist. "You have to understand, Ai. There was nothing we could do. He died happy, in his sleep. His soul is otherwhere. But if we reported it... Well, it isn't just *us*. Just read the newspapers. Keiko tells me it happens everywhere."

Ai shook her head. She shot out her arm, knocked the container onto the floor where the lid popped off. A gelatinous mix of yellow chicken, egg and onion spilled onto the floor. The chicken dead meat, the egg a scrambled mess, the onion sloppy worms.

"*Kodokushi,*" she said.

A lonely death.

Keiko opened her mouth to speak but Wami shook her head.

Ai knew what she had been about to say. That it wasn't like that. Just like her false memories weren't her true memories and her true memories weren't her false memories. None of it mattered. Her father was dead and she had abandoned him. It wasn't Keiko and Wami who were at fault. It was herself.

She left them at the table. Walked to her parents' bedroom. Closed the door.

She knelt by the side of the bed. Her head down. Not intentionally in prayer, but because she couldn't bear to face her father's milky eyes. His smell permeated the room. It was in the bed linen and the curtains. How could they have withstood it? She watched as the carpet darkened with her tears; like inkspots.

The following day she left her hotel – she couldn't bring herself to stay in the apartment – and walked to the temple of the peaceful dragon. Each footstep in clay, her passage hardening in her wake. She couldn't believe it. Didn't know what to do. During the night she had convinced herself that she wouldn't support Wami and Keiko, but come morning she knew that she would have to if they were to continue living in that apartment. And she wanted them to remain there. She wanted them to feel punished, trapped, for the remainder of their lives.

She also needed to give her father a proper burial. Which meant it needed to be paid for. And to pay back the money that had been falsely claimed. The pension that he had worked so hard to obtain and which had outlived him.

When Ai was a little girl her father had often taken her to *Ryōan-ji*. Yet it was as if she were seeing everything for the first time, as well as remembering everything as it was. The simple structure of the main building's interior, with its light brown colours, open space, and sliding partitions. The traditional temple gates. The gardens with their greenery, stunted trees, pink blossoms. The Ryōan-ji's *tsukubai*, a small basin of water for visitors to ritually wash their hands, cleanse their mouths; positioned so that you had to bend to reach the water, suggesting supplication and reverence. And then the *karesansui* rock garden, over five hundred years old.

Another memory:

Ai! Count the boulders.

She squeezed her eyes half shut in concentration. Behind her, Keiko spoke random numbers, attempting to distract. Wami laughed, pulled Matako close. They were a family. A happy family.

Fourteen.

Her father smiled. Shook his head.

She walked around the garden, viewed it from a different perspective. Counted again.

Fourteen.

She watched her father smile again. She loved his smile, but she wanted to make him laugh.

Again.

She wandered the periphery of the raked gravel garden, with its moss-covered boulders.

Fourteen.

When she turned, her father, mother, and Keiko were already descending towards the monks' quarters. A camera swung from a strap around her father's wrist.

It was much later that Keiko told her there were fifteen boulders, positioned in such a way that only fourteen were ever visible; except from above. It was only through attaining enlightenment that the fifteenth boulder could be viewed.

Today, she counted them again. *Fourteen.*

She left the garden and walked back to the *tsukubai.* Washed her hands, cupped brackish water into her mouth. As it was a weekday the visitors were few and far between. She decided to sit for a while, let yesterday's events pass over her through the tranquillity of the temple. Maybe she could still her muddled heart to make sense of it all.

She found a low stone wall. Reached into her bag through habit and almost lit a cigarette. Crumpling the pack, she held it in her fist. She could do with some *tonjiru* right now. The hearty miso soup was her comfort food, made her feel that everything was right in the world. If she remembered correctly, there was a small restaurant not far from here. Maybe she would visit it.

Her bag vibrated. She hadn't answered her phone since leaving the train. Even overnight. She knew Naoharu would want to know if she were okay, but she hadn't been able to tell him of her father's death. Needed to work things through for herself. Despite the evidence of the polaroids, she was no longer sure if she were close to him at all.

Leaving the temple, she was about to search for the restaurant when she noticed an elderly group of people dancing on a nearby patch of green. Music, a waltz, played loudly but not obtrusively. She watched their movements, some more fluid than others. After a while, she realised someone stood beside her.

"Old people dance because they are afraid of dying," the man said. "And that's why they dance, to stay healthy."

She turned to face him. He appeared to be in his late sixties, his face weathered and lined, yet somehow smooth despite that.

Before she knew it she said, "My father died yesterday."

He took her hand. His fingers were twigs covered in thin strips of leather.

"Come."

They moved towards the dancers. Ai was swept from her feet.

Later, when she revisited the boulders, she saw there *were* fifteen. Her guide pointed them out. One by one.

It was to be a long time before she returned to Hokkaido.

❀

This is the first of several Japanese-themed stories touching on what might appear to be quaint absurdities from a Westerner's perspective, but which I hope sensitively utilise their concepts to inform on both cultures. In this case, *kodokushi* ('a lonely death'), is a term for those who have died but have remained unburied for long periods of time; often because they have no relatives or – in some instances – because the family continue to claim benefits after the death. Here, one of my characters subsequently visits the zen temple Ryōan-ji where fifteen boulders are placed in such a way that only fourteen can be viewed simultaneously. It is traditionally told that only through attaining enlightenment can all fifteenth boulders be seen.

A Knot Of Toads

Insanity is doing the same thing over and over again but expecting different results
— Rita Mae Brown

A descent of woodpeckers

"Do you want me to take your photograph?"

The girl stands at Windermere's edge. It's the height of the season and Ambleside is rammed with tourists cramming themselves onto steamers and rowboats. Nationalities jostle in ways unthinkable only one hundred years ago. Tourist honeypots illustrate global integration even greater than the Internet. Drawn together for one common purpose: to see what is out there. Except me. I'm here for other reasons; for understanding. I'm here because there's safety in numbers.

I had watched as the girl cycled down the hill weaving her way between lazy pedestrians drifting into the road like leaf fall, before parking her bike alongside the low wall which overlooks this section of the lake. She had paused to take in the view. After ten minutes it was clear that she was alone. She fiddled with her camera, the *Hello Kitty* strap in bright contrast to the standard black. From a distance she stood out from the crowd. She didn't really belong. I knew if I waited long enough I'd see her eschew the tourist boats to continue her journey away from the masses, to find somewhere quiet where she could hunker down and appreciate the lake solo. But even so she had to be here just for the moment, because she wanted to take it all in: the good and the bad, the busy and the quiet. She was both a tourist and a traveller: she wanted to be an outsider who worked from the inside out.

My observations were rarely other than accurate.

It was when she began to dither, when she was on the cusp of leaving, that I approached her and asked that question: *Do you want me to take your photograph?*

She looked at me briefly. Already there was an imbalance between us. I had studied her for ten minutes, she had regarded me for ten seconds. Before I realised how dangerous I was I had used that line as the perfect chat-up for lone travellers. How else to start a conversation? You can't know that you have something in common. There has to be a reason to engage.

Do you want me to take your photograph?

She was a tourist traveller. Of course she did. She needed to prove today's existence, and no one else was offering and she never would have asked. It would be rude for her to say no.

She tucked a stray strand of black hair behind her right ear and smiled. "Yeah, okay, thanks."

I took hold of the camera. "This one here?" I always pointed to the wrong button. It added conversation.

She took the camera from me, turned it around. "No, this one. Just look and point. It's set on automatic."

When she handed it back our fingers touched for the third time.

I looked at her through the viewfinder. This was the hardest part. I didn't know her yet, but I would love her. I would love her with a crying passion that would tear me inside out, and I would hate myself for doing so; for doing this. For I knew within the week she would be dead.

Click.

Her face was framed in the parameters of the photograph. In the background, Windermere extended in all its vastness. I had managed to capture her carefully, she might be the only one there. It had to be that way. I couldn't have anyone else in shot.

"Again?"

She nodded. *Just to be on the safe side.*

I ran off a few more shots. My heart ejaculated. The damage done.

I handed the camera back. Again, that touch. I noticed her blush. I'm not an ogre.

She switched the camera from photo to view and flicked through the images. "Thanks."

"No problem." It was then that I asked her name – *Veronika* – and where she was from – *The Czech Republic* – and what her plans were for the evening – *Not much.* I suggested a nearby restaurant. She laughed and said I was very forward. I smiled. I had to be. I couldn't bear that she might spend some time alone.

That morning I had seen a descent of woodpeckers in the woodland beside my property. Depression was instant, my previously cheerful mood decimated at the sight of the birds scattering unexpectedly from the branches above. I didn't know how many woodpeckers formed a descent, but their collective noun itself wasn't important. It was the grouping that carried foreboding. The certainty that I was trapped with my destiny.

Later, back at my property, the tops of the trees just in view from my position on the bed, I caressed the insides of Veronika's thighs as she lay naked in front of me. Giving everything up.

A business of flies

When Natalie spoke it was obvious she was local. I always thought the voices of Cambrian females sounded how men would talk if they were women. She had a slight overbite which gave her mouth the appearance of a circus ring. She wore a thick woollen jumper over a white shirt noticeable by its collar. The jumper hung low, concealed her rear which was encased in blue jeans. She wore glasses and was squat and her hair was cut boyishly. She smiled when she thanked me as I returned the camera to her. Cambrian women were chatty and it was easy to engage in conversation. I had travelled north that day and we stood at the Castlerigg stone circle near Keswick. She had hiked there. Her walking boots were caked in mud.

"Do you come here often?" I laughed; and the returning smile suggested that I had her.

Inside I could feel love blossoming. In the moments that I knew her she would be perfect. My senses heightened, every movement, look, word, action would be magnified through pathos until it was heartbreaking. I couldn't deny there was a rush in it, but that wasn't why I had photographed her. It had taken me a while to understand that the animals were a sign. The next step was to prevent it from happening.

It had been unintentional. My journey to Castlerigg was purely recreational, to get myself out of the house. But then grouped against the stone wall where I had walked from the circle itself to stand and look at the surrounding crags I had seen a business of flies. There was nothing obvious about their grouping, no animal excrement which might have precipitated it. So it was clear they had grouped for me. I stood watching as they wove in and around each other, a ball in motion. When I turned back to the stone circle I scanned the tourists. It was almost impossible to take a picture of the circle itself without someone being in shot. If this was a challenge then it was similar to separating Veronika from the crowd at Ambleside. But I had to do it. I couldn't take more than one of them down.

I had read of Veronika's death five days after meeting her; four days after she had left the morning after our lovemaking. My heart a popped balloon as she cycled into the distance, held static until I had seen her face on the website and the *Oh So Tragic Death* headline. She had fallen whilst climbing Scafell Pike. Her relatives had been informed. I wiped tears from my eyes and snot from my nose before saving her image as a jpeg within the usual file. She had company there. Too many girls.

I asked Natalie where she was heading. I hadn't planned on doing any hill walking, and I was barely equipped for it, but I told her I was going in the same direction and after she shared her lunch with me we set off together. Many times I was desperate to pull her fingers into mine, to interlock the flesh that descended from the wool of her jumper, and to reassure her that everything would be okay even as I knew that it wouldn't.

We parted late that afternoon. She left to catch a train from Cockermouth and I had walked twelve miles with her by then. She waved goodbye with a cheery smile and a *thank you* for my companionship. We didn't exchange numbers. She was an innocent free spirit, caught up with the absoluteness of the world and uncomprehending any danger within it. I returned to Keswick by train, in the opposite direction, and by the time I had walked the three miles to my car where I had left it at Castlerigg the night was so dark that I only could confirm it was there when I was almost on top of it.

I sat in the vehicle for a while. Thinking of Natalie and the loss that I felt. The interminable despair. Then it hit me – an uppercut to my determined stoicism – and I sobbed over the steering wheel, tears running down the tight plastic in either direction, parallel waterfalls. My insides ached from love, hunger, and the fresh residue of Kendal mint cake. It was a while before I switched on the headlights and gunned the engine, forging light ahead of me as I drove, carving my way through a tunnel of darkness.

A skulk of foxes

None of the deaths were unnatural. In some ways this provided relief, yet this was coupled with an overarching terror of determination. Was I the catalyst or the conduit? What was the significance of the photograph?

Everyone knew that in some parts of the world to take a photograph was to steal a soul. For some time I had considered this explanation, although it didn't explain *my* role as photographer. Were the victims predisposed to end their lives this way? Or was it my finger on the button – on the trigger – which hastened their demise. How culpable was I?

Natalie joined the others in the file. Ironically, as occasionally happened, the websites used the photo I had taken with her camera. I flicked through the images of the other girls. It had taken me a while to realise what was happening. Three girls had died before I saw connections. Then – through research – I realised there were more. My pick up line had worked beyond innocent intention. If it could be called innocent, even as it was. I felt compelled to know the answer.

Which is why, when at dusk I had seen the skulk of foxes, I phoned the Youth Hostel in Windermere, desperate to know if they still had a bed for the night. The foxes' eyes were pinpricks of light underneath the oaks, haunting me with an intensity of expression which went beyond the feral; a sign I knew I couldn't risk ignoring.

There was no evidence to support it because I never took the risk, but each time I saw a grouping it felt imperative I immediately take a photograph in case it was *my* life at stake. Call it paranoia, call it what you will, but I had few puzzle pieces and most of them were sky. Beyond midnight I believed I would be lost. My rationale to perpetuate girls giving up their lives was so I could gather more facts to understand it. Perhaps then the phenomena would stop, before I was stopped myself.

A glow from the real fire lit the faces of a dozen travellers. I stood by the doorway and watched, trying to piece together the solo from the multiple; if indeed such a combination existed. I needed solo as an excuse for the photograph, but also because another person might link me to the death. Not that I could be considered a suspect – none of the girls were killed – but for my own sanity I couldn't be exposed.

I hadn't realised I was blocking the entrance until the accented *excuse me* of a New Zealander and a gentle pressure on my shoulder caused me to step aside. She smiled and I knew she was the one. In fact, I would have fallen in love with her even if I hadn't been compelled. Her button nose pointed upwards as if my presence close to it was the most natural thing in the world. She sat away from the others, a map spread out on a wooden table. When I walked over I felt like debris in a river, floating towards her effortlessly, sliding down beside her as though lodged against her in the water.

I compared Milford Sound to the Lakes, and she smiled and nodded and believed I had actually been there. Quickly I touched off the subject of New Zealand and asked what she was doing here.

"I've been travelling for a year, only four days left before I see my family again."

Firelight reflected in her eyes. Their colour was so intense I could believe it was natural. Her family who had waited three hundred and sixty one days would never welcome her back alive. Already I was crying, and when her concerned fingers touched mine I made some excuse about a recent death in the family. It hurt doubly that this simple lie added to the certainty of *her* death. The sympathy exuded made it easier to say, *Can I take your photograph?*, as she later stood outside smoking, pale grey trails rising skyways to a pale grey moon.

An unkindness of ravens

I may have given the impression that these deaths occurred more frequently than they did. That surely the police would link these girls and – if not make a connection to a killer – at least raise curious eyebrows before returning to their paperwork. But this is not the case. Two years separated Veronika from Natalie, eight months Natalie from the New Zealander. It would be another fourteen months till I saw the unkindness of ravens, a few days after my thirtieth birthday. No cause for celebration.

I had been twelve the first time it happened. Details were half-remembered, yet those that remained were sure. My cousin, Miranda Hutchinson, had been given a camera for her eleventh birthday. Film, of course, back in those days. She had squealed when she saw it. I remember that distinctly. Only that morning I had watched a skein of geese make their way across the sky and the sound reminded me of them. If it hadn't been for that, then maybe I wouldn't have made the connection.

She had stayed over at my parents' property as her mother was only recently out of hospital and she needed a daily lift to school. As there were only two of them it made sense for her to live-in. It was a Saturday and we had experimented shooting pictures. Everything was interesting to her: the way bark peeled backwards like a ballerina from a eucalyptus tree, the wooden slats of our veranda and the barely-glimpsed objects beneath, the expression our cat wore just after eating, and Miranda's feet stuck out on the jetty seemingly independent, odd socks disjointing the image.

"Do you want me to take your photograph?" I had said as she held the camera out facing her at arm's length.

I had no great interest in capturing her image, but I knew it was the only way she would let me use the camera.

That Thursday night Miranda and her mother had returned home and the following Friday morning she had run out from behind an ice-cream van and a car embedded bits of her against its fender and bonnet. The upturned cone slid down the windscreen over the horrified driver's face. I had been there to witness it.

Miranda was the only one I hadn't loved, hadn't wanted to touch in some way. But then I was only twelve and I didn't know. *I didn't know* the effect that life and death would have on me.

So when I bend forwards now and say *Can I take your photograph?* to the middle-aged lady in oilskins, shouting my words over the noise and the spray from the speedboat, I'm already prepared to feel the love. To be aware that my experience will be amongst the last human touches she has. I want to savour her, to lock her inside me, to have her realise that she is wanted as she veers towards the abyss.

"Of course." Her smile is genuine, as they always are. Never have I had a puzzled look, a step away, a warning off. Perhaps this is part of the curse – for I have come to believe it is such – that the victim makes no effort to escape the trap. Sometimes, I take solace that their compliance made them implicit in the act. Yet often that is swept away as quickly as this boat shooting spume in its wake, the droplets of water reminding me of that business of flies, back at Castlerigg stone circle.

Pain was already etched on her face. She was recently widowed. "This trip was planned before his death," she says, unexpectedly gripping my hands in hers and shooting staves of love up into my body like hot pokers. "I couldn't cancel it. It would negate him, somehow."

I spent a few days in her company, providing companionship and no more. I like to think that for Vivienne this was a peaceful death, an exit that she might have craved although wouldn't have initiated. Either way, the day following our parting she was gone. *Heart attack*, the paper said. For a moment I wondered if she were a blip.

But as always the evidence was there. The animals, the photograph, the conjunction of the two. And the fear of my own death was paramount, my compulsion to take that picture, to relieve my guilt. I imagine a psychiatrist might patiently explain that for me to survive when

Miranda had died – that my decision to dig deep for the ball of bubblegum that lay at the bottom of my screwball – that split second delay between me running out with her and then stopping – had monstered that guilt. Maybe, if I told a psychiatrist everything, they might even believe that this manifested the curse, that I was its creator and not just a participant. It is a decision I've toyed with over the years, even during barren periods when nothing untoward has happened, when I wonder if I've transcended the condition and that it is all finished with.

But then I know the animals are grouping. They are right behind me should I care to look.

A knot of toads

I've come to enjoy the collective nouns. *A murder of crows. A train of jackdaws. A clutter of spiders.* No doubt if I travelled I might see a mob of kangaroos, a gaze of raccoons, a fluther of jellyfish, a bask of crocodiles. Something anchors me to Cumbria, however, to my familial home. There's something earthy about British animals, something that binds them to the soil and in turn roots them there. I don't want to leave this area. I am afraid to.

The collective noun for girls is *bevy. A bevy of girls.* I do not want to see a bevy of girls. A bevy of *those* girls. And if I leave here I have a feeling they might track me down.

Adding to their group is the only thing that keeps me going, that keeps them at bay. Because I have come to believe there is no reason for what is happening. No magical answer. It just *is.* And it has defined me. If I no longer took a photograph after seeing an army of caterpillars then my self would unravel and I would have nothing, nothing at all.

I need this obsession to continue existing. It has subsumed any need for understanding.

This evening I saw a knot of toads. They gathered together with their lungs inflating and deflating, stretching their sacs to transparent bursting point before relaxing them again. I could see them as a knot, their entwining posing questions as to where one began and another ended. It has been six years since the last happening. Whilst since then I have seen flocks of sheep or herds of cows or packs of dogs, these animals are too commonplace to be a sign. Surely if that were the case then a crowd of people would send me mad. But I have avoided madness yet.

I focussed on the bulbous eye of one of the toads. It regarded me impassively. Later I will turn up – turned out and freshly washed – at the over-thirties night at the Crown in Kendal, and single out a singleton for a mating as deadly as a reversed praying mantis. I'm wondering whether when I take hold of their mobile I should hold it at arm's length, away from us, then lean my cheek against theirs and capture us both in one image. Would that break the cycle? Would it kill me? Would I dare?

Do you want me to take our photograph?

Only the male toad has the vocal sac.

I'm in love with everything I have lost.

❀

Several ideas for this piece came about whilst I was on holiday in the Lake District: the diversity of tourists at Ambleside, the line about Cumbrian female accents sounding like men would sound if they were women (not intended to be disparaging, this is my character's view not mine!), and the 'can I take your picture' line as an intro to picking up solo female travellers.

Meanwhile my partner had come across a list of collective nouns for animals and thought some of them would make good titles or jumping off points for stories. I agreed, and this idea knocked around in my head for a while like a fly in a glass box, until I realised that the outdoors-ness of the nouns would tie in with my Cumbrian story. I tried to avoid the obvious (a murder of crows etc) and a knot of toads suggested a complex immersion in nature to fit as a title, with other collective nouns as section headings.

The crux of the story is about how we apply meaning to meaningless coincidence, and how such rationalisation is ultimately pointless.

The Abduction Of Europe

The moment someone very important or even semi-important dies, it gives me a feeling, which is at once monstrous and reassuring, that this dead person has become 100 per cent Dalinian because from now on he will watch over the fulfilment of my work.

– Salvador Dali

I used to proclaim Christy Brown as my favourite painter. Then I found I could use my thumb to travel and life gave me fresh perspectives. At that age it was all about influence. My father hated the Irish and he hated the disabled. It wasn't even that Christy Brown was a *great* painter, but he was enough of a painter to annoy my father who couldn't paint with both hands never mind his left foot. He couldn't even *kick* with his left foot.

Our upbringing was as narrow as the terraced house we lived in: sandwiched between others, conforming, conformist. If the houses in our row were people they'd be queuing for food handouts with their shoulders hunched. And the people on our street looked second hand. They looked slept in. Yet outside our street there was another street and then another and another and before you knew it there was the whole world. All clichés are truisms: every journey starts with a single step.

Christy Brown's colours were vibrant. If rain fell as paint it might create his works: puddle-drops of greens, reds and blues. All the more remarkable because of his disability, his conquering of cerebral palsy. Back then there wasn't much of an expectation that someone with a disability could do much at all. Let alone paint, write, have affairs. If I chose Christy as a role model at the tender age of fifteen it was because I was nothing like him. It was the obverse that appealed. And it was precisely this that disagreed with my father. A father who had done nothing wrong, but had done little right either. Rebellion: it's what your youth is for.

I was watching a documentary on Christy Brown one evening when my father returned from work and muted the sound. We watched the screen in silence for a moment. Then he switched the set off.

"That's not real painting," he said, his tone low. "Without that foot he'd be nothing."

I remembered my father's unfinished canvases that littered the shed and the garage. I remembered my mum threatening to throw them out.

"What's real painting?" I asked.

"Dali," he said, "Dali is real painting."

"Dali was a loon," I said. The word was in vogue at the time. So was *vogue.*

"Dali could paint," he said. "You only had to look at him to tell he could paint."

I shrugged. This was my father's recommendation. It would be some years before I took it.

Then I regarded my father's face, framed it with my fingers, as I understood what he had said. Because it was clear just from looking at him that my father couldn't paint.

Some years later and the sun beats down on a head that has already lost too much hair. I look up at the corolla through my shades, like viewing a silhouette backlit through a pinhole camera. Sweat populates my forehead. I'm a long way from that terraced house, in distance, space and time. My thumb took me to many places and then it brought me here: Perpignan in Southern France, close to the Spanish border. I'm waiting with a mixed crowd of locals and tourists to watch the annual Sanch procession. Marianne should be with me, but Marianne isn't here.

The sound of a tambourine in the distance reminds me of rain. It was raining the night Marianne left. It's not a memory I like to recall. Then the procession turns a corner and comes into view, pops Marianne out of my head. There are twenty or so figures, in costumes designed like photographic negatives of the Klu Klux Klan: jet black with tall pointed hoods. Except for the procession leader, who is decked out in red as though challenging a bull.

Other than the tambourines' solemn beat the procession is silent. Some figures are barefoot, one is on his knees. I commit the ultimate sacrilege of the modern age and film it with my mobile phone. The act distances me from the ceremony. I am jettisoned away from Perpignan and the here and now and become part of a pixelated future where technology is the God and consumerism is the goal. Then slowly I float back to earth, find my feet again. By the time the phone is returned to my pocket the procession has passed.

I find a nearby café and order a brandy.

There's something about the French/Spanish border that's less about national identity whilst simultaneously obsessed by it. Not far from here the French town of Arles has a Spanish bullring. For most of the year the fights are *courses camarguaises* in which the bull isn't killed but a group of men attempt to remove a tassle from its horn without being injured. Over Easter, which is where we are now, the bullfighting turns Spanish. The bulls are killed and there is bull-running in the streets prior to the fights.

Easter: a celebration of death. Dali proclaimed he was immortal and wouldn't die. Dali believed the train station at Perpignan was the centre of the universe.

Dali is why I am here.

My father was right. You only had to look at Dali to know he could paint. But for those who needed proof, for those who believed money was his only goal and that his surrealist antics masked an inability, one only had to regard his *Basket of Bread*: a naturalistic still life which – if one avoids the multiplicity of socio-political meanings – is simply a fantastic piece of art in the most mundane sense of the word. Unlike other painters I could mention, Dali painted the surrealistic because he *chose* to paint the surrealistic, rather than being unable to paint reality. Dali simply painted what he saw.

Later in my hotel I fold back the white sheets and slip naked under their covers. Cracks in the ceiling resemble Dali's *Topological Abduction of Europe – Homage to René Thom*. I lay there and watch them do nothing: they neither retract nor expand. A couple of hundred metres away Perpignan railway station is silent. Somewhere I can't imagine, Marianne makes a noise.

My father disappeared at Beachy Head. It was somewhat ironic, because his later pieces were chalk on black paper. Thick lines leading nowhere, from one edge of the page to the other, always with the hint of destination but never anything concrete. From these chalk cliffs his life terminated, reduced to a figure amongst the twenty-two that died there that year. Along with San Francisco's Golden Gate Bridge and the Aokigahara forest in Japan, Beachy Head is a suicide hotspot. Having never travelled I guess my father thought local would cut it. Sometimes I wonder what his imagination conjured as he descended, the wind rushing against his face, ineffectually buoying him in the air.

Each of us carries their own epiphany. On the 19th September 1963 Dali experienced *a kind of ecstasy that was cosmogonic: an exact vision of the constitution of the universe.* A universe similar in its structure to Perpignan railway station. In 1983 Dali dictated a prophetic testament centred around four hallucinations he had experienced since the death of his wife and muse, Gala. Within these hallucinations, French mathematician René Thom appeared, convincing Dali of an upcoming catastrophe the centre of which would begin between Salses and Narbonne, a short distance from Perpignan railway station. That catastrophe would be the disappearance or abduction of Europe.

That catastrophe is also why I am here.

In the morning I avert my gaze from the Dalinian representation of the precise location of the end of the world and ignore the ceiling. I dress, breakfast on croissants, wonder whether it is morning wherever Marianne might be.

I met her in Germany. At Museum Ludwig in Koln. I met her standing before a Salvador Dali painting titled *The Railway Station at Perpignan.* I met her seventeen years ago today.

At the centre of an otherwise brown painting is a square of brilliant yellow light. Each corner of the square radiates a searchlight glow to each corner of the painting. Like my father's chalk efforts the effect is that the 'light' extends beyond the frame. Common Dalinian figures stand ghostly in the gloom: the faint outline of Christ, a pitchfork, the farm couple from Jean Francois Millet's 19th century painting *The Angelus.* Within the radiant square a figure is either falling away from us or falling towards us. Falling into Christ or falling from Christ. This was a discussion Marianne and I would have, later, in the coffee bar attached to the museum, after I tentatively asked her if she would accompany me and she tentatively agreed.

"My father thought he could paint," I began.

She nodded. "So did I."

"And?"

"And then you look at someone who *could* paint," she said, "and you realise your life is meaningless. That you will never attain such greatness, either by recognition or from the art itself."

My mouth hung open, about to offer a platitude for an artist's work I hadn't seen and to a woman I wanted to know. But she was right. There is so much art that shouldn't be, and so little art that is.

"You'll catch a fly," she said, smiling. Then reached out and touched my chin, closed my mouth.

I watched her sip her coffee.

"My name is Marianne," she said.

I told her mine.

"What are you looking for?" Her eyes were sly, possibly wild. I felt she was playing with me.

"In art?"

"In anything."

I thought. I wanted to be profound. "I'm looking for you," I said.

Her cup rattled in her saucer. "You English."

I shrugged. I looked out of the window. Clouds were rolling in. Clouds darker than those which were the backdrop to the painting. I was my father's man. I was ineffectual.

"It's getting dark," I said.

She laughed. "The weather. English again. But also, it's getting late."

I knew time was of the essence. In retrospect I see how the connection of quantum physics and the mind had begun to supersede psychology. Instead I said, "May I walk you home?"

Her shrug gave me everything, yet because it was a shrug it gave me nothing.

We stood. I caught the corner of the table with my coat and coffee residue ran round the racetrack of my cup.

"You know," Marianne said, after we had gone a hundred yards, "Dali believed he was immortal yet he died."

"He died several times," I said. "He died before he was born. He had a brother, also Salvador Dali, who had died three years before his birth. When he was five he was taken to his brother's grave and was told by his parents that he was his brother's reincarnation, which he later came to believe."

"I am my own reincarnation," said Marianne.

"Then he died when he broke with the Surrealist movement," I said, "and those former members began to refer to him in the past tense. As if he no longer existed."

45

"He also referred to himself in the third person," said Marianne. "Just like Marianne. She does that too."

The clouds had thickened and twilight was upon us. It was too dark to be sure if Marianne were smiling, or whether she had noticed my smile. My heart was pounding like a thunderclap.

"When his wife, Gala, died," I said, "he died with her."

Her voice was quiet. "Part of us always dies when we lose someone."

"Finally," I concluded, "he died a lasting death. Of heart failure in 1989."

"A final death," she said. "His death."

Marianne turned to face me, stood on tip toe and pulled on the collar of my coat. Her solitary kiss imprinted itself as a memory even before it was over. Then it began to rain, hard. I heard a laugh, saw a bus, and she was gone.

It was raining the night Marianne left.

During the years that followed, my father leapt to his death from Beachy Head and my mother, always in his shadow, faded to nothing in a retirement home.

Obsessions are what make us.

Obsessions undo us.

I might sneer at my father because he wasn't a great artist, but maybe he led a more genuine life than someone who was too scared to even touch a brush.

I waste my inheritance by remaining on the move.

Dali declared that the Iberian Peninsula rotated precisely at Perpignan station 132 million years ago.

Nostradamus spoke of *the grace of Perpignan betrayed.*

The visionary preacher, Vincent Ferrer, a century before Nostradamus, suggested an apocalyptic frenzy in the same location, a necessity once all sinners had repented.

I sit in the Perpignan railway station waiting room.

I rush out in front of a train.

Biographer's note: This account was found with H____'s belongings in his hotel room in Perpignan. He had arrived in Perpignan only a day or two beforehand, and it is fair to say that it was written in anticipation of his suicide which occurred exactly as this account describes.

The author's obsession with death around the time of Easter has been well documented. His father's death occurred on April 15th 1990 – Easter Sunday. His annual attendance at the Sanch ceremony was almost a pilgrimage. Previously banned by the church, the distinctive peaked, masked robe was historically used to protect the identity of prisoners being led to the town's annual execution. The intention was that bystanders could not determine who were prisoners, penitents or executioners and therefore wouldn't seek premature retribution. It might be that H____ felt his attendance at the ceremony was akin to being part of it, as though he were also robed so confusion might reign over whether he considered himself guilty or not guilty of the crimes he carried inside him. His mobile phone footage testifies that he attended that day. And it's possibly no coincidence that the brotherhood of the Sanch (*the blood*) was founded by Vincent Ferrier.

Also confirmed is that he met the enigmatic Marianne at Easter. His travel diaries verify the museum trip in Koln, yet as Marianne is untraceable we can only surmise the details. What is clear is that the meeting could not have taken place for more than an hour, yet it made an indelible impression on H____. Elsewhere he has compared her to a potential muse in the way that Gala was Dali's muse. Certainly, he blames Marianne for his lack of critical success. Her absence stymies his creative impulse; an absence of which she could never have been aware.

What will be often argued is whether – like the central figure in Dali's *The Railway Station at Perpignan* – H____ was falling into the light or falling away from it. Perhaps the simplest explanation is that he was seeking illumination. Some have said he found it. Others, that it was abducted from him. Either way, Europe remains.

Perhaps it is not without irony that the distance his father fell from Beachy Head roughly equated to the distance H____'s body was flung by the Barcelona-Paris non-stop express. What is certain is H____ experienced a personal abduction in Europe. A physical outing of the soul punched through the body by the movement of the train. Of course, without his father's fame his death would simply be an unfortunate occurrence, without any need of documentation other than through official means such as an inquest. As it is, this written account of his apparent jealousy of his father's work, his fame by association, his inability to find his own muse, his hackneyed fiction, his obsession with determining meaning through interlinking accounts of the surreal and the esoteric, and ultimately his fixation with Dali's assertion that Perpignan was the centre of the universe, is simply a passing footnote in this new addition of his father's biography.

❀

This story was originally written for an anthology titled "Dali-ances: The Salvador Dali Anthology" to be published by Obsolescent Press. However, whilst the story was accepted and payment received, the anthology has never appeared (in some ways, true to the spirit of surrealism!). All stories needed to be influenced by Dali in some way, and having already been obsessed with him from a young age it wasn't difficult to extrapolate that into this tale.

The Aniseed Gumball Kid

When Sandford's wife and child left, he quit his job and found employment on the opposite side of town. He didn't want to see those familiar places any more: the street, the shops, and especially the park. He changed his number and scrapped his car. He left his clothes in several black bin liners at a charity shop and restocked his wardrobe from the same store. He styled his hair differently and bought a different brand of toothpaste. Yet there were aspects of his life that bled in from the past that couldn't be avoided; such as the sky.

On sunny days, memories assaulted him through picnic blankets, warm sandwiches and uncanned laughter. On wet days he was hit by the sloughing of rain from umbrellas and the digital flicker from windows backlit by television sets. On windy days clinging onto his child's hand couldn't be avoided; that soft grasp. On other days, when the sky wasn't doing anything in particular, just looking *up* acted like a giant mirror into the past; as if above him the world ran as normal and his life was intact.

Sandford hadn't told his new workmates about his wife and child. He orchestrated conversations so that they never existed. On some levels this was true. For what is existence but memory? Without memory, the past is never present.

Yet he was also careful not to lie; he remained noncommittal. Because lying created false memories which then became true. As true as any memory is truth, and as false as any truth is but a memory. This way, like a rake being drawn across a sandpit, he kept it upon himself to erase his footsteps.

Not to start afresh. Because starting afresh would open old wounds through coincidence. One relationship would remind him of the other. A prepared meal has no allegiance to the cook, but to taste. Sandford saw himself as driftwood on an endless sea. A sea no more than two inches in depth, containing no monsters.

Limiting his world to that of his spatial awareness gave him fresh perspective. People, vehicles, animals: these all appeared to come to life at the peripheries of his vision. As though as he moved forwards he triggered a hidden tripwire that activated a marionetted diorama. These people, vehicles, animals held no life other than that called into presence by his being. Once out of sight they ceased to exist. He became increasingly sure of this during his time at the office.

Sandford had worked in a handful of offices during his life. None of which were remarkable, either through the nature of the work or the workers themselves. In his new office he realised quickly how the staff fell into stereotypes: the dumb blonde, the surprisingly clever blonde, the SF nerd, the fat guy with glasses who blinked too rapidly, the married woman on the verge of having an affair, the token ethnic, the knowledgeable female, the motherly female, the unattractive temp, the chummy boss, the avoidable boss, the workmate who thought you liked him and who considered himself a friend but who you would never see socially. And so it went on.

Over his spiced chicken wrap – he no longer bought fish paste sandwiches – Sandford catalogued his fellow workers and found each correlated with an identikit counterpart in a previous office. Beryl was Carolyn was Cynthia. Wayne was Dwayne was Shawn. Emma was Sharon was Melissa. Raj was Raj was Raj. From this only one deduction could be made: his brain held a finite template of stereotypes from which to draw new people. Similar circumstances created similar people. The more he toyed with the idea the more he decided to believe that was true. And the more he believed it was true, the more it became true.

After Sandford had been in the office a week he began to stray from his designated desk and spent more and more time at the water cooler.

The cooler faced a ground-floor window onto the street. Inside the office, people were obsessed with figures and targets and productivity and how to do things better. And those who weren't obsessed with those things pretended to be, until distinctions could no longer be made. Outside of the office, on the other side of the glass, life was completely different.

Men walked briskly or leisurely, not subjected to the demands of the workplace. Babies were manoeuvred in prams or pushchairs, unable to engage with the concepts of profit and loss. Cars adhered to speed limits, destinations unknown. When Sandford bent to his knees to generate water from the cooler, he found he could look through the plastic container and view the street anew, distorted. Shapes, rather than figures, flitted back and forth; a cloudscape of colour. Faces, bodies, were blurred.

When Sandford stood he experienced a slight dizziness, a rush of blood to the head, which he found difficult to attribute to any one sensation.

From the window – as well as the outside view, and the ghost-like ethereal half-reflections of his nearby colleagues – Sandford could also see marks on the glass itself where it was chipped or dirty or had had a static collision with a bird or a fly. It was this snapshot of reality, like a microscope slide, which began to fascinate him: not just the divide between one world to the next, but the falsely interstitial properties of the divide itself.

When his colleagues saw him staring at the window they couldn't comprehend what he was seeing. In fact, of course, what *they* saw was different.

Different also, was his opinion of those colleagues when they were outside the glass.

Some mornings, Sandford would arrive at work early, and then regard his workmates' transformation as they came inside from outside, shedding individuality and creeping into conformity. And occasionally, in the evening, he would stay later and then watch as they became themselves again on the street. They were chameleons, the lot of them. And he was no different.

For some time, this was his existence. In role as observer. A year – maybe two – passed. Those memories which did assail him, assisted by the ever present sky, became distorted like curled autumn leaves or melted snowflakes or oven burns, until it was impossible to know what had happened and what had actually happened. Most days, Sandford knew that what had happened had never happened. With this in mind, and with the rolling reality both inside and outside the office, he sublimated his life.

Then one morning – crisp, fresh, where the sky was a pale blue, the blue of someone's eyes that he couldn't quite recall – a gumball machine was installed beside the newsagents on the other side of the street. He had a clear view of it through the window, standing by the water cooler. The base was a deep pillar-box red, the middle section clear – filled with gumballs, the top also red. On the side that he couldn't see he imagined a metal dispenser with a money slot and a plate like a cat flap that you lifted to access the sweets. He imagined it thus and therefore it was true. Although his journey to and from work didn't take him past the gumball machine, he knew the flap existed and in some respects hindered access to the sweets as much as it ensured none fell onto the pavement.

Something about the dispenser tugged at something inside him.

When he stood by the water cooler, no matter what time of day, there seemed to be a kid standing by the machine.

At home, Sandford had started hoarding. In direct contrast to the life he left behind where memory was the enemy, it seemed that behind closed doors he needed to be crushed by every aspect of his new existence.

Free newspapers local to the area were stacked, unread, in date order beside the stairs. Cardboard food packaging insulated the loft, beginning from under the eaves and extending backwards to the trapdoor, gaining height in a roof-ward pyramid. Tin cans, bereft of labels – which were steamed off, flattened, and supplemented the carpet – stood head to toe flanking the hallway like suits of armour in a stately home. Glass jars took up shelving space in the living room: not wasted, their contents contained finger and toenail clippings, the weekly mesh from his hairbrush, spat toothpaste, excrement, and a slowly increasing pile of eyelash, pubic, and eyebrow hair. Each day created less space in the property, reaffirmed his new identity, and shouldered out those old memories like excitable women at a garage sale.

Sandford spent his evenings watching his reflection in the television. A genuine reality show.

Those letters that he received, those that had to remain unopened, were buried deep in the garden.

The kid at the gumball machine would reach into the pocket of his shorts, pull out a coin, insert it into the machine, turn the mechanism, push a stubby finger behind the metal flap and pop the gumball into his mouth.

Sandford would stand by the water cooler, his thumb pressed against the plastic lever, waiting whilst his cup filled to the brim. He didn't have to look at it, familiarity and sound told him when to stop. Instead, his eyes to the gumball machine, he watched the kid chew for a moment, before the boy extended a numb tongue like a black carpet before turning away.

Sandford assumed it was aniseed and so it became aniseed. Not only for himself, but for the kid, too. He assumed the kid liked aniseed, and so he did.

Sometimes, caught up in the moment, Sandford would actually say: "Hey, do you see that kid?" or "See that kid?" or "You see that kid?" But immersed with deadlines and projects and very important matters none of his co-workers paused to answer. Often they didn't look up.

The kid wore grey shorts, knee-length, pockets stuffed with what Sandford could only imagine were sticky handkerchiefs, bits of string, cats-eye marbles, discarded chewing gum, smelly coins, pencils, scraps of paper with ideas for big machines, conkers. And so they were. The kid wore a white school shirt that had seen better days, colour washed into it, the cuffs and collar frayed like a mini-Elizabethan. Sometimes he wore a blazer, other times he didn't. Sometimes he was with friends, sometimes not. Sometimes with a mother, sometimes alone. Yet whenever Sandford went to the dispenser, unfailingly the kid was there.

He experimented. On some days Sandford waited until he was so parched from taking telephone calls relating to product that his tongue flopped in his mouth like a fish thrown onto a beach; until he could no longer function without a drink and he could smell his interior self. On those days, when he approached the water cooler, the kid approached the aniseed gumball dispenser.

On other days, he had barely drunk from his cup before he was back at the cooler, his bladder bursting from the intake, repeatedly filling up and drinking, filling up and drinking, watching the kid feed the aniseed gumball dispenser just as frequently, just as methodically. Yet never looking up, never looking through that glass window at him, at Sandford, just standing there popping gumballs into his mouth and then extending his tongue.

It was on those days – on those frequent water days – that Sandford was more likely to talk or gesticulate to his colleagues. To say, half in jest: "That kid'll rot his teeth, chewing all those gumballs" or "Look at that kid. Do you see that kid?" But his colleagues, few of whom ever seemed to venture near the water cooler – preferring the coffee machine or the kitchen where they took turns to make herbal cups of tea – might barely look up and nod, before returning to their work. Their very important work which earned them the right and the money to be individuals. Or, so they believed.

One evening, Sandford returned home to find a free newspaper, some leaflets advertising pizza, kebabs, and a nearby Chinese takeaway, a plastic sack within which he might place clothes to donate to charity, and a handful of envelopes – some brown, some white – wedged behind his front door so that he had to put his shoulder to it to open it.

So many memories were trapped in the house that should the bricks and mortar and window frames and tiles be removed there would be a second house held intact within it. A house which Sandford told himself he could quite comfortably live within. And so he did.

Watching his reflection in the television screen he switched off his mind and drifted into a sleep containing dreams under which he had no control; they were effortless fractal fairytales that swam from past to present and into possible futures. Sandford often couldn't recall his dreams upon waking, but this evening the ferocity of the visions assailed him as though he were standing on a beach battered with twenty foot waves. Repeatedly images washed over him, drenched him to the bare nerve of consciousness, until he realised he wasn't standing on a beach at all, but before an office window from which fell consecutive panes of glass, as though he were the central figure in a flicker book with each pane a page, altering him as it fell, giving the appearance of movement.

When he awoke, he had a clear memory of his wife and child. The wife and child that had left him some time ago.

Because Sandford had slept fitfully, concentration failed him.

At the water cooler he realised his cup was overflowing onto his fingers at exactly the same time as he realised the kid was not standing by the gumball machine.

"Hey," he said to someone who was passing – Geoff? Jeff? Jess? – "do you see that kid who isn't there? Do you see that kid who isn't by the water cooler?"

Kev? Keith? Katherine? answered: "Water cooler?"

"Gumball machine. Gumball machine."

"Gumball machine?"

"Kid."

"Kid?"

Sandford returned to his desk, dripping water.

He took a sip. Placed the cup on his desk where it created a lagoon on the shiny surface. Returned to the water cooler.

There was still no kid by the gumball machine.

After thirty minutes, Sandford had twenty-nine plastic cups taking up space on his desk. Finally, he was getting noticed. But the kid still wasn't by the gumball machine.

Later, after the conclusion of the story, his work colleagues would tell anecdotes about the guy who repeatedly went to the water cooler one winter's morning when the heating had broken and so couldn't possibly have needed one cup of ice-cold water never mind twenty-nine. Invariably, they wouldn't remember Sandford's name, but they would compare him to other oddballs they had worked with in other offices, those who kept themselves to themselves and who eventually disappeared, often unnoticed even in absence until a few days after the event.

"There was that guy," they would say. "Do you remember? That guy with the plastic cups. At the water cooler."

And others would say, even those who worked in different offices, "Yes, that guy." Adding credence to the story from false memories.

But on this day: on the day after the dream of his estranged wife and child, on the day that the kid didn't return to the gumball machine, on *that* day, Sandford had felt compelled to walk out of the office – through the glass that changed everything – towards the newsagents on the other side of the road. As he walked, his memories of other offices, of other street scenes, of who and why he was, were pulled together until all the realities were folded up over his shoulder like a knotted handkerchief held to the end of a stick. Everything contained there.

With each step a new reality closed around him, a pressing reality not dissimilar to the contents of his house, with one significant difference: he was no longer burdened.

Each step was lighter. The sky above threw itself open, freshly painted with soft gleaming clouds.

The gumball machine shone like a beacon, the contents black as tar.

As Sandford approached, it increased in size; so that when he stood where the kid had stood the top of the machine was head height. He reached into his pocket, a pocket stuffed with bits and pieces, crammed with his memories, and pulled out a coin. It was large and bronze and not of this time. He inserted the coin in the slot and turned the metallic handle. Within the mechanism the coin dropped, and then reality shifted for one of the gumballs and it fell into the dispenser with the sensation of vertigo. Sandford eased it out, sniffed it, then popped it into his mouth.

The taste was strangely familiar.

Sandford looked around for the kid in the shorts, but only noticed a series of faces pressed against the office window across the street, so indistinct as to appear sketches on the glass.

He stuck out his tongue, blackened and numb, and turned away to wait for his wife and his child. Who would be along shortly, some time in the future.

❀

My memory of writing this story is a little hazy. I know that I found the title written on the back of a recipe pinned to our kitchen corkboard, and that subsequently the title has been claimed as my partner's. I also remember the story sprang from the title alone.

"The Aniseed Gumball Kid" tells the story of an office worker who has become estranged from his family, who clings to a halcyon vision of reality which doesn't match the situation he is actually in, and who becomes obsessed by a kid he views at a gumball machine through his office window. The kid becomes a representation of everything he wants to be. That's it in a nutshell, but it's also more nuanced through typical office politics, how reality in any office is a self-contained world confirming to its own rules, and about how loneliness can affect the mind.

Eskimo

Everyone thought Eskimo was the bravest man in Shikoku, but Tamotsu knew he was simply the most stupid.

Sometimes Tamotsu would sit in his favourite *katsuo tataki* restaurant and watch other diners eat. With tuna fish pinned between chopsticks they would feed their faces as they spoke, not fully appreciating the city's most famous dish, simply taking it for granted. Halfway through the meal they would unbutton jackets, heave bellies over the top of tight-fitting trousers. Watched in isolation, divorcing the act of eating from the visual spectacle, they looked ridiculous. Still, Tamotsu did not think they were as stupid as Eskimo.

Sometimes, when Tamotsu *was* Eskimo and he stood in his blue costume on top of one of the tallest buildings in Kōchi with his cape billowing out behind him, his feet perched the edge of a precipice, looking down at the tiny traffic and feeling no fear, he knew without any doubt that not only was he the most stupid person in Shikoku but he was also the most stupid person in all of Japan.

And then, just when he thought he couldn't get more stupid, Tamotsu fell in love with Summer Snow.

Summer Snow was Canadian, twenty-four, born of second-generation hippie parents. She loved the Beatles at the precise moment that they were finally going out of fashion. Tamotsu watched her amongst his group of friends as he arrived late and she had somehow arrived early, at the wrong karaoke bar, lost, and then adopted by his crowd. Pulled back in a tight ponytail, her hair accentuated her face by its absence. Her eyes were round, wide. Her lips a faded rouge from alcohol diluting lipstick. She gripped the microphone and sang *Paperback Writer*, badly. Tamotsu wondered if she were making fun of them, because she sang it with a faint Japanese accent. Or perhaps she was just a chameleon child, wanting to mix in, to not be out of place.

Tamotsu was late because he had rescued a mother and child from a burning building close to the Obiyamachi shopping arcade. With smoke down to the floor and a ceiling bulging, almost collapsing, overhead, he snatched the child from a back room, its face pushed into the cold of the refrigerator, and then returned for the mother who had lain sideways against the exit, her hand outstretched but too weak to turn the handle, her body pressed against it hindering rescue.

The firefighters had congratulated Eskimo, patted him on the back. Tamotsu had shrugged. "It was nothing," he said. And indeed it was.

When Summer Snow looked at him, directly, as he entered the booth, it was *something*.

She made space beside herself and he sat, whilst she continued murdering the song. Tamotsu wondered if his broken English – much of it learnt from pop music – would be enough to start a conversation. Instead tongues were loosened with alcohol and language didn't matter. Neither did cultural difference. Nor the fact that Tamotsu was a superhero and Summer Snow just an ordinary human being.

If Tamotsu had had his wits about him, maybe he would have realised that ordinary human beings – with all their foibles, vulnerabilities and misunderstandings – were the most dangerous foes of all.

By the end of the evening, Summer Snow couldn't stand. She held onto Tamotsu who decided he didn't care if others were watching, and even if he did then he knew he could activate Eskimo. But he didn't need to. And when Summer Snow finally fell into a taxi after they had exchanged telephone numbers he watched the vehicle become smaller and smaller, from full-size to toy-size to indistinguishable to nothing until he realised it was raining and his clothes were soaked through.

Hailing a taxi for himself, he shivered all the way home.

If Tamotsu were ever to write an autobiography he would confirm that being a superhero was never something done by choice, it was something which happened upon you.

Shikoku, the smallest of Japan's main islands, was the only one without a volcano. So when Tamotsu visited the volcano Sakurajima in Kagoshima Prefecture on Kyūshū he was a little careless. Even so, he couldn't be held to blame for the minor eruption on March 10 2009 which spewed debris up to 2km away. When they found Tamotsu, huddled inside a boulder which appeared to have trapped him like an upturned shell, it was declared a miracle. But Tamotsu knew the boulder had not been hollow seconds before it descended on him. A force had been present – whether from the boulder or himself – that had cushioned the blow. From that point onwards, Tamotsu was a superhero. Even if at that moment he didn't realise this.

Perhaps it was sheer fear, the knowledge of imminent death. Perhaps a superhuman feat requires something in return, an exchange of power. But regardless of the cause, Tamotsu could now switch off fear, blot out bad feelings, caution, any of the emotions which held the non-super-human race back. So it wasn't bravery which meant Tamotsu could rush into burning buildings and reunite children with their families, but sheer stupidity because physically he could be hurt just like the rest of them. It was purely that he no longer cared.

Tamotsu had released his *nom de guerre* to the media shortly after stitching together the requisite blue suit. Fatman had suggested he be proactive, after his experience with the newspapers. 'Believe me,' Fatman had said, the contours of his costume clinging badly in places indicative of his attempts to lose weight, 'you need to control the press in this city, get in there first. I would have chosen *The Avenger*. Believe me.'

Tamotsu had nodded. *Eskimo* sounded good to him. Cold, cool, foreign, distant. And he did have a particular trick of saving humans from burning buildings.

None of this made him feel better about himself. He was stupid for journeying to Kyūshū, stupid for getting in the way of the erupting Sakurajima, stupid for not dying when the rock should have hit. Now he had a compulsion for danger without any safety mechanism, would always put others before himself, build an igloo around his natural instinct to flee, and whilst admittedly he did good it felt as though it were by default, without heroism, without meaning. He became trapped within others perceptions of him, of his alter ego.

Of course, like all secret identities, Tamotsu was the only person who knew he was Eskimo. And likewise, Eskimo was the only person who knew he was Tamotsu.

Summer Snow called the following day. She couldn't speak Japanese but he knew it was her. All he understood was the name of the karaoke bar, and all she understood was that he said *yes*.

He couldn't help but give a little bow when he saw her, outlined against the back of the bar, before gesturing to a nearby café where it would be a little less noisy.

For an hour or so they attempted conversation.

Then Tamotsu took her to his favourite *katsuo tataki* restaurant and instead of staring at the faces of stupid diners he hardly took his eyes from Summer Snow's expression as she tasted the lightly seared and seasoned tuna and realised that she was enjoying every mouthful.

They continued a semi-silent friendship for over a month before Tamotsu had learnt enough English to ask Summer Snow for a kiss and before Summer Snow had learnt enough Japanese to respond that she would be happy to grant him his request.

Volcanic sparks lit their irises.

Meantime, Eskimo pulled a driver, white-shirt bloodstained, glasses broken in two, from a burning car. He made headlines rescuing a party of schoolchildren lost on Mount Ishizuchi, despite the lack of fire. And he averted an attempted rape by dispatching a crazed knifeman in an alley near Urado Bay. For his wound, he had to apply the stitches himself. The rapist died in a subsequent fire.

With each stitch he cursed himself for being such an idiot.

Summer Snow saw the marks. By this time, their language was almost conversational.

"Hey, what happened?"

Tamotsu shrugged. "Accident at work."

"In the insurance office?"

"I slipped. Glass window. You know how it is."

"I know how it shouldn't be. Did it – does it – hurt?"

Tamotsu said it didn't hurt. And he was right. Because at that moment he was Eskimo.

One of the rules of being a superhero was that you didn't need the suit to be a superhero. You just had to be careful. Because if you were a superhero without the suit then your secret identity would be revealed and you would have no defence against Mechagodzilla. Snowman he didn't need to worry about, as Snowman had been defeated by a fall into a volcano. The irony wasn't lost on Tamotsu. But he did need to worry about Mechagodzilla.

One night, after he had kissed a line tenderly from Summer Snow's neck down to the base of her spine, after he had wondered for the first time about the future and what possibilities it might contain and how their relationship might be viewed by prospective in-laws, he asked her how she got her name.

"Hippy parents. You know the hippies, right? They just thought it sounded beautiful."

"It is."

Summer Snow leant her chin on a pyramid of fingers. "Your name, Tamotsu, what does it mean?"

He translated: *protector, keeper.*

She smiled. "Really? Are you going to protect me, Mr Tamotsu San?"

Tamotsu was less sure of protecting her as he was of keeping her. In the darkness of his room her eyes sparkled, and suddenly, impetuously, he decided to declare his feelings.

It was then, in the excitement of the moment, that he switched on the light which she had always insisted be off and saw the bruises at the base of her spine and on her buttocks.

Stupid stupid Tamotsu.

"It's not you, Tamotsu. I love you."

The words spilled around Tamotsu's head like the tiny silver balls in those children's toys which you had to roll into the eyes of a cat, or become sequins on an Emperor's costume, or with which you had to find the exit from a maze.

They had sat together, crosslegged for two hours, Tamotsu's face immobile, his lips bitten, as Summer Snow explained her desire to be beaten. A wish to be submissive. A desire and a wish which, despite her true great love for him, was greater than that true love. A desire which existed before him and which had existed during him, but one which would never exist after him because there would never be an *after him* within which it might exist. The explanation exhausted both Summer Snow's knowledge of Japanese and Tamotsu's knowledge of English.

It was only when Summer Snow had left, her eyes puffed as though inflated, once Tamotsu had promised that this knowledge would make no difference to their relationship, that he relaxed his Eskimo powers and let his emotions overtake him, fighting back tears just as he allowed them to fall.

There was no question that he might abandon her.

Tamotsu stood on the top of Mount Ishizuchi, willing Mechagodzilla to show up and fight. But Mechagodzilla would never, because he was fictional and the only supervillains Tamotsu ever had to worry about were those who were ordinary human beings transfixed by danger and power and greed. From the *Roof of Shikoku* Tamotsu contemplated what he should do, how his knowledge of Summer Snow impacted on their relationship. Truth was, he knew he could blot it out, lock the knowledge away inside him and pretend it had never happened. And in due course, it would have never happened, because Eskimo would see to it that he never knew.

There was no question it might stop. Summer Snow spoke words of *need* rather than *want*. That was clear in both English and Japanese.

"It's not cheating," she said, pushing a stray hair out of her eyes, looking like a little girl. "It's not even sexual. It's completely different. It has nothing to do with me and you. I will never leave you."

It was the biggest battle for Tamotsu. For the superhero and his alter ego. For the need to know and the need not to know. Summer Snow thought he should attend a meeting of like-minded individuals, so he would understand. But Tamotsu didn't need to understand. Understanding wasn't an issue because it was understanding which hurt. More so when, during those nights where passion and love were too much to be yielded against, he would play a torch over her sleeping body and note the changes, the new bruises, raging purple on her skin, the older ones yellowing, fading, like paperback pages left in the sun, and that understanding cut into him just as the remembrance of cancer cut into the heart of a patient in remission.

There were some nights that despite how hard Eskimo worked, Tamotsu just couldn't ignore the pounding of blood in his temples.

It was on those nights that Tamotsu knew it didn't matter if he was brave or stupid, because he was not in control of his own destiny. That destiny was held by Summer Snow.

"It's Eskimo!"

Tamotsu ran into the restaurant, decorations aflame, pushing tables from side to side as he made his way into the kitchen, eyes searching for the chef who had seared the tuna just that little too much. One foot skidded on a piece of raw fish dropped on the floor by a fleeing assistant. Tamotsu slid into a metal shelf unit holding various polished pots and pans and held his hands over his head as they rained down in a barrage of silver reflections speckled with flickering orange glows.

When he finally pulled the chef from the wreckage the cheers were muted. Still, Tamotsu thought, he would live.

Intolerable.

Detachment.

Hurt.

Indifference.

Acceptance.

Devastation.

His emotions fought within him. Clouded his duty.

Another month and he asked Summer Snow, in a burst of love, if she would join him on *Sjikoku Henro*, a thirty day pilgrimage around eighty-eight temples. Participants wore white jackets emblazoned with the words *dōgyō ninin*, meaning *two travelling together*.

Summer Snow declined.

"You have to accept me for what I am."

You have to accept me for what I am, thought Tamotsu.

She shifted, as though uncomfortable. Tamotsu wondered about bruises. "I want you to meet Tsuneo."

"Tsuneo?"

"You know who he is."

Tamotsu did, indeed, know who he was. Tsuneo was the man who inflicted the bruises on Summer Snow, who laid his mark on her whether it was sexual or not.

"I think you would understand," Summer Snow said, "if you spoke to him."

Tamotsu thought he would understand if he pierced the neck of Tsuneo with a Samurai sword but instead he nodded and pulled Summer Snow close until he could feel the fire within her body stoke the fire within his.

Just for a moment, when Tamotsu agreed to go, he did wonder if after all he was the bravest man in Shikoku.

Summer Snow held Tamotsu's hand. Tamotsu held Eskimo's hand.

In a small room at the back of a tiny bar Summer Snow's secret life sprawled before them.

Mostly, people were sat around drinking, talking, conversations ranging from share prices to marital status. It could be any bar in any part of the city. Except for the dress of the clientele: the chokers, the impropriety, the occasional lack of clothing, the ropes that bound. Summer Snow introduced him briefly to Tsuneo who had bowed without embarrassment or shame. Eskimo worked hard. Tsuneo had been about to speak but Tamotsu had pulled away. Summer Snow followed him into a corner, where he stood with his back to the gathering, like an insolent child, a dunce.

"Don't be rude," she implored. "I want you to feel it as I feel it."

"I'm trying to block this out so I don't have to feel anything," Tamotsu said. Emotions curled inside him like newspapers in fire.

"If you can't watch, just listen." Summer Snow stepped away.

So Tamotsu listened. He heard the eruption of Sakurajima, the crashing of the rocks around him, the screams of those caught in the disaster which then mingled with all the subsequent screams of those he had saved and culminated in his own scream. A long silent scream which was surpressed by Eskimo and despite his willingness to accommodate Summer Snow he knew that to survive there was only one thing to do.

Tamotsu built himself an igloo. As he mentally slotted each brick into place he found he was removing himself further and further from the bar, from the world, from the practitioners of acts which he could barely understand, and from the undoubted love of Summer Snow. Until, with the last block, he was totally cocconed from each of the sounds, each of the events, each of the emotions that surrounded him.

Eventually, once Eskimo had everything locked away, and Tamotsu was safe from hurt, humiliation and devastation, yet also protected from the frailties and confusions of genuine love, there was silence. Tamotsu was no longer superhuman, nor was he merely dead. He was alone.

His work done, Eskimo fell from Tamotsu leaving a charred, brittle structure that collapsed onto the floor like a bundle of sticks which could never eat in a *katsuo tataki* restaurant or sing *Paperback Writer* or defeat Mechagodzilla or love.

A structure that was neither brave nor stupid, but one that had merely been human.

❀

The story stems from a simple premise. What if the 'special power' of a superhero was that he was unable to feel fear: meaning he would do rash acts of heroism simply because he wasn't afraid to step in where others would shy away? What if this power extended to all emotions? And what if his alter-ego were to fall in love. Would his superhero-self need to step in to protect his regular-self from being hurt?

The Last Mohican

Each morning when Laura was alive she used to lay my clothes out on the bed whilst I had breakfast leaning against the front door jamb; looking down the row of terraced houses on our street: a cigarette.

Now I watch from a chair in the corner of the room as Tatyana – one of my regular carers – pushes her soft hands into my underwear drawer searching for a sock matching the one she has draped over the bedpost. She tuts under her breath: "Can't you fold them into one?" despite being aware it's my granddaughter who does the laundry. The two of them have a good relationship though, and she doesn't like to argue.

Through the thin curtains sunlight glows as though viewed through a yellow toffee wrapper. It's the 4th June, 2069: a Tuesday. It would be a good day to be outdoors, drawing heat from a cigarette to kick-start my lungs, just as the day draws fire from the sun. But the blue morning light can't be sullied with smoke, the ban isn't only national but personal.

When Tatyana handles my underwear I wish I could feel a pull of attraction, even lust. Instead memories fold into each other of Laura, head over heels as though falling down a stairwell. The little things: her half-smile tilting her head, the energetic way she danced, mouthing song lyrics in the mirror. I push out the thoughts of the later years. They only serve to make me feel lonelier than I already am.

Tatyana is talking: "A big day, Mr Read, no?"

I nod. I want to talk but I know there's a cough brewing at the back of my throat, and I don't want the embarrassment of hawking up phlegm. Instead, I continue watching as Tatyana lays my clothes on the bed. Socks at the end, then black skinny jeans with my underpants laid where the crotch would be, a torn white t-shirt with *Punks Not Dead* scrawled over it with a permanent marker, and my favourite long black leather jacket hung on a stand. I dislike how she places the clothes as though I can't remember how to put them on, but I suppose it doesn't really matter considering it is Tatyana who will be dressing me anyway.

Finally, at the back of the underwear drawer she pulls out a metal box containing what I consider to be medals, my badges of pride. In the old days, when there was war, there were 11th November Armistice celebrations at the cenotaph. Those old boys standing proud with polished medals over their lapels. At the time I used to wonder how they could commemorate those battles that they fought, as Spitfires flew passed strafing the crowds with noise instead of gunfire. Now, today especially, there is some kind of understanding.

What didn't matter was what you had done or that you had survived it. What mattered most was that you were there.

Tatyana takes the badges out of the box and I try to ignore my irritation at the fingerprints she will leave on their smooth surfaces. I'll be polishing them again later, before the event. She places them down on the side table beside me. I let her choose, and she chooses rightly: The Damned, The Buzzcocks, The Fall, The Stranglers, Joy Division, and – of course – the Sex Pistols.

Technically speaking, The Stranglers and The Damned shouldn't be included, of course. Them being Southerners and all. But apply that logic and the Sex Pistols wouldn't be there either. And that wouldn't cut it. Besides, being punk means that the only conventions are that there are no conventions. No doubt the major newspapers will run articles at great length on what it means to be me – the last survivor of the Manchester Lesser Free Trade Hall gig of the 4th June 1976 – but I won't read them. Once this year's parade is over I want to be *over*. There's no fun in being the last man standing. And anyway, Laura is waiting for me.

Later I'm downstairs. Tatyana is at my feet, but not in supplication, she's re-threading the laces on my black monkey boots after having applied a polish that sends memories up my nose faster than a sniff of cocaine. The yellow and red alternate spikes of her Mohawk haircut nudge against my knees. She finishes and looks up, smiles through black lipstick, her lip piercing gleaming in the low wattage energy saving lightbulb over the kitchen table.

"Done," she says, with that accent of hers that reminds me how global punk became. Not that the Eastern Europeans really understood it, even if they had more to rebel against than we had.

1976: Britain was run down, rubbish piled high on the streets, electricity flickered intermittently due to strike action, unemployment reigned, and the education system taught you to keep your place. What did Rotten say? *Out of all that came pretentious moi and the Sex Pistols and then a whole bunch of copycat wankers after us.* Well, he would say that, and he had the

68

right to say it. But whatever way you looked at it the Pistols were the catalyst for what had been brewing for a very long time. And – surprising us all – it worked. It bloody well worked.

The front door opens and my only surviving son, Steve, shoulders his way through. He's approaching eighty himself, but a six-pack of beer is held within the crux of his arm. Behind him come his two daughters, Magenta and Columbia, their husbands, Gary and Clive, and my two great-grandchildren, Scooby and Iggy. For a moment there's a cacophony of noise but Tatyana – bless her – quietens it without looking like she's imposing; although I do see her place a hand over her heart at the same time as she holds a finger to her lips.

Shortly afterwards, Chrissie, my daughter also arrives. I try to look through the crowded kitchen to see if she's brought anyone with her but as usual it appears that she's alone. I remember buying her white X-Ray Spex t-shirt almost three decades ago, and it still looks good on her. Just like the music, these things were built to last.

"We're all here," Steve says, cracking open the first of the beers although it's just after ten in the morning. "So's the press. They're three deep outside."

"It's an important day," says Tatyana, speaking for me. I realise then there's as much pride in her voice as there is from my own children, perhaps more so. I guess for my kids I was a father, whereas for Tatyana I'm approaching an icon. Even if I was never an actual musician.

History splits us into two groups. The Southerners and the Northerners. The Southerners had the Saint Martins College gig and we had the Manchester Lesser Free Trade Hall. Ok, so the Southerners got the Pistols first, on the 6th November 1975, and out of that came Billy Idol with Generation X, the scream that was Siouxsie Sioux, and the rest of the Bromley Contingent, but the Pistols hadn't even played any of their own material before the plug was pulled. To all intents and purposes they might as well have been a covers band. Whereas we got a proper gig, and out of that we got the Buzzcocks, Joy Division, The Fall, and eventually The Smiths. Oh, and Paul Morley. Journalists were always wankers. You just had to look at the way they treated The Stranglers. But the point is the most important gig in the North had been played. There couldn't have been more than 40 in the audience, but it was the 40 that mattered. Although reading about it for years afterwards you would think there were thousands present. Add everyone together who claimed they were there and you'd have the half-million who were at Woodstock. Tell anyone though, size doesn't matter, it's what you do with it that counts.

Spiral back ninety-three years, scratch the surface of memory.

Laura is fourteen and I'm fifteen. We're standing opposite each other in the grey hallway at school, in two distinct groups of boys and girls. Matt, the long-haired Adonis that he is, nudges me and says: "Hey Pete. You ain't had a girlfriend yet? What's with that." I shrug. I hadn't really thought about it. I remember my eyes scanning the crowd of girls. They were alien to me. Then I was about to mumble something placatory when I caught Laura in profile, at the back, looking to the floor. Something tugged inside me, as though all my interior organs were laced together and they had just been pulled tight.

"Who's that?" I said; my voice sounding different, as though I were hearing it recorded.

"Who's what?"

"That. *Her.* At the back."

Matt looked over. "That's Laura," he said. "Fuck knows what she's done with her hair."

What she had done was cut it short and dyed it black. It made her stand out like a Negro at a Klu Klux Klan convention.

"You like that do you?" Matt continued. Then before I could answer he'd crossed the divide between the boys and the girls and was whispering something in Laura's ear. That was the first time I saw the half-smile.

Four weeks later, after we'd been going steady for a while, I held two tickets for a gig at the Lesser Free Trade Hall. The Sex Pistols supported by Solstice, some heavy metal rock band from the Midlands who everyone then forgot. But Laura couldn't go. Her parents forbade it. So it was me who caught the revolution and whilst she attended the second gig six weeks later there was always a wedge between us – just like the dividing line in the school corridor – that I could never actually cross. She didn't hold it against me – how could she? But it was there.

It remained that way through the following eighty years, four children, several grandchildren and the two great-grandchildren. Even now I get sad about it. She had the ticket. She should have gone. I don't even remember what happened to that spare. I just know that I didn't sell it and if I had it now then it would set my family up for life.

Through the window I can see the reporters, the white vans of the television crews, and the other equipment that I don't quite understand now that technology has passed me by. I'm holding a warm can of beer in one hand, and my head in the other. A few sips of the beer have settled in my stomach like oil on water. I'll put it down somewhere discretely when I get the chance. Alcohol doesn't agree with me any more, but I can't let my family know that.

I remember the first time I saw Laura naked. We had pulled aside a corrugated metal sheet that half covered the entrance to a deserted warehouse in Moss Side. I don't think either of us knew what our intentions were other than just to get away and be together. We were outsiders, we knew that: at home, at school, in the city. People looked at us askance. There was no edge to us; I won't pretend we knew violence. But the difference was there and we could feel it beyond the pull of puberty.

Laura wore a mohair jumper, black and red, like Dennis the Menace. When she pulled it up over her head I remember being shocked that she wore no bra. Her tiny breasts appeared as pale clay moulds against her skin, the nipples even paler. Cupped in my hands the centres of my palms connected with a jolt. She reached around behind her and undid her pleated skirt that fell to a floor covered in brick dust and odd pieces of rusted metal. I remember pulling down her white knickers until they were around her ankles and standing back and looking at her and not knowing what to do.

Another day she touched my penis until it hardened and I came with my head arched back looking at a bright blue sky through the jagged smashed glass of broken windows. I swear a bird flew across the view; but as a silhouette I couldn't tell if it were a dove or a raven.

Tatyana used to hold me as I went to the toilet, but she doesn't do that any more. I now have to sit down regardless, but I don't miss her touch, which I know embarrassed us however matter-of-fact she made it.

My other carer, Daina, is as rough as they come. My skin bruises easily and I won't show my family but Tatyana tuts when she sees it although she says there's nothing she can do.

If my body has had a chequered history then so did the Lesser Free Trade Hall. Finished in 1856 – well over two hundred years ago – it's been a public hall, a concert hall, a bombed out World War II shell, another concert hall, a hotel, and now a museum. Certainly it doesn't have the extended kudos of a venue such as New York's CBGB's, but at least it remains standing.

I always thought it pertinent that it was built on the site of the Peterloo Massacre: that date in 1819 when cavalry charged into a crowd of 80,000 who had gathered to demand a reform of parliamentary representation, killing a handful but wounding more than 700. And that in 1905 the Women's Social and Political Union activists, including Chistabel Pankhurst, were ejected from the building during a meeting from which began the militant WSPU campaign for women to vote. Maybe there was something in the ground that echoed upwards and instilled the crowd during the Pistols gig. And if that sounds like a contrivance, then I'll answer it's just my memory assimilating how such a tiny event could have triggered both a musical and political revolution that has led us to where we are today: a free country independent from the constraints imposed by the capitalism and faux democracy lauded by America and the rest of Europe and the ever-emerging Third World Countries. We welcome all and repel none. We have true power held by the masses where individuality can make a difference. And a government unbound by convention or artifice: where each decision considers the rights of everyone. Unequivocal freedom of expression.

"You alright, dad?" Chrissie is on her knees, beside me, and I realise I've been rehearsing parts of my speech in my head in my own little world; the eye in a storm.

"I'm fine," I say, my voice crackling like burnt leaves underfoot. "Just reminiscing."

"You're lucky you've still got your memories," she says, and I know she's thinking of Morrissey, who, until last year and for the previous six years before it, was the only other survivor to join me for this march. I barely knew the man. We had exchanged but a handful of words over the years. But he had a right to attend, just as all of them did. In the final years, of course, he didn't even *know* he was there. What was it that they used to say about the Sixties, that if you can remember them then you probably weren't there? Much the same was true about any decade, because despite the drink and the drugs or the lack of them, memory will be your ultimate enemy. The loss of it an erosion of everything you know, of history.

Chrissie's right. I am lucky I have my memory. And this is it, now:

Despite what you might think from the myth and stories that sprung around afterwards, the only thing you could have been sure of at the gig was that you were about to witness something you'd never seen before. And whilst perhaps half of the audience went on to do something within the punk movement, that didn't alter the fact that for the rest of us, the schoolboys and schoolgirls, the people who worked for the Manchester Dock company, the plasterers from Denton, the *ordinary* people, it was no less than remarkable.

The front that was the Seventies: the propping up of tired systems, the patching up of old establishments, the inherent class system, the popular rock music that was a soporific opium to the masses, the traditional values of inherited decency which no longer belonged to our age, the outrage that anyone might question *anything* – all this was about to be torn down.

I'd be lying – and I will lie to the papers, the television, later today – if I said I could remember the gig note for note. So many gigs have been and gone in the intervening years. For a time I even tried to forget it. I wanted my first gig with Laura – the Pistols second, on 20th July 1976 – to be my moment of epiphany. But history is a brush with tar that will never wash off, and I remember enough of the gig to know I was there. And that's the important thing. I know I was there and I can prove I was there.

Everyone says they remember where they were when Thatcher's government came down. Of course, we were all post-punk then, but the ragged sentiments from the three-chord thrust were still running through our veins. And by that time we had the whole country behind us. Whoever said the revolution starts at closing time had been right. We had a black and white TV in those days, but I swear you could see the orange flames flickering at the Houses of Parliament.

The rest, as they say, is history.

I'm exhausted by the few questions I answer leaning over my garden gate, a veritable Medusa's head of microphones pushing towards my face. The parade itself will follow in an hour's time, but for the moment I bask both in the sunshine and in my moment of glory. A glory tinged by sadness, of course, not only for Laura who would have been proud of this moment, but for all the fallen soldiers I've left behind: Pete Shelley, Howard Devoto, Ian Curtis, Morrissey, Peter Hook, Mark E Smith and the regular gig goers. Not to mention those who were crucial to the revolution: Ian

Dury, Poly Styrene, JJ Burnel, Joe Strummer, Dave Vanian, Captain Sensible and Steve Severin. And of course, John Lydon himself. The only one that ever really mattered, because he was smart and he knew it. No wonder the old government had tried to suppress him. He was a dangerous Molotov cocktail that threw himself back into the audience.

Later, with Tatyana taking my arm, I walk a few faltering steps at the start of the parade, my monkey boots reflecting the harsh light off streetlamps in monochromatic photography, my long black leather jacket moving in a soft wind around the tops of my knees, my t-shirt proclaiming what we always knew, my jeans hugging my legs like paint. Of course, after those initial steps I'm back in the wheelchair, deafened by the accompanying applause. It's fitting that the parade takes place at night, around the time that the gig would have occurred all those years ago, but also it conceals my frailty from the harsher light of day.

I look out into the faces of the crowd, almost half with hairstyles extending skywards like space rockets. Of course, back in the day, hardly anyone styled their hair like that. Few wore bondage trousers. Few had safety-pins pushed through their noses or earlobes. What we had was what we stood in. I remember one of the thousand documentaries about the punk revolution where an Irish record shop owner recalled his amazement at seeing the Undertones on Top Of The Pops *wearing their own clothes*. Yet every movement has a uniform and so long as it's funded by the independents and not the multi-national companies that seem to have sewn up the rest of the world then that's fine with me. In my day, we removed the logos from our clothes. I've heard in some countries the population is now physically branded.

By the time we've reached the Lesser Free Trade Hall I'm exhausted. I stand again, receive the applause. I think of those November Remembrance parades of yore, watching a dwindling number of ex-army men year after year after year. Now, I'm one of them, but representing a worthier cause. What will happen, though, after I'm gone?

For I was only there. After the gig I married Laura and we had our kids and I went out to work for the rest of my life like everyone else. And I built my world around myself. And – like the best of them – I remained me. But I held no greater role at the gig than a cook might have in a forgotten army. And after me, what comes next? Could tonight be another catalyst, or will another group come and usurp us. Steve told me a rumour that a collective known as the New Romantics are waiting in the wings. But after 93 years of successful revolution, and with myself in my one hundred and eighth year, I can't quite believe that.

They call me The Last Mohican but it's a misnomer; yet the media like a sound bite even if we're a long way off Bill Grundy.

Much later, back home, with only the crumbs of meat patties, sausage rolls, crisps and tiny orange flakes of cheese remaining on the paper plates; with the bin choked by flattened beer cans emptied by the adults and squashed Kwenchy Kups drunk by the great-grandchildren; with the echoes of my extended family's goodbyes resonating in my ears; and with Tatyana upstairs making my bed, I close my eyes. And when I open them I see Laura.

She's sitting across the table from me. Her elbows create circles in the tablecloth and her head is resting in her hands.

"How did it go?" she asks. As though her voice is coming from a long way away. From the other side, perhaps.

When I sigh I feel something unpick my heart, a stitch unstitched.

"It was ok," I breathe. "But I wish you were there."

"You always wished I was there," she says. "My bloody parents."

I force a smile across the table, across the years. How different would it have been if she had been there too? Regardless, I would have remained the last one standing. The last one standing even as I sat. Even as I watched the crowds pogo to God Save The Queen at the end of the parade: from the Lesser Free Trade Hall right around the country to the museum dedicated to the sins of the past which was once Buckingham Palace.

I reach out across the table, fingers outstretched.

Laura does the same.

When we connect, the music is there. A simple beat with a simple lyric. And it's just as valid as ever. Because punk – true punk – isn't just about nostalgia. It's about being us, now. And being us, always.

I won't hear Tatyana return downstairs.

❀

Having had my formative years defined by punk in the late Seventies, the music and can-do attitude has remained an inspiration. It was only a matter of time before I wrote a punk story celebrating that. I recall watching a Remembrance Day parade where it was mentioned the veterans attending were fewer and fewer due to old age and death. It struck me that eventually there would be no one left who fought in the First World War and – as my own years are advancing – I applied the same thought to those who remembered punk. From this I developed an alternate reality story where the punk revolution extended beyond 1976 and created a viable, punk-fuelled society. I needed an event that could be annually commemorated for this society, and the classic Manchester Lesser Free Trade Hall gig which the Sex Pistols played near the start of their career and which proved a catalyst for many aspiring bands was perfect. It was a gig that has gone down in legend, with the number of people claiming they were there seemingly over and above the venue's capacity.

So there was my story. We join the final survivor of the iconic gig at the anniversary of the event as he muses over a life intertwined and forever affected by punk.

Bullet

I searched for my girlfriend armed with a copy of Kafka's *Bullet*, a false map, and certain knowledge of the gateway to her dreams.

On the table bar halved pistachio shells were lined up like coracles on the shore of the river Teifi. Their contents mushed to a paste in my stomach, I wheedled stray pieces of nut from behind my gums and swallowed. The exterior of the shells were salty. I had held them in my mouth for as long as possible before splitting the shell between my teeth. Each half reminded me of Ava and I. Hesitantly, I picked up a pair and fitted them back together. Even though it appeared the rearrangement was complete, I knew that the interior was hollow.

I swept the shells from the bar into my open palm and then dropped them into the bin. The barman smiled, gap-toothed, dark-skinned. I dropped a twenty baht note on the counter and stood. Two dogs were sniffing each other behind me, their fur patchy, their tails erect. I walked around the corner, back through the market where a butcher pierced and then squeezed intestines blanched white from one plastic bowl to another. It was getting late. The sun was obscured by the height of the nearby buildings, and twilight infiltrated the stalls. The products were stored underneath them, their wooden surfaces covered with bamboo matting and hard pillows in readiness for the traders to spend the night.

Turning onto Samsen Road I made my way to the main backpacker area of Bangkok on Khao San Road. Cutting through the forecourt of the police station on the corner I emerged into tourists following the ancient beatnik trail. Mock Rastafarian colours and dreadlocks separated the long-term travellers from those who had just arrived. I wove my way through the stalls and restaurants, the guesthouse frontages, the familiar souvenirs, the tuk-tuk drivers, the catcalls and the taxis. Slipping into Orm restaurant halfway down Khao San Road I ordered some Mekong whisky and ginger chicken. When the meal came it was Westernised, but I enjoyed it anyway. I sat watching the world evolve in front of my eyes, the hustle and bustle in one of the busiest streets in Asia. Then I wondered where Ava must be, so I opened the book and searched for her.

"You're so far out you're indoors."

Ava had laughed, her long blonde hair shaking at the sides of her head. She swigged from her Singha beer, some spilling down the corners of her mouth. Her eyes sparkled with the sheen of a blue tit's tail feathers. She reached one of her long skinny arms towards me and ruffled the hair on my head. "Cheer up," she said. "Maybe it will never happen."

"Maybe *what* will never happen?"

"Whatever it is that you're morose about."

She became distracted, looked from side to side, her attention snatched away from me once again.

"I've been thinking," I said. "If the tide is out on one side of the world does it mean that it is in on the other side."

Ava returned her gaze to me as though seeing me for the first time. "It doesn't work like that. The tide is out on both sides. The swell is in the middle of the ocean; like this." She made a movement with both hands, sweeping them towards each other and then up in a mount before they met.

"How do you know this?"

"I know everything."

We had known each other for two weeks, been an on/off couple for two days. We had travelled up to Ayutthaya, the former capital of Bangkok, and hired an overpriced tuk-tuk from the train station to the old temples. Climbing the spirals we had marvelled at the dearth of tourists, played hide and seek, and photographed ourselves by a large stone Buddha head that had been subsumed by the roots of a tree. On the train journey back Ava had fallen asleep, her head on my shoulder, her blonde hair falling into my fingers which were open on my lap. I touched her hair as she slept. Later she told me she had dreamt she was Rapunzel, recently released from her tower. Shortly afterwards we made love for the first time; Ava on top.

We visited the usual tourist spots within a short travelling distance from Bangkok: the bridge over the river Kwai at Kanchanaburi, the large golden dome at Nakhon Pathom, the royal family's favourite beach resort at Hua Hin. After three weeks together I felt that I had begun to know her. To know her better than anyone else I had ever known.

It was at the top of Wat Arun, the temple of dawn, that Ava returned to my comment about the tides. The sides of the temple were decorated by tiny mosaic pieces of crockery. We had speculated on the length of time it must have taken to complete the work, as the humidity seeped into our clothes and returned the daily stink to them despite the earliness of the hour.

"My description of the tides," Ava had said, her eyes blinking rapidly, "could that be an analogy of you and me? That when we are out we are both out, and when we are in we are both in."

I shook my head. "I have no idea of what you're talking about."

"There's a word you won't know," she continued. "Antiscian. Do you know what Antiscians are?"

I found myself shaking my head for a second time.

"Antiscians are people who live on the opposite side of the world from each other, whose shadows at noon are cast in opposite directions. That would be you and I."

I looked out over the expanse below us, the tourists milling to have their photographs taken with their heads pushed through the wooden cut-out faces of traditional Thai dancers; the locals buying incense and kneeling to pray, the sticks burning upwards in their pressed-together palms; both tourists and locals alike applying thin gold leaf to their foreheads. I touched the faint burr of gold on my own head, and then noticed Ava had a square of it intact like a discarded sweet wrapper.

"I never want to be on the opposite side of the world to you."

"Cheese!" She laughed, then her expression became serious. "We are often in opposite worlds," she said. She wouldn't expand on this when I pressed her, when I tickled her, when I brought it up again with a lump in my throat just after we had made love.

Following Ava's disappearance I found a recent translation of Franz Kafka's *Bullet* in a secondhand bookstore on Samsen Soi 2.

I wasn't sure what had drawn me inside. In truth, I was wandering aimlessly, the previous Ava-lost days had been spent in a haze of Mekong whisky and all-night bars; the multi-language babble of tourists soughing against my ears like the lap of the sea against the shore, or the mysterious rush of air within a shell.

Maybe I wanted to also lose myself, in fiction if not in fact; but I was drawn to the cover which pictured a bullet, standing on one end, it's tip red like the point of a lipstick. I realised then that the bullet/lipstick analogy was deliberate. Kafka's long lost novel was pulp crime noir and the image fit the contents perfectly. I picked it up, held the substance of the work in my hands, remembered – as I always do – that a writer had sat solitary in a room to create a fiction that was distributed worldwide. I believed there was an intimacy in fiction which didn't exist in other mediums: film, sculpture, even the fine arts. I resisted flicking through the pages and instead reached for my wallet and paid for it immediately. Returning to my wooden room in a small guesthouse on Samsen Soi 4 I lay back on the bed and read as the pages flickered with life beneath the slowly spinning ceiling fan above me.

I sucked on pistachio nut shells as I read, turning the pages slowly. I remembered reading in the Bangkok Post how Kafka's incomplete novel had been found in the possessions of his long-time friend Max Brod's great great granddaughter. The style was different from his other work, in terms of the actual telling of the story. However, the story itself, of how a private investigator known only as K investigates the murder of his girlfriend against the possible cover up of a slew of faceless government officials, was reminiscent of much of his existentialist writing; with frustrations, ennui, and misdirection at every corner.

And I couldn't help but feel, with the turn of each page, the procession of each word, that the book had been written with myself and Ava in mind; that we were – in fact – the main characters within the novel and that to finish it would reveal the circumstances of Ava's disappearance.

Because of this certainty, I read at an even pace. I didn't want our lives to end.

Ava had leant against the metal back of her chair at the guesthouse dining table, tipping it so that the front legs were at an angle off the floor. She ate chilli-cakes with one hand whilst navigating the large pages of the Australian newspaper, The Age, with the other. "Listen to this," she said. "They've discovered that there's an island in the South Pacific which doesn't exist, even though it appears on nautical maps. It says here *that the supposedly sizeable strip of land, named Sandy Island on Google maps, was positioned midway between Australia and French-governed New Caledonia. But when scientists from the University of Sydney went to the area, they found only the blue ocean of the Coral Sea. The phantom island has featured in publications for at least a decade.*" She looked over the newspaper at me. "How cool is that?"

"It's pretty cool," I said, thanking Mai as she brought over my toast.

Ava sat forwards, folding the newspaper in her lap. "Maybe we should go there."

Later, when she had returned to her room to shower and brush the taste of chilli-cakes out of her mouth, I picked up the paper and read further: *A spokesman from the service told the paper that while some map makers intentionally include phantom streets to prevent copyright infringements, that was not usually the case with nautical charts because it would reduce confidence in them.*

When Ava disappeared, I scoured the offices of Bangkok cartographers until I found one that admitted adding Samsen Soi 5.5 to a street map which he then promptly sold me for 200 baht. I returned with it to Khao San Road and opened it in front of me, as the regular hordes of tourists were regurgitated and absorbed into taxis and tuk-tuks and the swell of life pressed on regardless.

There was something else that Ava had said, something else that resonated within me as a possible source of her disappearance.

We had taken a tuk-tuk with a Dutch couple through the night-darkened streets of Bangkok, weaving in and out of cars, motorbikes, and buses; as though we were tiny fish in a massive ocean, swimming alongside tuna, wrasse, sharks, and the hulking dark shapes of whales. The Dutch couple – and, in truth, Ava – had spuriously wanted to visit the night markets at Patpong with the unstated intention of popping into one of the sex clubs that lined each side of the street. I had objected, after she had already made the arrangement, as we were pointlessly changing our clothes in our room before leaving.

"You're a prude," she laughed, reaching for my penis tucked in the soft material of my underpants.

"I'm no prude," I said, flipping around under her outstretched arm and pulling it behind her back whilst snaking the fingers of my other hand into the front of her knickers, "but I don't see any justification for perpetuating the profits of a dubious sex industry."

"You're just jealous," Ava said, snatching my hand out of her clothing, spinning around and bending my own arm up behind me. I couldn't see the reason behind her words, but as the pain bit and she didn't relent I laughed and agreed I was jealous until she let me go.

The jealously only manifested itself in the tuk-tuk when the Dutchman stole obvious glances at Ava's poorly-covered figure, at the swell of her tiny breasts, and the golden down on her legs. His partner sat beside him with an amused expression on her face, as though she had seen it all before and was content to be an observer.

We left the tuk-tuk and tipped the driver. He roared back into the street, the guttural engine noise an attractor for his next customers. The stalls were lit with bright white lights, their canopies also white, the goods beneath imitations of branded wares that some people paid a lot of money for back home. I suddenly felt sickened by it all, the ugly face of capitalism and the unnecessary want for products which were meaningless other than fashionable accessories. As we walked through the markets we were beckoned into the sex clubs with their lurid neon displays and promises of ping-pong shows. Eventually, at Ava's insistence, I found myself hustled into one of the establishments with the Dutch couple in tow. We found ourselves seated at a round table. The air-conditioning was freezing and Ava wrapped her arms around her chest whilst watching naked girls shake barely legal bodies at elderly businessmen. We were inside only two minutes before leaving our drinks behind and ejecting ourselves back into the dry night air. The Dutch couple had remained inside.

"That was awful," I said.

Ava nodded. "I was reading earlier that when last year's Japanese earthquake struck it shortened the day by two milliseconds. Surely that time can't be made back, so with all the earthquakes that have ever happened does that mean we are living in a different time?"

I shook my head. "What is it that you've been drinking."

She smiled: "I've been drinking life."

K turned up the collar of his jacket. The night hung in spiders' webs punctuated by the speckled lights of the city. He moved through the streets like wading through molasses, the black substance of the night clinging to him at every step, a resistant force keeping him away from the truth about his girl.

I lay the book spine upwards, pages spread down on the bed, like a suspect forced to lay outstretched on a floor. I glanced up at the ceiling fan, following one of it's blades as it circulated, then closed my eyes and opened them, realised the blade I had been following was indistinguishable from the others. Did it matter which of the blades I watched, which of the Ava's I attempted to find, which route I took: whether a genuine street from the map or the false street inserted by a copyright wary cartographer? Did it only matter if we were living in the same time and it was possible to still find her. Did it matter if I found her at all? Had she, in fact, existed, or was she a human island placed within a sea of people just to confuse the casual traveller?

I sucked on a pistachio shell, placed my tongue inside the concave interior, flipped it and felt the nub of the convex side press against my teeth. Biting hard, shards of shell splintered inside my mouth, cut my gums, and forced me choking towards a bottle of water.

I reached for the book again. There were but a handful of pages to finish.

K sits in the bar, watching one of the heavies crack walnuts in his bare hands. The other heavy's face looks like a walnut itself, a broken fairground mirror distortion of what a face should really resemble. He sees both of them notice him. They stand. Advance towards him.

K rises from his chair, backing away to the door that leads to the rear of the bar and thereafter into the street. Before he reaches the door, strong arms grab him from behind. He tries to turn but is thwarted. The identity of his captor remains a secret, for now.

I push the book into the back pocket of my jeans, shell the last few pistachio nuts and crush the kernels into a paste in my mouth, washed down with the last swig from the warm bottle of Mekong. When I leave the small room I don't lock the door behind me.

I take the steps downstairs two at a time, exit through the mosquito screen door, wave to Mai behind the till who is counting baht received from the next batch of travellers, and then turn right onto Samsen Soi 4.

The sun beats high directly in the sky above me. The back of my neck is scorched red and I consider returning for my baseball cap, but decide against it. This will be a day without returns. I emerge onto Samsen Road and walk beside pineapple and papaya sellers until I reach the entrance to Samsen Soi 5. I have the map in my hand. I glance up at the sign and then walk further along to Samsen Soi 6. There is no alleyway between the two soi's.

I run my finger along the map. The alleyway marked Samsen Soi 5.5 – the false alleyway – is equidistant between 5 and 6. I pace the distance, then return, halving it. With my back to the main road I face the concrete wall that separates a shop selling bicycle parts and a residential dwelling. I look at the map again, make sure of myself, and then with the hot whisky still coursing inside me I walk towards the wall.

K's girlfriend had her throat cut from ear to ear, a false bloody grin where her pearl necklace had hung. K knew theft wasn't the reason behind her murder. The missing necklace was misdirection for the real necessity for her to disappear. The search for her killer had been blocked by officialdom and paperwork. K had walked many empty corridors within dozens of bureaucratic offices to get to where he stood now, arms pinned by his sides, in front of the only man who could provide him with all the answers. It was obvious what had happened, now he thought clearly through all the clues: the misspelling of the route she had taken, the time of her murder that had been advanced to allow an alibi to be created, the positioning of two candlesticks on either side of the globe that was illuminated from the inside casting shadows about the room, the bullet which looked like a lipstick, the kiss of a fist.

K shook himself free from the arms of those who held him. He advanced towards the person behind the desk. Thumping one hand down onto the walnut surface he confronted his adversary. "I know," he shouted. "I know everything there is to know."

Franz Kafka's manuscript ends here. It bears no title. In conversation he used to refer to this book as his 'night novel', but I have called it Bullet *after the surname of the main character. Kafka never wrote the concluding chapter, and when I once asked how the novel was to end he regarded me contemptuously. The sole copy of the manuscript has the word 'I' replaced by 'K' on every page. There is no truth in the rumour that the uppercase* I *had broken on his typewriter and that he used the nearest equivalent.*

Ava returned from her unexpected trip to Chiang Mai with a thread of guilt running through her veins which – if pulled taut – would tie her in a knot from which there would be no escape. She shouldn't have allowed herself to be persuaded by the Dutchman, but then she was easily persuaded, open to suggestion. Sometimes it felt like her whole life had been written for her, but in a language she couldn't understand: as though in the babble of tongues of those trying to build the Tower of Babel.

When she returned to their room off Samsen Soi 4 she found it already occupied by other travellers. She asked Mai about him and was taken to a locker under the stairwell where his backpack, clothes, and other accessories had been stored. Amongst his possessions were the copy of Kafka's *The Castle* that he had been reading, together with an empty bottle of whisky with a slip of paper pushed inside the neck, and a newly-bought map which Ava didn't recognise with the alleyway Samsen Soi 5.5 circled with red lipstick.

Ava rented a room and examined his belongings. She pulled the piece of paper from the neck of the bottle, and rolled it flat on the bedside cabinet, holding each corner down with one of his possessions: his watch, the bottle itself, the map, and the book.

On the piece of paper a large heart had been drawn in the lipstick. In the top right hand corner of the heart his name had been written, in the bottom left hand corner of the heart her name had been written. An arrow punctuated the heart, dividing it in two: their names either side.

Ava ran a hand through her long blonde hair and absentmindedly picked up a pistachio nut and cracked it between her teeth.

Later that afternoon, armed with the book, the map, and a total uncertainty as to what she was doing, she left the guesthouse and counted the soi's that led off Samsen Road until she stood equidistant between Soi 5 and Soi 6. A crack ran along the wall between a residential dwelling and a bicycle shop. Ava stepped up to the wall and ran her fingers down the crack. Something had been pressed into it, something like flesh: dark and wet. She felt the mechanics of her heart stop.

Feeling self-conscious she pressed her ear to the crack in the wall. Maybe the sensation was simply similar to the false noise of hearing the sea through the whorl of a shell, but if she closed her mind against the traffic sounds and the incessant chatter of the Thai's on the street, Ava could have sworn that she heard breathing.

She stepped backwards, smartly, away from the wall and clutched her hand to her heart which had resumed its regular beat. Finding her way to Khao San Road she ordered a beer and opened his copy of *The Castle*. The novel was incomplete. She picked out a lipstick from her shoulder bag and began to write. There was unfinished business to settle.

❀

Very occasionally, story ideas arise from dreams. The ending to my story, "Beyond Each Blue Horizon", came at the denouement of a dream where I opened the curtains and found an entire city had been erased. Over the years, I've nicked bits and pieces of dreams for other stories, although I think it's important to ground them in reality and not simply – to paraphrase surrealist film director Luis Buñuel – to pad out the fiction. In this case, the thrust behind "Bullet" came specifically from a dream. I remember I was travelling in Thailand searching for someone I had lost. I believed I held a guidebook in my hand, but when I glanced down to see what I was holding I saw it was a copy of the novel "Bullet" by Franz Kafka.

Now, obviously, Kafka never wrote a book called "Bullet", but it crossed my mind what it might have been like if he had. That sense of altering reality that I got from the dream intrigued me, as did the search for someone. I put the idea to one side and waited for something else to happen (generally I get two ideas which mesh as one story) as it usually does.

Some time afterwards I read a news story about an island which has appeared on nautical maps for decades but which in fact doesn't exist. As part of the article it mentioned that some cartographers deliberately add false streets to maps in order to protect copyright (what a fantastic idea, that information can be falsified by those I would have thought are sticklers for precision!). Of course, putting together the dream, the false map, Kafka's missing novel – which acts as an indication that what we are reading might not actually be true – and the missing person suddenly drew the story tight like a drawstring. I had everything I needed: location, purpose, misdirection, and my favourite device, the unreliable narrator. Just how much we shape reality from our experience is something that has always interested me, how we seize on the familiar to try and understand the unfathomable. I guess this is the heart of the story, although it is open to several interpretations.

A Life In Plastic

Oki usually took his green tea quietly. At one of his favourite establishments they brewed it at the table. He would watch as the waitress put approximately three grams of loose green tea into a ceramic cup with a filter. He preferred the taste of *sencha*, and the waitress would stand quietly as the water she had boiled cooled for several minutes before pouring it over the loose leaves and covering it. Again, they would wait for a few minutes, depending on the newness of the tea, then she would remove the cover and the filter and place the cup in front of him.

He always admired the colour before inhaling the aroma, then taking a sip. The tea rolled over his tongue as he savoured the subtle scent of the sweet grass. He would nod at the waitress and she would return to her station, whilst he returned his gaze to the department store opposite.

There was a young girl who reminded him of his daughter that he sometimes saw window-dressing the mannequins. Today she wasn't there, or maybe it was too late. She usually performed her tasks early in the morning, often Thursdays. Oki decided not to wait too long. The store next door to the tearoom had been refurbished as a record shop, and it was their opening day. They were blasting music by Ayumi Hamasaki and if he watched carefully he could see the vibrations flutter the tea in the cup, individual ripples which touched the shore of his tongue.

He stood and beckoned the waitress over, dropping coins into her open palm. Then he left the establishment, glanced once in the direction of the record shop and swiftly crossed the road until he stood in front of the department store.

It was her work. That much was clear. There was a cleanness to her touch which was almost a trademark, yet it was often matched by a quirkiness that was decidedly kooky. In the traditional salaryman's suit facing Oki a yellow handkerchief had been folded into the breast pocket in such a way that the corners resembled petals. He placed one hand against the window, aware that he was soiling the sheen with his fingerprints. Then, sighing once, he placed his hand into his trouser pocket and turned back to the street. Hailing a taxi, Oki departed for work.

In his thirty-third year he had one child, a girl, Keiko, with a partner he hadn't intended to be serious with. The girl's parents had pressed for them to marry, but she had also known that their relationship wasn't fated to work and had resisted. Oki should have known then that her stubbornness was a sign of great strength, and in retrospect he should have pursued the relationship and made it honourable. As it was, he hadn't seen his daughter until her first birthday. From a distance. She took a step and fell into the arms of her mother.

Oki realised then that the woman was indeed a mother and therefore no longer and never would be his girl again. Even if they were reunited.

He sent a letter to his daughter's grandmother seeking permission into the child's life. With a gentle persistence the woman convinced her daughter that the child should be aware of her father. The first few meetings were tentative, then regular. When Keiko was six it was agreed that Oki might take her on a long weekend to Ōkunoshima.

The subsequent day the record shop had tempered its enthusiasm and Oki was able to enjoy his green tea in relative peace.

As he took his first sip the girl stepped into the window display, creating an association of the tea's sweet aroma with her presence. He watched as she unbuttoned the yellow handkerchief mannequin, slipping the jacket off its shoulders. Involuntarily, Oki shivered. He imagined his own jacket slipping from his body. As the girl folded it in two and placed it on top of a cardboard box she looked directly across the street. Oki held his gaze, sure she hadn't seen him. And even if she had, she wouldn't have understood that he was watching.

Some people were interested in speculating what might happen should a mannequin come alive, but for Oki the reverse was true. He wondered what it would be like to *be* the mannequin. He couldn't imagine his emotions any more distanced than they already were, yet would like to try.

The girl crouched and unzipped the mannequin's trousers, slid them down smooth white legs. Oki had seen a television programme which had shown how mannequins were produced. Many of them had detachable limbs and torsos. A large proportion of mannequins had the same legs and lower body, whether they were male or female. Only the face, fingers and breasts, or absence of breasts, were necessary to distinguish their gender.

Two months after he had first seen the girl who resembled Keiko in the department store window he purchased a mannequin for himself. It had taken another month for him to unpack it from the box.

Oki hadn't been sure what to expect, but imagined disappointment. The mannequin's structure was inflexible. There was some movement to be had from swivelling and positioning the limbs, but it was clear once the structure was complete that this wasn't what he was looking for. The mannequin might be immutable regarding its emotions, but even something emotionless needed a heart.

The task wasn't to recreate what he had seen in the privacy of his home, but to find himself thumping against the safety glass of the department store window as the girl he decided to call Keiko dressed him.

The day was crystal-bright. With Keiko's small hand in his they caught the Sanyō Shinkansen train to Mihara Station, then took the Kure Line local train to Tadanoumi Station. A smiling cartoon rabbit greeted them from a sign for the island and they walked the short distance to the terminal before catching the twelve-minute ferry to Ōkunoshima.

Oki had taken Keiko to the island because he didn't know where else to go. He wasn't used to being around children, few of his friends had married and those who had children tended to keep themselves to themselves. The island, with its over-zealous population of rabbits and numerous walking trails, seemed a good destination to bond with Keiko. So far their occasional meetings had established an uneasy camaraderie and Oki felt they needed something specific to themselves and devoid of maternal influence which they could reflect on in later life and identify as theirs and theirs alone.

Other than the rabbits and the walking trails the island held a dark history. From 1927 until 1945 it had been home to a chemical weapons facility that produced over six kilotons of both mustard and tear gas.

When Oki remembers it now – holding Keiko's hand as the ferry surged towards the island – he can no longer picture her face. She looks up at him blankly, the skin as featureless as a tan stocking spread over a mannequin. Her long black hair streaks away from the direction of the island as though in fear. It pains Oki that he cannot remember how she once was, that he has supplanted her face onto the face of Keiko the window-dresser and then aged it. Yet that is the only way he has been able to deal with the tragedy that unfolded.

Keiko squeaked at the sight of the rabbits. She chased them along the forecourt to the entrance of the hotel, their multiple bodies, from Oki's perspective, splitting into twos and threes, skittering into the undergrowth. Rabbits had been used in the chemical munitions plant to test the effectiveness of the weapons during World War II, however those rabbits had been killed when the buildings were demolished. According to official reports, the rabbits which now overran the island had no connection to those involved with the weapon tests.

Oki called out to Keiko and she returned her hand meekly into his. They checked into the hotel and Oki ran a bath as Keiko explored their room, emptying her backpack and placing the contents into a cabinet alongside her single bed.

Oki stood in the bathroom doorway, steam billowing behind him as though he were a monster stepping out of the mist. In that moment the privacy of the hotel room astounded him. Outside the four walls there might be no one in the world, but inside the cramped space he and his daughter quietly existed.

He had never felt more alone in his life.

Keiko had arranged two mannequins facing each other. One had an outstretched hand whilst the other, a gloved female, held her fingers close to the side of her face.

Oki stood with his back to the tea room, the street separating him and the department store. Cars were grid-locked. He imagined hoisting himself onto the roof of the nearest Daihatsu and stepping across the four lanes like a squirrel hopping across a stream on turtle backs. He watched with decreasing detachment as Keiko gently positioned the mannequins, her right hand held out ready to steady them if they tilted, her left hand smoothing down the clothes so they gave the appearance of a fit.

If his daughter were standing beside him he was sure she wouldn't see the connection between her and this older woman. True, he had extrapolated the years onto her, but she had already been created in Keiko's image and he considered he had simply found her rather than appropriated her. There was nothing sexual in his gaze, in his admiration of her slender form and the delicacy in which she performed her job, one she obviously loved.

If there was any emotion, it was that he was proud of her.

Oki crossed the street, placing his hands on car bonnets, feeling the heat from their engines. He stood directly in front of Keiko standing within the window display. She didn't notice him, simply continued with her task like an actress forgetting an audience, or – more simply – a worker focussed on the work in hand. If she were to acknowledge the window then she would fail in her task. For Keiko to succeed she had to imagine the window to be a blank black wall. This would explain why she failed to acknowledge him.

That evening Oki dug out the Swiss Army Knife he had retained from his camping days and began to peel back the hard plastic from the arm of his mannequin. It came away like shaved wood. On an unobtrusive part of his right shoulder, where the limb would be concealed by his office shirt, he glued the fragment of plastic to his skin.

Keiko soon found the speed of the rabbits detrimental to her enjoyment. The morning after her arrival she sat on the front steps of the hotel with her arms folded across her chest.

Oki remembered that she had asked for her mother.

Ōkunoshima had little – in retrospect – to pleasure a child. Even for an adult the six-hole golf course couldn't hold attention for more than a morning, and the Poison Gas Museum had limited appeal. One of the two rooms was devoted to donated artefacts from family members of the workers who had lived there. A display explained the inadequate conditions; how the gas would leak due to poor safety equipment. The second room held illustrations of how poison gas affects the human body through the lungs, eyes, skin and heart. Keiko looked at the images with scant understanding. In the afternoon they took one of the walking trails, passing the ruins of the gas manufacturing plant that were blackened and eyeless, their windows put out many years ago.

Oki spent some time examining the dilapidated building. Barriers were erected to prevent admission, but enough could be seen from the trail to imagine how life might have been. He considered the effects of war – not only on those who might be the recipients of a gas attack, but also on those who did the manufacturing. Sometimes his elder colleagues talked about war in terms which emphasised the immediacy of living a life constantly undermined by death, but Oki imagined it probably wasn't like that at all. In all likelihood, living in war would resemble being numbed. A desensitisation of emotion.

He began to wonder whether he would have liked to live in wartime, while Keiko ran after rabbits without any idea of what she might do should she catch one.

When Oki's colleagues mentioned how stiff he was looking at work, he held back a shrug and mentioned a recurring back problem.

In truth, the shards of plastic adhering to his skin restricted his movements. He had to be careful that none of them dislodged and fell through his shirtsleeves to the floor. That had happened on one occasion and he had quickly kicked the offending shard under his desk. That wasn't so easy now fifty percent of his legs were also covered in plastic, and even if the glue he had used recently was of greater strength there were no certainties to be had.

Even drinking his favourite green tea held difficulties. The regular waitress appeared to have noticed, as on two occasions concern had crossed her face and she almost broke the customer/staff relationship by querying his health. Oki had been touched, and for a moment regarded her as more than a waitress. In effect, they had been companions for some months and he wondered if that might extend to years. Whether he could court her. Whether she might become his wife. Whether they would have children. But then the memories of Keiko rushed back and he erased the future by closing his eyes.

All that remained were the tiny pricks of the edges of the plastic on his skin.

Oki wondered what he might have been should he have married Keiko's mother. He wondered about the life he didn't have.

At night, dissecting the mannequin, he began to consider that it possessed more of an identity than he did. It was no longer a factory-identical model. Oki had ordered a male, but the genitalia were smooth.

Now the gouges in its structure had come to resemble the scars invited by emotional distress; the invisibility of the soul made manifest on the visible body. Whereas Oki was transplanting those scars onto his form, both absolving and absorbing them. It was similar to a deletion of history.

For twenty minutes Oki had lost Keiko at Ōkunoshima. Transfixed by the shells of the buildings, he had turned his back on Keiko far longer than he should have. He didn't blame himself. He was not used to being around children. He should have realised that they had no fear, no conception of time, nor of their elders' concerns for them. Yet when he turned around and saw that she was missing, those abstract concepts of fear and time were riveted into the core of his being. As his fear increased so time slowed, as though he were forced to savour its intensity as a punishment for being remiss.

After those long minutes, when Keiko was returned to him by no more than a bend in the trail, squatting beside a rabbit hole and poking inside with a stick, Oki bent down and clutched her in his arms and vowed never to allow those circumstances to happen again.

The following morning they returned to the mainland. The wind was once again in the same direction, and Keiko's hair blew around her face from behind, revealing and hiding, revealing and hiding, until they reached the land and took a taxi to her mother's house where Oki formerly handed over his responsibility once and for all.

It might only have been two years ago but it was easier for Oki's conscience to imagine Keiko grown up and independent.

He needed to order another mannequin for parts. He had put on weight since first seeing Keiko in the window. Some of the plastic required buckling to make it fit. Unlike in phenotypic plasticity biology, where an organism has the ability to change its phenotype in responses to changes in the environment, Oki acknowledged his procedure was less natural. But that didn't mean it was any less effective.

On the morning before the substitution he stood directly before Keiko in the window. All of his body hidden by his clothes was covered by ill-fitting, often overlapping shards of plastic from his mannequin. None of this was evident from the outside. He simply resembled an almost forty-year-old undergoing a midlife crisis as he watched Keiko self-consciously dress the male mannequin in the display. He saw the curiosity in her eyes as she darted glances towards him, noticed her attempt to spy his reflection in the glass rather than view him directly, to try to understand – obliquely – where his attention fell. She wore a skirt that stopped just above her knees and Oki smiled at how beautiful Keiko had become. A human tear ran down from his right eye at the intervening years which had been lost. Yet it was a solitary tear, and he knew in his heart that if he had taken a greater place in Keiko's life, those tears would have been more damaging and more frequent.

He was about to leave when Keiko turned and stood still. Her limbs coalesced into a typical mannequin pose with almost fluid precision. For an instant she was perfect, and then her eyes dropped and her posture sagged. She forced a smile, then shrugged and exited the back of the display via the little door she needed to stoop through to use. After a moment a security guard poked his head through the same door, and after another moment Oki found himself sitting inside a taxi. He didn't look back to check if the guard had left the building, if he was standing outside the store.

That night Oki applied the last of the plastic to his face. He lay on his futon, eyes closed. He knew it would never happen, but he imagined breaking into the department store and replacing himself with the main male mannequin in the display. He watched as though from a distance, perhaps with the smell of green tea in his nostrils, as Keiko entered the display window and dressed him.

It was difficult to breathe.

Oki slipped into a fantasy whereby his subterfuge was evident and he was hauled from the display and thrown into a furnace. The heat melted the plastic until all that remained was his mouth as a blistered O.

Yet he had no illusions that this was an improbable ending, and that, in truth, when Keiko touched him, there would be nothing at all.

❁

This was one of the few occasions where the title changed after I had written the story. The original title, "The Plasticity of Identity", was taken from a review of another of my stories, "Drowning In Air", which appeared in Strange Tales IV. The reviewer being Peter Tennant of Black Static. As soon as I read the phrase I realised I wanted to write something with that title, but when Tartarus Press accepted the story for publication in Strange Tales V, they suggested I change it as it seemed a little clumsy. As it happens, "A Life In Plastic" is probably a clearer representation of what the story is about.

This piece is one of my Japanese stories, and is partly set on the island of Okunoshima, an island where Japan produced poison gas during the Second World War which has since become a haven for rabbits.

The plastic serves as a metaphor for the disconnect the main character has with emotion, particularly with regards to his estranged young daughter, but also with a preoccupation he finds with a window-dresser who resembles how he considers his daughter might look when she grows up. There is a gradual transformation of himself into a mannequin as the story progresses, as he decides to distance himself from his daughter after holidaying with her on Okunoshima.

Burning Daylight

We all get the injection on the same day. We're looking around the gym hall trying to impress. One line of girls, the other boys. The girls' line is the longest and hairs tingle on the back of my legs as I sense the competition. I'm in trunks; straight out of the swimming pool, just enough time to dry. Mason's in front of me and he's still wet. But then he never swims properly, just lies on the bottom of the pool and dreams, accumulating water.

"Today's the day," he told me, a grin on his face as we joined the line.

I shrugged. I was good at hiding my ignorance. My parents never spoke to me about puberty. I had been sick during the induction course and had missed most of it. My only information had been gleaned from half-heard conversations, nods, winks, and enquiries after the health of my father.

"Does it hurt," I wondered. The line had yet to move. We were waiting for Dr Thirst to arrive. Mason had said he knew he would be late. But Mason was my counterbalance: the amount I didn't know was weighed against the amount *he* didn't know but which he said he knew. Together, we were in perfect harmony.

I looked around the gym. The horse had been pushed to one side, the blue roll mats leant against one of the walls. The apparatus – such an intriguing word – was stacked at the far end of the room resembling a scrap metal yard. Both of the beams were now parallel like bars. All that was left was the plimsoll squeak of the polished wooden floor. The ropes were laced through the climbing bars.

I thought of the number of times I had raced around the gym, just one boy amongst the others, sweat pouring down my back, my muscles aching, as Sir played fish with the football, hurling it towards us as we leapt and dived out of the way. Until only one person was left. The person that was never me.

"Survival of the fittest," Sir had said, before one last fling at the boy remaining standing. He wasn't allowed to flinch: his reward being a surer shot than any of us had taken. "Of course," Sir said, "we all get hit in the end."

We shuffled as we waited, not used to staying still very long. The swim that morning had been intensive, and at the end we were hauled out of the pool. I remember swimming over Mason, glancing down as he lay on his back. He exhaled as my shadow touched him, and a bubble of air floated up and broke the surface rankly behind me. I felt the swell of it touch my legs.

Soft conversation fluttered around the air, like the hum of wings. The girls in line exchanged glances with several of the boys. Truth be told, there wasn't much to tell us apart. All rippling with muscle, tanned, steady on our feet. Even if I often felt the runt in the group I knew I could hold my own. Yet when it came to glancing at the line of girls I did so shiftily, not having the confidence to openly stare and leer.

Mason nudged me. "Coral fancies you." I pretended not to hear. The next time I looked up at Coral it was clear that she had just looked away.

Coral had blonde hair, blue eyes. Her skin eased over the confines of her bathing costume, which in itself shone with a pseudo-wet sheen. I liked Coral. I couldn't say I didn't. If she liked me then hopefully our futures might be sealed, but I knew in the rush of it that it wouldn't be easy. I'd overheard plenty of the boys say that sometimes you just had to take what you got, what you could catch.

A hush descended over the hall which echoed back at us. The gym door had opened and in squeaked Dr Thirst accompanied by the nurses. He pulled a small trolley behind him: a canister attached on two wheels. The teachers followed behind: Sir and Miss. Sir walked to the head of the boy's line and Miss stood at the front of the girls. They lowered their heads and automatically we followed suit. I could hear Dr Thirst positioning the equipment. Then there was a moment of silence. And then:

"May you be thankful for what is about to happen."

Dr Thirst's voice was thin, reedy. Mason said it sounded like someone had tried to strangle him once and had damaged his vocal chords so that they were more constricted than they should be. He showed me how a whistling noise could be made by slitting a hole in a blade of grass and then holding it between your palms whilst blowing through it. That's Dr Thirst's voice, he had said. And we laughed, although my laugh was tinged with a fear that I couldn't identify.

Dr Thirst continued: "Remember, all your exercise, especially your time as little naiads in the pool, has been focussed to bring you to this moment: the acceleration of your lives in the greatest experiment the world has ever known. You may find the transition curious, emotionally painful, even; but remember there are hoards of boys and girls outside of this school banging on the gates trying to get in. You are the privileged. Make no mistake of that. And in the following twenty-four hours you will know the truth of my words. May..." *and here I thought I could detect a slight smile in his voice* "...none of you forget that. It will be brief, fleeting. It will fly..." *another smile, surely* "...but it will be intense and it will be yours and it will be special."

We looked from one to the other, even across at the girls, our heads still bent. Had Coral's gaze just lingered on mine for a moment, or was I imagining it? In truth, I was a little tired. I had been awakened early for the swim. My parents had hovered over my bedside. I was aware of them before they woke me. They had been speaking in low susurrations. I thought my mother had been crying. When I opened my eyes I saw she was rearranging the books on my night stand. There were the high school staples: *Animal Farm, Brave New World, 1984,* and Kafka's *Metamorphosis* which I hadn't had time to read.

"Time to get up little one," said my father; with a trace of affection that I had never before heard.

"Today's the day!" My mother's voice wavered, undermining its intensity.

That phrase echoed throughout the morning, repeated by the other boys, Mason, and now Dr Thirst. "Today's the day," he almost chortled. "You could, in fact, make a case that *today* is the *only* day!"

Sir and Miss raised their heads, and as if with a hive mind we did the same. Their expressions were a mixture of excitement and sadness. Trepidation ran through me. I wished I hadn't missed those lessons, wished I felt a greater affinity to my parents so that I might have broached those difficult questions, wished I had the courage to ask the other boys to explain their couched insinuations and to expand on their innuendos. I wished I had done all that before, because it was a fact I couldn't do it now.

"Let the experiment begin," Dr Thirst announced rather theatrically. The two nurses, one male for the line of girls, one female for the line of boys – *did that suggest coercion?* – unwrapped rolls of white plastic perforated every couple of inches with tear-away strips containing needles for us tearaways with which they would administer the drug.

The injections proceeded like a military campaign. A boy/girl stepped up, their right arm was swabbed with alcohol on a spot between the elbow and the shoulder, the needle inserted and the syringe depressed, the minor bubble of blood wiped away with cotton wool, the boy/girl patted on the head and sent sideways to flank the hall as the next one of us was beckoned forward.

I estimated there were up to one hundred boys in the hall and at least one hundred and thirty girls. Yet the whole procedure couldn't have taken more than an hour. We were buzzing by the time the last few girls remained in the queue. I kept scratching the hole that I couldn't even see. A transformation was taking place, that was clear. I had a desperate need. And through that need, Coral appeared even more attractive than she had but a few minutes before.

After what seemed like an age the final girl stood against the gym wall. Dr Thirst tied a facemask behind his head and nodded to Sir and Miss and to the nurses. From their pockets they produced identical facemasks and attached them; Sir and Miss fumbling with some difficulty. It was clear they hadn't done this before.

I looked adjacent to Mason who was fairly hopping from one foot to the other. The more I watched him, the faster he seemed to go; until eventually all movement became a blur. I blinked, rapidly, but there was no effect. His legs were no longer visible, their speed fantastic. I shook my head to dislodge the thought but only succeeded in blurring everything in my vision. Bile rose to the back of my throat and I choked it down. Under the influence of the injection I realised I could hear Dr Thirst again, but unlike everything else which had speeded up his voice had slowed down. In fact, it was almost normal.

"Remember," he said, calm, but also with a detectable excitement, "this is what you have been bred for."

There was a *whoosh* and whatever was in the canister showered into the air. Gas or liquid I couldn't tell, but my vision clouded and I blinked – one two three times – before closing my eyes completely and inhaling the sweetest most intense sensation I had ever known.

Both my penises hardened.

If Sir or Miss or the nurses or Dr Thirst remained in the gym then I had no conception. We ran: the boys towards the girls, the girls towards the boys. All I saw were faces and teeth, hair and earlobes, bodies and legs, arms and feet, discarded swimsuits and membranous wings. We ran sporadically, flitting, flying, darting en masse, our brains hardwired for copulation. I held out for Coral, I swear I did, but the first gonopores I saw that laid open for me belonged to Martina and I dived in, my penises connecting like pistons in a finely oiled machine and we bucked and rode and came and separated and headed off yet again, the only certainty being the certainty that all life was contained in this day and to falter, to hesitate for a moment was suggestive that all might be lost.

Yet if this day *were* a day – and the movement of the sun across the upper windows of the gym suggested this was the case, as did Dr Thirst's pep talk and his constant megaphone shouts of *Hurry, hurry. You're burning daylight!* – then it was the longest day, the sweetest day, the most perfect day with a duration way beyond the twenty-four hours we had been promised. Mason had once said that at the point of death your entire life flashed before you, but this was the opposite: at the point of our birth, of our true birth, of our emergence from the swimming pool and as survivors of the fish, our future life fast-forwarded for us. In a flash. So that I knew when it was over I wouldn't be sure it had ever happened.

I copulated with Amanda and Tanya, I failed miserably with Julie – our parts didn't gel, I beat myself almost raw at the door of the gymnasium with a frightened yet entranced Miss trapped like a specimen on a microscope under glass unable to tear herself away from the utter intensity of my lust, and finally I coupled with Coral, her gonopores sore, almost withered, yet for me the most important of them all. Afterwards we lay sideways, our arms entwined in each other's, gazing idly at those still filled with the determination to further the species; until we, also, were stirred into action again, and flitted off, away from each other, into the gonopores and onto the penises of others.

Finally, after what seemed like a decade, all activity in the gym settled, the lights turned off, and I dozed and dreamt.

I graduated. Celebrated. Courted. Loved. Worked. Partied. Copulated. Married. Conceived. Copulated. Conceived. Raised. Celebrated. Travelled. Aged. Lost. Failed. Slid. Fell. Suffered. Gasped. Died.

I woke. Years had passed. Somehow I was no longer in the gym but by the swimming pool. At first I thought the surface was dark, but then I realised it was littered with bodies. Those of my classmates, some face down and unrecognisable, all naked. Bobbing between each, like the Styrofoam floats we had first used when learning to swim, were objects which I realised were eggs. The girls had deposited them on the surface of the water before collapsing into it themselves, no longer having the strength to fly.

My own time was near. I knew it. Yet I had had a good life. A long, pleasurably-filled existence. I had Dr Thirst to thank for that, and his two nurses and the hard manner of Sir and the soft concern of Miss. I had nothing to be ungrateful for. It was all as it should be: survival of our species, the thrust of evolution.

I lifted my head a final time, Coral staggered into view. She had always been a poor swimmer, like me. Maybe that was why I was drawn to her. As I watched she extruded eggs from her two oviducts as long packets, which adhered to each other as they were in the process of leaving her body. They wouldn't fall. I could sense the desperation in her body movements; but finally she tipped forwards into the water, her wings extended, and squeezed out the eggs as she died.

I'm sure I heard applause, from Dr Thirst, the nurses, and from Sir and Miss, as I began the final slip through the end of my world, a peeling away of my reality and a replacement of my consciousness with nothingness. It would be a lie to suggest I wasn't afraid; but at least I was satisfied. I could rest easy that our children had been laid. That the continuation of all I knew had begun. Our purpose fulfilled.

❀

Most of my fiction stems from the title, and rather embarrassingly I must confess the term *burning daylight* came from the TV show, "Dog The Bounty Hunter", where Dog – as usual – was trying to track down a bail jumper and time was running out. "C'mon, we're burning daylight here!" he shouted, as I scribbled down the title (I will point out I was watching this during a day job lunchtime and it was not a programme of choice!)

For a while I wasn't sure what kind of story it might relate to. "Burning Daylight" initially struck me as a potential vampire story, but I don't write many of those and it didn't appeal. So I began to think of the concept of burning daylight in Dog's context, that of wasting time. What wouldn't want to waste time? Something that didn't have much time. Like, for example, a mayfly.

In my story the main characters might quite simply be mayflies in a human context or humans in a mayfly context. Either way, the pulse is for procreation at a fantastic rate!

Making Friends With Fold-Out Flaps

All the best fairytales begin back to front. They start with a death, usually parental, and end with a birth; if not a physical birth, then a re-birth either through marriage or the sloughing off of past evils. That's how all the best fairytales start.

My mother said that when I was born there was a plague of rain. The drops hitting the glass windows of the hospital like locusts. She was eight floors up and could only see the sky and the silhouette of my father standing against the window. He had looked away, was watching the rain intently, with passion.

She said this: "Have you never seen rain before?"

She wasn't sufficiently dilated for me to arrive, but even so it irked her that the outside world seemed more important than the miracle that was about to take place in the room.

Of course, there are two sides to each story, sometimes more. My father told me he had gone to the window to close the curtains, to keep the outside world out and to reduce the moment of my birth succinctly within the four walls of the room. That he might have waited awhile to watch the rain was simply part of the process. He told me he wondered if it would still be raining as I was born. Whether some of the drops that left the clouds would do so before I arrived and then hit the ground after I was here. He wondered whether I might be born within the time it took for that to happen. Within the life and death of a raindrop.

These disparities in the story, from seemingly reliable narrators, just indicate how difficult it is to cut away all the bullshit to get at the truth. We distort memory and then believe it. Or we deliberately conceal it.

Gavin used to say I was an obsessive perfectionist. I would argue that I just sought the truth. Truth itself is perfection: unsullied by lies. I don't care what the truth is, but I want to hear it. Regardless if it hurts. If I were a perfectionist then it was to get at the truth. We had these arguments that rolled around into themselves until we'd get lost and have to fight our way out. They were theoretical arguments, most of the time. It was when they weren't that the relationship began to break down.

Maybe it was the oft-told story of my father's silhouette, but I became intrigued by the word and latterly by the subject. When I was a young child I would buy magazines where you could cut out figures of girls and then dress them in a selection of paper clothing, with tiny flaps appended to each garment that could fold around the shoulders or ankles of the figures. Perhaps it was testament to my later artistic nature or simply a bit weird, but I would use these templates and transfer the shapes to black card; dressing each black silhouette in black silhouetted clothes. Whilst some see the colour black as a colour of concealment, I saw it as truth. Black is black, no arguments. Accepting, of course, that black is a colour.

My parents were open to my behaviour, although nowadays I'm sure a child psychiatrist would be considered appropriate. Yet with their help I succeeded. My memory has lost the truth of the exact date, but sometime during the 14th June to 29th August 1972 I visited the National Portrait Gallery's *Exhibition of Silhouettes* and once there became beguiled by the shadow portraits of those famous before the popularisation of photography, immortalised by artists such as Beardsley or Nicholson, Dulac or Gill. I loved discovering that the word silhouette itself was derived from Etienne de Silhouette, an eighteenth century French finance minister who amused himself by cutting profiles from black paper. Holding my father's hand I moved from image to image, transfixed by simplicity, by honesty, by truth.

There is no need to embellish a silhouette, no artist's concerns of *getting the light right*. It is, to put it simply, black and white.

Maybe I embraced punk for the same ideals. That embodiment of truth. A few years after the exhibition, once I had become a terrible teenager, I produced a school fanzine which through financial necessity had to be monochrome. At the same time, the striking cover image for The Stranglers' *Black and White* album resembled a silhouette. I was always struck by the position of Hugh Cornwell, whose downturned posture made it appear he were headless. I left school and entered art college. If it wasn't for the complexity of relationships I imagine I would still be sane.

The bonus with silhouettes is that they are one-dimensional. But people aren't. The truth embodied in a silhouette is lacking from that in a person. With them, it's not so much about the surface, it's about the things people keep hidden: their thoughts, their repressed desires, their understandings, their internal organs. To get at the real person you have to undress them, utterly. I could equate this to locating the kernel within a fruit or a nut, or a grain or seed as of a cereal grass enclosed in a husk. Or – to use the computing definition of the word – the kernel is the main component of most computer operating systems; it is a bridge between applications and the actual data processing done at the hardware level. The kernel can provide the lowest-level abstraction layer for the resources that application software must control to perform its function. It was the lowest level that I was interested in.

"I don't like my body any more because it reminds me of you."

Gavin looked up; looked *at* me over his glasses. I used to find this appealing, now it was irritating. "What's that supposed to mean Hilary?"

We were sitting outside under a summer sun, around a circular metal table with two beers warmed from the bottom upwards. I had just exhaled an extremely long pent up puff of smoke.

I sucked on the cigarette again. "You're all over me. Forensics would find your fingerprints everywhere."

He closed his eyes. "Can't we talk about this another time?"

"Displacement activity," I said. I drank some beer. It wasn't refreshing, beer never is. I ran my tongue around my teeth. "We've lost it."

He placed the catalogue to Gunther Van Hagen's *Bodyworlds* exhibition on the table. "What's that supposed to mean?"

I took the catalogue, quickly rubbed off the slightly sticky residue of beer which had pooled near the spine. "This is Frank's, you should take good care of it."

Gavin shrugged. "We should take good care of each other."

I drank more beer. Gavin didn't know I knew about Teresa.

It was August 2002. We had spent the past five years living together in a tiny rented apartment close to Brick Lane. We hadn't a lot of money so we'd had to save for several months to pay the entrance fare to the exhibit. Frank had let us borrow his catalogue. In some museums it felt like the catalogues were more expensive than the exhibits.

I had graduated from silhouettes just before I was due to join St Martins College of the Arts. As a leaving present my mother bought me a copy of *Gray's Anatomy*. "You'll be needing this," she said.

Henry Gray almost post-dates the period from 1770 to 1860 when silhouettes were popular, but only by a few years. He died from smallpox at the age of 34 in 1861, and the first issue of *Anatomy* had been published only a few years earlier in 1858. For me, the addition of colour to black and white drawings was where the lies began. The colour put flesh on the bones.

Still, it was fascinating. The difference between smooth outer skin and the mess of internal organs kept me occupied artistically for many a year. There were obvious discrepancies between what is seen to be a person and what they really are. My first exhibit was a selection of paintings using clothing catalogues as a guide. The paintings were triptychs. On the left hand panel I pasted a cut-out from the catalogue (I tended to use the lingerie pages to be more salacious, something I would learn to regret), and in the right hand panel would be a representation of the same figure, but posed without skin. The central panel was the equivalent silhouette.

Critics discussed whether the panels should be read from left to right or from right to left.

It clearly shows how we live clothed, pass through the silhouette of death, and emerge as visceral bodies, ran one review.

Hilary Parsons shows how we are born in flesh, become transmuted by the template of society, and emerge as potential fashion models, ran another.

But all I was doing was mixing things up, making things different. I had no agenda. I just liked what I saw.

Gavin was at that first exhibition. Or so he told me later. Of course, I believed him, but after a while I wasn't sure of the truth.

Some people say you can only trust someone once you know them completely, yet from experience I would say you can only distrust someone once you know them completely. If you start from the position of trust, you then have to work your way through to the kernel of truth.

Trusting someone and knowing the truth are two separate things.

When we finally made it inside the *Bodyworlds* exhibition I was blown away. Gunther van Hagens' process of plastination made utter sense. To use a much maligned artist's phrase, *it spoke to me*. I regarded the horseback figure, the gentleman playing chess with his brain on view, the woman carrying the foetus with utter fascination. If only I were clever enough, or moneyed enough, to have a plastination company of my own. Van Hagens knew people. He knew the truth. And however much he might refute it, quite plainly it was art. The most beautiful art I have ever seen.

As we moved from exhibit to exhibit I examined the hard kernel of truth about Gavin that had been revealed to me by Frank. I transmuted the figures in the displays with images of his eviscerated body. What would Gavin look like as a mass of red arteries, repeatedly branching into smaller and smaller vessels reaching every extremity? How would his muscles appear with the skin stripped away from them? How would he appear with all the water and fats removed from his body and replaced with plastics? That was something I wanted to see.

After a while I had lost interest in *Gray's Anatomy*. I wanted something alive. I was considering moving from painting and collage to sculpture. I needed the semblance of life, if not life itself. When Gavin made himself known to me it seemed an opportune moment for life studies. My parents thought he pulled me out of books and into the real world. I supposed I agreed with them, but it was only in retrospect that I realised it wasn't what I had wanted.

Some people equate the *real world* as different from a *fantasy world*. But both accumulate the same lies as each other. It makes no difference if one member of a couple lives in the real world and the other in the fantasy world, or the other way around, or both in the real world or both in the fantasy world. Lies clothe the truth in every instance. Even myself, I am but a multi-coloured coat of untruths. I shake my body like the boughs of a tree and lies fall from me like leaves. Yet new ones grow all the time.

Life studies with Gavin were intense, vigorous. He admired my *enthusiasm*. Truth was I hadn't fucked anyone before and he showed me how. I became the depository, suppository for his definition of what a woman should be and should do. I can't say I was innocent, I can't claim to have been defrauded, but I abused myself chameleon fashion in order to please him. The love that I had thus mutated me from Hilary Parsons to Hilary Swainthorpe. If I had looked closely, if I had admitted the truth at the time, I would have dissected the a, t, h, o, r and p from that surname and discerned the truth so much earlier.

To use modern analogy, people aren't flat screens. And whilst they project personalities like the multitudinous lies that emanate from television sets, there is always more – much more – beneath the surface.

Gavin bought me my first anatomical flap book. They actually predate *Gray's Anatomy*, some dating back to the 16th Century. Quite simply these illustrated scientific guides took their name from the moveable paper flaps that can be lifted to reveal hidden anatomy underneath. Perhaps more so than *Gray's Anatomy*, which presented body parts simply as they were, the *revealing* aspect of the flap books touched an aspect of me which took delight in exposing the hidden.

I created two more exhibits using the flap books as a jumping off point. By necessity, these were interactive; something that appalled my agent and promoter. *How can we keep them from becoming damaged before they are sold?* I had to compromise – another idea of Gavin's – by creating originals in glass cases which were accompanied by miniatures the general public could play with. The first exhibit was simple: lift the silhouette to find a naked body beneath, then lift the flesh to find the organs, then lift the organs to find the hidden organs, and so on, until the final flap was lifted and you were returned to the silhouette.

This exhibit garnered moderate success, although not as much as my triptychs. The following year, however, came the work cumulatively titled *Making Friends With Fold-Out Flaps*, which essentially was the same idea but with the exposed cadavers beneath the smiling cartoonish characters of children's books. My promotional idea of inserting some of these innocently into public libraries caused an outrage and made front page headlines in the *Daily Mail* and those other rags. The originals sold for record prices. I buried my smirk beneath smiles.

Maybe it was then, during that brief flurry of money, that Gavin – who had appointed himself as organiser of our financial affairs; we had recently become married after all – began his twelve year affair with Teresa; an art student with such a blank canvas that only her body could guarantee her success. As for the exact date, I imagine that will never be known.

Frank told me as he slid the catalogue of the *Bodyworlds* exhibition across to me from the other side of the sofa.

"I know you've been intending to go to this," he said. "Do you want to borrow my catalogue?"

I almost snatched it from the purple material that it had begun to sink into.

"Do I?" It was hard to keep excitement out of my voice, even though I was getting too old for that. From silhouettes, to catalogue poses, to static anatomical drawings, to pop ups: the only logical step was to create works in the flesh. Damien Hirst had beaten me to it, of course. But even he had failed to see the inherent truth that could be exposed in such works. He hadn't stripped back far enough. His sharks and his cows remained what they were. They failed to transcend their corporeality. I felt they were no more than sideshow exhibits for a world which suddenly viewed Victorian values as a cultish anachronism. As an aside, the obsession with steampunk disgusted me. What I wanted was *real* punk.

In 2011 Gavin came into some money. I hadn't made much from my art for a while, Hilary Swainthorpe was long forgotten about. I had been making plans to leave Gavin for almost ten years, but had become debilitated by a fear of becoming emotionally crippled. This is what lies will do to you. They will cloak your fears until you only see the cloak and no longer the fear. But you need to see the fear in order to face it. You need understand the fear of the known.

By that time his relationship with Teresa was ever more obvious. I had met her several times. We'd had an awkward moment at her fifth gallery exhibit where an excess of free red wine had led me to acutely declare my utter contempt for her artwork which I said *bastardised love and vicariously emphasised the parasitic nature of humanity*. It was obvious to those present that I was referring to the artist herself, their affair was a known secret, an open deceit which was only not revealed in full because of a tacit agreement to withhold the truth.

I had a feeling that without the shreds of my own finances to cling onto that Gavin would finally abandon me, so I persuaded him to give me a birthday present which I knew he would see as a final send-off, an assuaging of his guilt. So in July of that year we travelled to Durham in North Carolina in the good old U S of A, and attended *Animated Anatomies: The Human Body in Anatomical Texts from the 16th to 21st Centuries* in the Perkins Gallery at Duke University. My exquisite relationship with the flap books was complete.

"Given today's technology, these are so outdated," yawned Gavin. I watched him repeatedly check his mobile phone.

"It's about going back," I said, "to a time where everything was only begun to be known. The truth is that nowadays we believe we know everything, whereas the truth is that we don't know the truth."

"You always talk in riddles."

"Conversely, you never have anything interesting to say."

The barb made him look at me askance, but he quickly composed himself. It was then – and only then – that I knew I was going to do it.

The curator of *Animated Anatomies* was an interesting woman called Valeria Finucci. She held my attention through a short presentation. Something that no one had been able to do for some time. She was pleasant looking with a cream jacket over a brown blouse. Her hair colour matched her top. I realised she was probably my age, edging fifty. She was exactly the type of woman who was so intelligent and normal that Gavin would have found her unattractive.

I found myself doodling. And then I transcribed her words beside the doodle. She showed me something.

"Flap books illustrate bodies immersed in the intellectual, aesthetic, technological, philosophical, gendered, even religious culture of the time in which they were produced. In the interchange between the doctor/anatomist and the illustrator/technician, the body parts that emerge acquire a life, and a beauty, of their own."

She was right. It was the relationship between the artist and the subject which needed to be dissected to find the truth.

On the plane home I couldn't help smiling at Gavin. If he felt any concern, he didn't show it. Maybe because at that stage I had learnt from him so well and had become such a consummate liar.

My final exhibit will attract more than casual interest, more than scattered applause. I've yet to decide how to show it. I haven't had an agent for the last five years – there being so little to be agented. Gavin had arranged a few minor showings – retrospectives they called them – of what remained of my earlier work. But the shock value had gone. The interest was benign. Art is of its time and my latest piece isn't hypocritical, it's hyper-critical. It perfectly represents the age we are living in – the age *I* am living in – yet at the same time absolutely encapsulates the everlasting lie of human existence, both the universal and the personal.

You see, all the artifice of life is but clothing to mask the surety of our deaths. Everything we do, all our routines, our faults, successes and failings, our society deep in its heart, is nothing more than a camouflage distracting us from our future non-existence. That is the truth we all have to share. That ultimately we are nothing.

I have done my best to embalm Gavin's body; although it's rudimentary, I must admit. This won't be a permanent exhibit. I have painted each and every one of his internal organs black. He lies within the coffin like a silhouette. If you lift up each flap I have cut into his flesh, then you see only blackness beneath. You reveal the blackness, over and over again, including the blackness of his heart. And it is there that you find the simple truth of it.

❀

Another story where the title came first and dictated the piece. In this case, my youngest child had a board book titled *Making Friends* and the selling point of the title was the sticker *With Fold-Out Flaps*. Running these phrases together provided a totally different connotation. In addition to this, I'd picked up a copy of the National Portrait Gallery's *Exhibition of Silhouettes* at a jumble sale and had been thinking of writing a story about silhouettes for some time. Somehow these ideas conjoined perfectly.

The Frequency Of Existence

The aim of every artist is to arrest motion, which is life... and hold it fixed so that 100 years later, when a stranger looks at it, it moves again – William Faulkner

When Valerie was into *reiki* she was hands on all the time. It was a fad. Something she only took seriously for so long as it took to bore her. Unlike *my* personal interests, which were permanent, embedded, Valerie only did things by halves.

I once asked her why she had such an old name for such a young girl.

"The young eventually become old," she said. "One day it won't seem so odd."

She was right. In the far-flung future all the Brianna's, Kaylee's, Brooklyn's and Khloe's would be great-grandmothers and trends would spin and turn and the youngsters would all be Valerie's again.

But generational variations hadn't been the focus behind the derivation of her name. Her mother had been fascinated by Valerie Solanas, the radical feminist journalist who had attempted to assassinate Andy Warhol convinced that he might steal her work. Valerie's own mother was in the feminist movement and she saw Solanas' arrest as an indictment of male dominance. Herself a painter, thereafter she exhibited carbon copies of Warhol's work with large X's painted over them, negating the image. Unlike Warhol, she remained in obscurity. Upon her death, no traces of those works were even found.

Valerie herself – *my* Valerie – drifted from unsuccessful project to unsuccessful project. Unlike my parents, who had been solid working class types and had instilled in me a work ethic that took decades to shift, Valerie's flibbertigibbet mother forced her into dissatisfaction with everything. Not quite a nihilist, all her ambitions were fated to be thwarted by men. Including me. Not that I had much to do with it. Although on occasion she considered me wholly responsible for my sex.

I had been interested in photography before Valerie, afterwards I became obsessed with it. She found me one day with my back on the park grass, my camera skywards, photographing clouds. With my eye attached to the viewfinder her head loomed into view. Short fringe, long at the sides, her brown hair was a bob-cut grown out. She had dyed it black, her eye-lids Kohl reflectors, her lips unpainted. I thought her clownish, she considered it cool.

"Why are you photographing the sky?"

I put the camera down, shifted onto my side and leant on one elbow, grass blades began to dig into my skin and would leave me with curious tribal-like markings.

I had been tempted to say, *because it's there*. But considering this strange girl had deigned to talk to me at all I found myself honest. "We don't look upwards enough. I'm capturing what most of us miss."

She lay down on the grass beside me, her medium-length skirt riding halfway up her thighs. "It's a miracle up there," she said. "We view it, we pretend to understand it, but the sky isn't even blue. It's just that molecules in the air scatter blue light from the sun more than they scatter red light. Simple."

I glanced over to her rucksack that rested beside her. Its white shape was covered in song lyrics, bits of poetry, and what I recognised to be parts of Gregor Mendel's Laws of Segregation and Independent Assortment. It was then that I knew I hoped to like her, whatever the cost.

There was no doubt there would be a cost.

"It's all up there," I said, understanding that I would soon fall into cliché and she might up and leave.

Instead she closed her eyes and I seized the moment.

"What are you looking at now?"

"I'm looking at me," she said. "Me from the inside out."

Later we shared a Hawaiian pizza and a bottle of Shop's Own coke. Television flickered in those days. Digital was a thing of the future. My camera contained film that needed to be developed, but I had plenty I had prepared earlier. Moving the pizza box onto the floor and insisting we wash our hands we returned to the sofa and I showed her my flicker books.

At first she laughed. Then her expression became serious. She fast-flipped the cards through her fingertips – I noticed the ends of her nails were bitten to the quick – watching the clouds scud intermittently across the sky. She repeated the movement: once, twice, four, eight, sixteen, thirty-two times until I had to ask her to stop. My head couldn't take the repetition. Once, strobe lighting had brought on an epileptic fit. My flicker books had the intent of taking me to the edge but never over it. Valerie brought the edge closer.

When I was a child a practice went around our school of inducing a faint. Mark told me the process: "It's simple. You get out of a hot bath and crouch in the steam on the floor. Take ten deep breaths and then hold it. Suddenly stand. You'll see the lights, all kaleidoscopic. Cold sweat will break out on your forehead. If you're lucky, you'll fall over. Everyone's doing it."

He was right. They all were. I cracked my skull on the side of the toilet basin and was never the same again.

Valerie looked at me, expectantly.

"If you take the motion out of existence what do you have?" I asked. "And if you try to put it back again, then what? That's what my work is about."

I don't know if she really got it, but she said she did. "Photo me," she insisted. "Break me down."

I shook my head, but she was serious. Later she said that what I captured in my photographs was exactly what she had been striving for in her paintings. But I'd seen those paintings and they certainly didn't have the clarity of photographs. They didn't have much to them at all.

She walked back and forth, like a tiger in a cage, wearing a groove in my deep pile carpet that reformed afterwards like a meadow after rain. I took photo after photo, believing them to be wasted, knowing I was only doing so in the hope of getting her into bed. But she left early and I was left with a bag of half-eaten dry roasted peanuts, *Omnibus* on the telly, and camera film pregnant with her image. I developed it myself at college the next day, flicked through her movements, watched her advance towards me and then away. Jerky movements, like that of a puppet, or as though I had watched her whilst repeatedly blinking. She mapped the frequency of her existence. Yet it was within the interstices, those pauses between each click of the camera, where she wasn't actually there at all that eventually defined her for me.

For a while I didn't see her. We had exchanged numbers but whenever I rang her flatmate insisted she was out. After a while, I realised the accumulation of time spent talking to the flatmate was greater than the amount of conversation I'd had with Valerie that extended day in the park. It was just as I put her absence down to deliberate avoidance and decided to move on that I saw her again.

I was at a *Portishead* gig. The music wafting over me subliminally whilst my mind found itself elsewhere. Whilst not strobing, the stage lights had enough of a flicker about them to emulate that effect in a range of primary colours. As though she were formed from them, Valerie advanced out of the mostly-stoned crowd towards me, her movements mirroring those in the photographs I had repeatedly looked through until their edges had furred. She spoke, but her words were borne away, absorbed into the music. When she leant in closer I smelt alcohol on hot breath. Her lips brushed my ear, patterned goosebumps down the entirety of my right side from my shoulder to my leg: *Let's get out of here.*

We leant against the side of the building. She had bummed a smoke off the security guard and had taken a few drags before offering it to me. I had declined. She flicked the ash scattershot, the embers curling away into the dark like miniature fireworks. For a while she was distracted, looking out into the night before glancing towards me and then away. I realised she expected me to speak.

"So," I said, "what have you been doing?"

She pulled me into a kiss, the cigarette leaving an iron taste on my tongue. "Thinking of you, idiot."

I could have mentioned the many times I had called, yet they seemed irrelevant now. The time between our first meeting had telescoped to this moment, as though it were but an extension of the same day. As though we had been flicked through, jerked forwards in time.

She returned to leaning against the wall. "You need to look at my paintings. Did you develop those photos?"

"The ones of you?"

She nodded.

"I might have."

She smiled. "Of course you did. C'mon, let's have a look then."

The cinematic Lynchian music of *Portishead* diminished further as we walked farther away from the building, until it deteriorated into tinny reverberations and finally winked out altogether.

There are many times now past when I wished I had stayed and got my money's worth at the gig. That loss wasn't the only price I paid.

She drank milk straight from the bottle until it dribbled down the sides of her mouth and ran in rivulets over her chin. At any other time it would have been a turn off, but with Valerie it oozed the erotic. Moments seen in her once, but never since.

We had returned to mine, got the photographs, and headed over to hers. I didn't actually know the address, yet it turned out she lived only a few streets away. "If I'd known this, I would have dropped by," I said.

She ignored me. Flicked through herself, fascinated by the semblance of movement. "I read a short story once," she said, "about a girl who might not have been there. Her name was Annie May Tedd. Animated. Get it?" She reeled off the name of the piece, but I had to admit I had never heard of the author. "This reminds me of that story."

"Are you really there?" I joked.

In answer she showed me her paintings, tried to convince me her works on canvas matched my efforts on celluloid. I made all the right noises, but without bigging up my art we both knew I had it and she didn't. On another visit I believed I saw coloured scraps of canvas amongst the black ashes in the fireplace. I certainly never saw the paintings again.

She moved onto photography. A bad move. Then onto sculpture, music, fiction. Whilst the potential was there, the impetus was short-lived. I could see her impatience seeping into our relationship, and as a result found myself holding back emotionally each and every time we reached a place of no return. So we never got to that place, and always we returned. Sometimes I wonder what we might have found there.

She encouraged me to photograph her frequently; put herself in the picture, so to speak. If she couldn't be the artist then she must be the model. I was reminded of her namesake, Valerie Solanas, afraid that she would be coveted, yet needing acclaim all the same. Even when one's authority over their art is 100% retained, the very act of sharing it with an audience transforms its ownership. At some point, you have to learn to let go.

I photographed her removing her clothes, stripping from all to nothing; I photographed her dancing, running for a bus, mesmerised by how her features were always different yet always the same. I photographed her advancing at me with a knife, a staccato *Psycho* scene. I once set up the camera on a tripod and took repeated images of us making love by pressing a rubber bulb, yet the pull of the mechanism had altered the angle and when the images were developed they depicted only a wooden headboard over which shadows merged and reformed on a dirty white wall. It was my best work.

When her flatmate left Norwich for Manchester, Valerie suggested I move in with her. She saw the hesitation before I acknowledged it myself.

"That's it then."

"Sorry."

"I said, *that's it then.*"

I noticed she had curled her fists in anger.

"You're kidding, right?"

A day later she laughed it off. That was when she knocked on my door, falling into my room with an armful of reiki books spilling out of her grasp. "Sorry about yesterday," she said, plonking herself down on my sofa and carelessly scattering some photographs I had been arranging in flicker book order. "I was stressed. Now I'm in tune with my inner self."

I found it hard to believe someone could master the art of alternative medicine to heal all their psychoses so quickly, but I didn't say that. Instead I said, "Apology accepted. Mine offered too. It's just that I'm so settled here..." but she was no longer listening. She sat flicking through the books as though she could absorb their information that quickly, gleaning all the important details whilst bypassing the inessentials. The comparison with my self-made flicker books was evident.

"Did you know that the word *reiki* derives from a Japanese word meaning *mysterious atmosphere*, which in turn derives from a Chinese word meaning *supernatural influence*? I'm drawn to that."

I was convinced she had only just read the statement, yet for the remainder of the afternoon it was her mantra, as though she had studied the meaning in those words since she had first been named after Valerie Solanas.

She experimented on me. Eased the pain I had in my back that came and went, so that instead it went and came. Relieved the headaches that I previously had around her. I admit that I never complained at the touch. As boyfriend/girlfriend we had been more off

118

than on. Now that all her tactility was multi-purposed she stopped the echo of her mother's feminist rants, evolved from needing the upper hand, and refrained from claiming I treated her as a piece of meat every time I reached out to hold her. Momentarily, reiki or not, we became attuned to each other. With her skin on mine I fell into reverie, glimpsed the passing of clouds beyond my closed eyelids, watched shadows create and uncreate in the corners of every room.

I began to measure my existence as moments spent with Valerie. The longer we were together, the more tangible I felt. When we were separated, I found myself slipping away.

Yet this was just a state of mind that I fostered as an artistic fallacy. It *suited* me to have that belief, to endow myself with that *mysterious atmosphere*. In truth, when I wasn't with Valerie I was continuing to prepare my portfolio for my final year art show. In retrospect, I can't believe I was so stupid, but youth has much to answer for. Just as age does not hold the answers and simply raises the idiotic repeat of why why why.

Pinning my flicker books to the temporary white plasterboard in the art school hall I edged the uncertainty from my head in the belief that I had remained true to my art, hadn't compromised.

On opening night, a glass of red swirling in a shaking hand, Valerie didn't see it the same way.

"Perhaps I haven't been entirely honest." I tried to duck out of her vision, but her gaze held me imprisoned like laser beams. She flicked through the books of other girls: both those before and after her. Not indecent, nor girlfriends, the majority were other artists whose bodily forms and manifestations of their own work surrounded her. Yet I had somehow broken an unstated condition that she was the singularity, both the instigator and the perpetrator at the heart of my show. Instead she realised she was one of many, at least, artistically. No one was to blame, just hypocrisy. She turned on one heel and I never saw her again.

Thirty years later her twisted expression haunts me.

It was as though her lipstick had been applied against the grain, forcing a grimace unnatural yet anticipated, a red bruise darkened by wine.

It wasn't that she didn't return my calls. But I didn't call. The inertia of failure mimicked the interstices between the photos in the flicker books, the moments of inaction, the frequency of non-existence. I was afraid. Should I contact her she would demand explanation, or even worse she wouldn't. I was hampered because I believed there was nothing to explain. I had blindly, assuredly, shuttered her out; placing my art first, blinkering myself to the consequences. In retrospect, regardless of her flaws, she had given me her honesty. It is that honesty which I now seek in my work.

Valerie has been and gone, a flicker in the past. Since then other girls have shadowed the peripheries of my vision, one begat me children and then left with them, another put up with me for as long as she could before abandoning me to my art. Now I spend my days in a run-down flat whose rear window faces the ongoing traffic on the M1. A simple motion detector ensures my photographs are taken for me, as I lay on my bed, half-naked, listening to the almost-noiseless digital camera capture headshots of the near-side passengers in the cars that bat along the tarmac.

The cars themselves are the flicker books. We are all digital now. I don't develop the photographs. At a certain point during the day the sun catches the light from the car windscreens and flashes it brilliant against my ceiling. I count the instances: once, twice, four, eight, sixteen, thirty-two times until I can feel my epilepsy that has lain dormant for so long start to come into focus and I find myself jerking on the bed like a shock treatment patient.

And as the cars increase their frequency, I find they increase my existence and anchor me to reality. When I do eventually stir, scratch myself, pick up a discarded t-shirt from the floor, and make my way across to the camera as the sun descends I understand that unlike Valerie Solanas *my* Valerie succeeded in killing her artist, regained the integrity of her work. However talentless she might have been. However much she viewed herself from the inside out.

In the blackness of the night, the digital screen images are hyper-real. Yet they remain representations, all the same. I search but will never find the face of a grown Valerie, even if by some miracle she is captured there. I am an artistic moth, blinded by the bright light of a camera flash. Willingly searching for something lost, something that isn't even there to be found. Watching a succession of faces: of passengers, not drivers.

This is how the story ends. One man's lament for the innocence and arrogance of youth.

❁

This piece is a curious one as I can't quite remember how it came about. I know I 'found' the title whilst flicking through a library reference book in one of my day jobs, seeing the phrase and jotting it down. I remember deciding on the name Valerie at random when writing the first paragraph and then remembering Valerie Solanas (who had attempted to kill Andy Warhol) and then extrapolating that character into my character's life as I continued writing. I remember being interested in flicker books and the spaces in between, and the idea of a flicker book (or series of photographs) depicting the frequency of existence. But this is one of those pieces whose story develops as it is being written, where I had no plot in mind and only afterwards I can see it was about the fractal nature of relationships and how we grant some moments in life a power and potency which they may not, in fact, have. How we linger over broken relationships and find it difficult to move on.

The Stench Of Winter

The body was found at the edge of the woods in a shallow grave littered with the wetness of mulched leaves and a solitary crisp packet.

It had been there some time. Perhaps six months. It could be this girl. Or it could be that girl. They said. It could have been any girl. The newspapers thought it didn't matter because she was blonde and probably foreign and could be any one of a half-dozen blonde, missing, foreign girls.

But it did matter. It mattered to the girl.

And if no one else was interested, then she had to be.

She heard them on the other side of the door.

"Do you know what you look like when you're asleep?"

"No, of course not."

The voices were male. One older than the other.

"That's right. No one does. But everyone *thinks* they know what they look like when they're asleep."

"So?"

"So they make noises, they sigh; they do anything but lie there and just *be* asleep."

"So she's not asleep?"

"No, she's not asleep."

Initially her movements were stiff. When she looked back at the ground she remained there. A man in a white all-in-one suit regarded the body curiously. She had come through the mouth. Yet all the features were indistinct. *Everything* was indistinct. She saw the world as if reflected in a steamed mirror.

The face of the man with authority, for example. Two black olive pit eyes, smudged around the edges. A hint of brow, of nostril. A general outline of shape. She might have torn at her hair if it were possible. How might she identify her murderers if she couldn't see them?

Snow added to the blanket of confusion. Everywhere she turned, other than at the base of the tree where she had lain, the landscape was disguised. And the snow was still falling, her memory disintegrating with each flake.

She saw herself fading out of existence.

Later, newspapers suggested names like Melka Wójcikówna or Krystyna Wiśniewska. Both were blonde. One age 17 the other 29. She felt she was Krystyna Wiśniewska because the words felt right in her head. This was confirmed by DNA from bone marrow in her right thigh. She became aware of these discoveries as they happened, as if there were a synaptic link between her and the investigators. Mostly, she wasn't there. When she was, familiarities crowded her.

She remembered one winter in Katowice. She woke early on the sixth of December to find that *Święty Mikołaj* had filled her boots with candy. She ran to find her mother who hugged her tight. "Can you wait until Christmas Eve," she said. "*Święty Mikołaj* will visit again."

She had nodded her head understanding it was true and false simultaneously. It was her age which caused the dislocation. An age where everything was possible.

Now she doesn't move through the air but the air moves with her. She watches the autopsy dispassionately, without sadness. Similar to the older girl who watched a younger sister squeal at candy, she had moved onto a different age.

What they wouldn't find, she thought, was the thin piece of *opłatek* that she had on her body when she died. The Christmas wafer embossed with the Virgin Mary holding Baby Jesus had long since disintegrated. For a while, she focussed on it so hard in the hope that its memory might burn its way into her flesh. But it never had.

Another memory: somewhere she released a cage of birds in the knowledge that they would be caught again.

And once more: standing outside St Mary's Church in Katowice. An appointment.

Those were the days when winter smelt like cinnamon with a hint of pine. When the wetness and force of rainfall kicked bacterial spores upwards and the moist air carried them to waiting noses with their distinctly earthy after-rain smell. Those were the days when she sprayed herself with perfume and policemen did not have to smear vapour rub under their noses or wash constantly for several days after her contact; even expelling her smell out of their own bodies following touch.

Despite no longer being corporeal, the stench of her autumn into winter in the soil remained.

Clearly she saw the path of her trafficked self from that meeting outside St Mary's Church through the hidden compartment of the articulated lorry and into the house where she thought she would remain for the end of her days.

It was only later that she realised the lorry had been necessary so no one knew she was in England, despite her eligibility to travel just like her boss had done.

Finding the house again was a matter of trial and error, like walking through a heavy mist to a destination unknown. Sometimes she faded in and out, just as she reached it. This fading was a dreamless sleep. The passing of time only evident from a change in the weather or location.

Once, when she caught the date on a newspaper she realised months had past. Another time she thought they had returned.

Occasionally she would think lucidity: *I am investigating my death.*

Sometimes she was just curious.

She began to think of herself in the third person as a way of confirming and reiterating her identity. This simple procedure solidified her.

Krystyna waited outside the entrance of the house. After some time two men walked down the steps. One was older than the other. There was a girl between them; arms linked. The girl was not Krystyna and Krystyna did not recognise her.

She watched as they entered a black car, tinted windows. The older man sat in the back seat with the girl whilst the young man drove. Krystyna followed at a distance, as though on a conveyor belt, or tethered from the back of the car to a skateboard. Down a long avenue, trees were budding. Green stems promised yellow tips. The sap was rising. She saw three gentlemen unbutton their coats as they began to play bowls in a park. She saw the cuckoo make its getaway. She saw two halves of the same lemon on a windowsill. She saw the car turn and disgorge its contents at her former place of work. A hidden place.

The girl who was not Krystyna walked with her head down. Krystyna knew what she was doing. She was counting money inside her head. She decided not to follow her into the building.

She blinked and she was back in Katowice feeling for money under the tablecloth amongst the hay. The fried carp placed at the centre of the table smelt good. She could almost salivate. White and blue bowls of *borscht* were at each place setting. Bobbing in the borscht were little parcels of *uszka*, dumplings filled with wild mushrooms and minced meat. She wasn't to know it, but this was a feast that wouldn't be repeated. Her father bore down on the table, smiling. Within two months he would be dead and their family would desperately need money.

She hadn't seen anyone else like her.

Certainly not her father.

When the wind picked up she was borne away. She watched the older man and the young man return to their car from the safety of a tree. Then the wind blew again and like a bedsheet ghost she fluttered off the tree and over their windscreen.

The car continued driving without impediment.

Krystyna spread herself over the shield, tucking into the surrounding edges like fitted fabric. From here, the mouths of the men were open: teeth white, golden crowns, pink tongues. Well fed. She came from a mouth, she wondered what would happen if she entered one.

She screamed at them, and they laughed back but they weren't laughing at her they were laughing at each other.

Without expectation she left them and when she returned the car was empty, parked by the side of a *Polski sklep*.

It wasn't possible but it was summer. She could feel the heat on the windscreen. She was illuminated

She remembered walking around the shopping promenades in Katowice, in the old centre and marketplace. Her mother had told her that much of the original architecture had been demolished in the 1950s to make way for modern communist buildings. There was an arm linked in hers, one of her girlfriends, Weronikia. She closes what she thinks are her eyes but she sees herself anyway, entering a shop where she will choose a dress that one day will be unzipped by a trembling Englishman forty years her senior who will fail to penetrate her and who she will masturbate over her breasts.

And even though she doesn't look hard enough, she knows that the dress cost more than the act.

It is impossible for Krystyna to know how many days have passed or *if* days have passed.

She hears the song *Greensleeves* played on a broken xylophone and then realises she is listening to hold music and that she is inside a phone.

There is a click.

Someone speaks in Polish. "Yes, this is Tomislaw. No, we do not know of Krystyna Wiśniewska. No Krystyna Wiśniewska is known here. Yes. Yes. We have already told the police this information. No Krystyna Wiśniewska is known here. That's right. No Krystyna Wiśniewska is known here. No Krystyna Wiśniewska is known here. Yes. Yes. That's right. No Krystyna Wiśniewska is known here."

Krystyna slips out of the phone. Wonders what she is. How long it will las...

She walks through the park. Kicking leaves. Age indeterminate. Her memory is false here. This is not Katowice and she never walked a London park. Dog walkers pass through her and she realises it is no memory, especially when they do not feel her breath on their necks. Nor when their dogs refuse to bark. So much myth in death which she has discovered is not relevant. In the distance she sees a child holding a helium balloon and she runs towards it with the speed of an express train. The balloon pulls out of the child's hand and she holds it as it floats skywards, then she releases her grip and continues to float, her heart heavy from the sounds of the unnecessary cries from the ground.

But she cannot retrieve the balloon for she had never actually gripped it.

Wind takes her further. London is spread below, the overview of the Thames creating repetitive music in her head. She wonders how she will return, wonders if she might float over the channel and thenceforth over country country country. Wonders whether she might then see her mother and younger sister; impoverished.

She doesn't want to see another Christmas dinner.

Atmospheric pressure conspires to return her groundwards. She imagines her toe touching the parkland with all the precision of a ballerina.

Krystyna meanders. One day she focuses and tries to see it all.

From the ruck in bedclothes wrapped around a disfigured foot, to a recurring dream of a lost voice, to steam in a bathroom, to the chatter of the girls as they talk about their experiences in hushed voices finding solace in what can no longer be called shame because they are no longer in control of their actions. From a look that the older man gives the younger man, from stained underpants and the wet odour of discarded cigarettes, from the television in the room which is only set to one channel, from the imprint of a shoe in soil, from the milky fluid circling in the opposite direction within the flushed condom; to the money which scorches her hand because it remains there so briefly, to the coins she hides vertical within some of her toes, to the notes which she folds and inserts in her anus, to the brick which the men discover in the girls' communal bedroom, the one that can be removed to find their stash, their hopeless getaway fund.

She sees the body of the carp on the plate, the skeletal bones running through it as if it has sprung itself open. She sees the *borscht* like dark blood, the *uszka* like organs. She sees dessert – a *makowiec*, a poppy seed roll – containing a colour twist like a question mark. She sees her father, dead before Christmas, leaning over the meal with a smile on his face and the daylight right through him. She sees her mother and sister frozen in place, unmoving mannekins, as she circles the table and wonders whether she's seeing the past the future or the present.

"Yes, this is Tomislaw."

Krystyna sees the telephone. Hears her mother's tinny voice at the other end. A miracle. Then she hears: "Of course. Of course. Her sister. Yes. Of course."

A weight thuds into whatever is Krystyna and she collapses through the wooden floorboards, through a thin layer of cement, through topsoil, through the light coloured eluviations, through the clay and mineral-rich subsoil, through the regolith with it's roughly broken stone and lack of organic matter, all the way through to the bedrock where she remains and against all the laws of nature germinates.

A thin covering of snow blinds the eye like tinfoil in the sun.

There is a sleeve inside winter that enables a return to the past.

Krystyna aches between her legs. She looks down and the young man is there. His fingers inside. He looks up, smiles, and pulls out a twenty-pound note. When he flips her over she sees the feet of the older man, Tomislav. He wears black shoes with pointed tips. The leather is embossed with a floral pattern. She feels the younger man part her anus and she grunts, hard. One finger. Two fingers. But the note is deep and it doesn't matter if he finds it because she has already heard she will be made an example of and she is already dead.

They tell her to get up, dressed. To get her coat. She is hurried through the Christmas party where the other trapped girls attempt smiles and Tekli passes her the *opłatek*. She takes it even knowing this cannot be true as she was murdered in August, and the heat outside confirms this as she is bundled into the car and they begin their drive to the woods with one of Tomislaw's hands over her mouth whilst the other is up her skirt like some kind of awful goodbye gesture to her womanhood.

Broken, she lies within soft earth.

She hears them on the other side of the door of life.

"Can you imagine what you might look like when you're dead?"

"I've given it no thought."

"Of course not. No one does. But anyone can *imagine* what they look like when they are dead."

"So?"

"So they lie still. They hold their breath. But they can't hold it for as long as they might if they were dead."

"So she's not dead?"

"No, she's not dead."

Krystyna heard the sound of the shovel more than she felt it.

"Now she's dead," she heard.

She exits through the sleeve of winter. There are crumbs in her palm. Like flakes.

She stands again, looks down at the body of Krystyna Wiśniewska who is not Melka Wójcikówna.

She wonders what happened to Melka Wójcikówna.

She decides to find out. She accepts that there is nothing more she can do.

Which is a pity, because if she hadn't accepted it then she might have understood it.

Fate has a habit of befalling those who expect it.

And Krystyna reeks of fate. It is her personal stench. That of her own avoidable winter.

❀

A few years ago I was aware of a news item about a girl's body that had been found on the Queen's Sandringham estate. I can't recall the exact details, but I certainly remember that the way it was reported seemed to suggest that because she appeared to be Eastern European then it didn't really matter. I'm sure this wasn't the intention in the article, but there was a sniff of it to be had. For me, the death seemed all the more tragic because of this.

I began to wonder who would care to investigate a death if the authorities didn't. I considered the one who might be most interested would be the dead girl herself.

I aimed for a delicate balance in the story, for the girl to investigate her own death but through the veil of past and present, a remembering of her being trafficked to the UK as a sex worker, but also warm memories of her family and Christmastime. And I also wanted her experience to be fragmented. Whilst she might be considered a ghost it isn't the case that anyone can see her, she can't affect anything, the baddies don't get their comeuppance and they remain unaware of her continued existence. Tragic as that might be, I thought this approach to be more realistic than a standard vengeance story. Real life (and death) just don't have happy endings.

A Pageant Of Clouds

Eiji gradually spent less of his time in daylight, until eventually it was none.

He wasn't averse to the sensation of sun on his skin. There was warmth to be had in a two-way process. In the old days his skin felt *projected* towards the sun, as though it were giving back something that had been taken. However he found that the light illuminated as much as it shadowed, and increasingly it was within those shadows that he wanted to live. The transparency of night provided hiding places, smudged him into anonymity. By sleeping during the day, he effectively erased its existence.

Eiji considered himself a noctilucent cloud, that rare meteorological phenomenon which could only be observed when the sun was below the horizon.

He had worn away his parents' objections. Initially they had resisted efforts to cease his education. They had encouraged his friends. They insisted he eat with them. Yet repetition is a strong tool, and by sleeping during the day and watching television all night Eiji achieved the degree of separation that he desired. To begin with it hadn't been a conscious decision, more an erosion of normality. Eventually he became subsumed within that routine and his parents no longer sought to dissuade him. He knew of the expression, out of sight out of mind. He had reached a plateau where he was this to his parents and he was that to the rest of the world.

He remembered Kokura although he had not been outside the apartment in over two years. The waterfront town had been redeveloped, with new bridges, pedestrian walkways, and restaurants and shops. He wished he could pretend the transition of the old town into the new mirrored his withdrawal, as if to create one you had to negate the other, but when he allowed himself honesty he knew it was simpler than that. He had become *hikikomori* when his girlfriend left him. Everything since then was soft disintegration.

He stretched his limbs. The futon creaked. Standing, he looked out of the window. It was impossible to avoid night pollution where there was civilisation, and it wasn't clear to him whether the lack of stars was due to cloud cover or the inability to see them though in plain sight. Across town, apartment buildings were stacked like TV sets, as though by looking into those windows he viewed the entirety of Kokura as a bank of CCTV. But he wasn't interested in other people. Bending to his knees he opened the door to his room, found the food which his parents had prepared for him, and pulled it inside before he could attract attention.

His mother had cooked his favourite: *jiaozi*, Chinese dumplings. She had filled the dough with ground meat and vegetables, crimped the sides and steamed them to perfection. He speared one with a chopstick and bit. It was still warm. Together on the tray was a soy-vinegar dipping sauce alongside a hot chilli sauce. Eiji dipped into them alternately, savouring the different tastes, the textures. He remembered eating in the Amu Plaza, within the Kokura Station building. Amaterasu would have been with him, glancing into his eyes as she bent her head to eat. He grimaced at the memory, almost pushing his meal aside, but hunger took sway and he consumed the remainder of the dish. Rubbing his eyes he returned to the sky.

The night clouds were fading. Either that or the twilight's shift to darkness served to further illuminate the constellations. Stars became visible. Eiji considered the fact that those objects existed day and night, that despite their slow materialisation to the naked eye they were constantly in the sky. He likened this to his own appearance. His anonymity didn't mean that he had ceased to exist.

He turned on the television, flicking through channels until he found a rerun of *Densha Otoko*. He identified with the main character, a socially reclusive male who wins his love through the help of an online community. Until recently, Eiji had also maintained a vigorous online presence, yet gradually he had retarded from this, as if any contact with the outside world could only prove painful.

Noctilucent clouds were not fully understood. They only formed under very restricted conditions; their occurrence a sensitive guide to changes in the upper atmosphere. Eiji shifted on his futon, sat cross-legged, became absorbed within the story on the television.

On the 6th August 1945 Kokura had been the backup target for the *Little Boy* atomic bomb. Should Hiroshima have clouded over, Kokura would have been hit. Eiji considered this carefully. If Kokura had been hit, he would not have been born.

He had raised this with Amaterasu. She had been born in Harajuku, Tokyo, and subscribed to the fashion of the district. Whereas Eiji was conservative in dress, Amaterasu wore garish colours, mixing tulle skirts with white leggings decorated in red hearts and teal Dr Marten boots.

"Don't take it too seriously, Eiji. It was a long time ago."

"My grandparents were living here. They would have become no more than atomic shadows."

"But they didn't. They only died recently."

"Does it matter, if they died at all?"

Amaterasu shook her head, waved to a group of friends. "C'mon, let's go to Cha-Cha Town. There must be an event in the plaza."

Eiji shook his head. "Aren't we sitting here?"

Amaterasu sulked.

They maintained a pose, as though being photographed.

Then Amaterasu lay backwards on the concrete. Eiji remembered the sky being a deep blue. In his memory, Amaterasu floats against the backdrop of that sky, rather than the grey concrete. She spins as if in a pop video.

He remembers the touch of her fingers on his lapel, straightening his shirt. He remembers kissing her mouth; just enough to catch a breath.

He wants to be outside again. To leave the apartment, to resume his education, to find a job. But the crushing disappointment of his parents has become an anchor. Eiji can barely exist.

Sometimes, changing the tense of himself, is the only way to stop being alone.

The television show ended. Eiji stood at the window again. Many of the lights in the apartments had been extinguished. The sky was now pregnant with stars, some of them stillborn. He blinked: once, twice; hoping to spark a falling star into action. Not that it would be a star, but the visible path of a meteoroid as it entered the atmosphere. Shining at the moment it encountered death.

He was reminded of the *Beagle 2*, a British landing spacecraft that had formed part of the European Space Agency's 2003 *Mars Express* mission. The craft had been expected to land on the surface of Mars six days after being deployed from the Mars Express Orbiter. What happened was that it disappeared for eleven years. Eiji wondered where it had been.

His room was like a space capsule. He remembered reading a story online about a couple who stocked up with provisions, sealed their room and imagined they were journeying into space. It didn't have a happy ending. When he had spent a year in his room he had heard the doctor talking to his parents on the other side of the door.

"He is tormented in the mind. He wants to go out, but cannot. He wants a friend – or a lover – but can't."

"There was a girl," he heard his mother say, but her voice tailed off to a whisper.

The doctor continued: "It may seem to you that he is alone, but in reality he is not alone. A recent survey for the Cabinet Office suggested there are 700,000 *hikikomori* throughout the country. It's a modern disease."

"Is there a cure?"

"You must try to engage with him. You have gradually allowed him to hide away. You must now re-establish contact, but it cannot be done quickly. He will rebel against you."

Eiji recalled hearing his father comfort his mother. He couldn't see her, but he knew she was shaking. This caused a further withdrawal. Eiji made a vow never to speak to his parents again, for fear of distressing them.

Noctilucent clouds were composed of tiny ice crystals, existing higher than any other clouds in the Earth's atmosphere. Whilst the source of both dust and water vapour at that height are not known with certainty, the exhaust from Space Shuttles had been found to generate miniscule individual clouds. Eiji had spent some time reading about their formation. There were some reports which suggested they did not exist until the eruption of Krakatoa in 1883.

Eiji opened his fridge and pulled out a bottle of *Ramune*. The traditional bottle was stoppered by a marble, and Eiji pushed it inwards, tilting the bottle and taking a cool draught of the lemon-lime drink as the marble rattled around inside. On some occasions he considered himself the marble, on other days the marble was the lost Beagle 2, and sometimes it was Kokura itself, cocooned by clouds.

The eruption of Krakatoa was the equivalent to 200 megatons of TNT, about 13,000 times the nuclear yield of the *Little Boy* bomb. Eiji wondered that if the eruption had indeed created the atmospheric conditions for the development of noctilucent clouds, then what creation might have been wrought in Hiroshima as a by-product of destruction.

One day, before he became *hikikomori*, he had invited Amaterasu to meet his parents. Beforehand they had discussed Amaterasu dropping her *Harajuku* style, and to some extent she had complied. She arrived wearing a pale blue kimono decorated with pink telephones. In one hand she carried a giraffe plush bag, in the other a small box of candy for Eiji's parents. She wore mismatched shoes with mismatched laces. Eiji initially felt the disapproval of his parents as the heat of an atomic bomb, but gradually they cooled and towards the end of the visit Eiji's father was making encouraging remarks about Amaterasu which only later Eiji found distasteful.

After they had eaten, Eiji's parents retired to another room, allowing Amaterasu to spend some time alone with Eiji. It was not permissible for Eiji to take her to his bedroom, so he retrieved the book he had been planning to show her, and laid it flat on the floor between them.

Amaterasu regarded the black cover, with its central mushroom image.

"What is this? *100 Suns.*"

Eiji turned the first page. "The book is a compilation of one hundred photographs of atomic detonations from the era of above-ground nuclear testing between 1945 to 1962. The photos have been selected by a man called Michael Light. I always found his name to be ironic."

Amaterasu said nothing, but watched as Eiji turned the pages.

"Those in colour have a raging red intensity, whereas those in black and white symbolise the line between life and death. See, how close these American VIP's are to witnessing the blast." Eiji pointed to the photograph of the 81 kiloton detonation at Enewetak Atoll in 1953. "There they sit, on their Adirondack chairs, wearing protective goggles as the explosion lifts 250,000 tons of radioactive reef material to a height of 35,000 feet."

Amaterasu shook her head. "You have memorised this?"

Eiji was proud. "I look at it constantly."

"But why?"

"Look at this 11 kiloton detonation in the Nevada desert in 1957. You see the force, the dust, the formations. It's like a pageant of clouds."

"I don't understand," Amaterasu said. "What interests you in such destruction?"

Eiji closed the book. "I had hoped you would share my enthusiasm."

Amaterasu stood. The colour of her hair matched the telephones on her kimono. Upon standing, one of her shoes caught the end of the kimono and it tugged downwards, briefly exposing her skin stretched taut at her manubrium, just below her throat.

Following Amaterasu's dismissal of his fascination, Eiji had taken a trip to the Yasaka Shrine at the main entrance to Kokura Castle. Whereas the castle had been destroyed and redesigned many times since it was first built in 1602, the shrine could be considered authentic.

For a few moments he was alone. He remembered the story of the Kokura lord whose eyes were damaged by a falcon leaving the shrine, and he closed his eyes reverently whilst deciding how to pray. Gradually Eiji overcame his reticence to seek solace with Amaterasu. Upon leaving the shrine he was overwhelmed with the feeling of having done something terrible, something wrong.

Eiji realised he was different to many *hikikomori*, who tended to be first born sons. He was second born, perhaps should not have succumbed to the pressures which his elder brother had already surmounted, yet from his reasoning it was living within that shadow, coupled with Amaterasu's reaction, which caused him to implode.

Unlike his elder brother, Eiji had been given the freedom to explore his creative side. It was expected he would not inherit the family business. He was secondary to his parents' business plans. As he watched the glimmerings of sunlight begin to reclaim the horizon, he remembered the film theory course he had dropped out of at university. There was a cinematic technique, called day for night, which was used to simulate a night scene whilst filming in daylight. Eiji considered this was now his existence.

He had taken one last chance with Amaterasu, grabbing her wrist as she ran between classes, almost spinning her around in a balletic movement to rest between his arms, like drawing a spinning top close to his chest.

"On the 9th August, 1945," he said, "Kokura had been the primary target for the *Fat Man* atomic bomb. But on the morning of the raid, the town had been obscured by clouds. The Americans had orders to drop the bomb visually, and not by radar, and so instead they diverted to the secondary target, which was Nagasaki."

Amaterasu stared at him, her wide eyes heightened by mascara.

"Should Kokura not have clouded over, it would have been hit. And I would not have been born."

Amaterasu wrestled her wrist free. She ran, shouting "You must rid yourself of this obsession."

He saw that she had the power of a falcon. Gently, he rubbed his eyes.

Eiji read that after eleven years the *Beagle 2* was discovered intact on the surface of Mars. Images suggested that two of its four solar panels failed to deploy, blocking the spacecraft's communications antenna.

He remembered an early lesson, from a childhood long before Amaterasu. *Mizaru, kikazaru, iwazaru.* See not, hear not, speak not.

One interpretation of the saying was that it suggested one shouldn't dwell on evil thoughts. Another intimated it signified a code of silence within gang culture. Still another perceived a lack of moral responsibility on those who feigned ignorance.

That evening – following Amaterasu's rebuke – Eiji desceded into the state of mind which eventually made him *hikikomori*.

The sun blistered the horizon. Eiji watched as the contours of Kokura, previously absorbed by the shadows of the night, began to reveal themselves. He considered the sweeping rays of the sun akin to the atomic fervour of the bomb, wiping out night's existence through its inevitable power. Eiji shielded his eyes, but the damage was done. Closing his blinds, he huddled under the windowsill, waiting for the explosion that had already come.

❀

This story came completely out of the blue. I found the time to write one evening, having been struck by some cloud formations earlier that day. Searching for the collective noun for clouds gave me the title. For some time I also wanted to utilise a book titled *100 Suns* that I owned, which contained photographs of controlled atomic explosions. This idea joined with another one I had been toying with, the increasing phenomena of (mostly) young Japanese men becoming reclusive and confining themselves to their bedrooms. Adding to this the city of Kokura which could have been the target of the atomic bombs which were eventually dropped on Hiroshima and Nagasaki depending on the extent of cloud cover, and the story wrote itself in one sitting.

Always Forever Today

It's time for life to give back to films all that it has stolen from them – from Rise and Fall of a Small Film Company (1986), *directed by Jean-Luc Godard*

You *could* say that it began when Donald Utting first visited the cinema at age fourteen. Or you *could* say that it began when Donald Utting first met Shirley Thomas at age twenty-four. For both those occasions, you *would* say that it was the greatest show on earth.

It was late Autumn in both life and season when Donald Utting – film critic, journalist, biographer – received an invitation to write an extended essay on which film he might consider to be his most influential. The destination for such an article, said his agent, Kelso, would be inclusion in a book of similar essays from equally revered sources. Donald needed to give the request no further thought: it was a done deal. His absence from such a work would be tantamount to an obituary. What did occupy the remainder of his morning was the question as to which film deserved his attention.

Once he had made his decision – Woody Allen's *Annie Hall* – his agent contacted him again to tactfully point out his mistake. The remit was not *the most* influential film according to his opinion, but *your most*. In other words, the collection of essays was intended to illustrate the power of cinema by the impact on the lives of the contributors. His choice should have *personal resonance*. The essay should be *part film study, part autobiography*.

Donald ran a hand over what had once been a full head of hair but which now offered no resistance to such movement. It was clear that the question now was not what he *should* include, but what he *could* include.

He recalled an occasion when he had dined with the author George Target, who had provided some advice on writing autobiography: the first unexpurgated version should be immediately burnt, the second mildly censored to be locked away for posthumous publication, and the third published in a whitewashed cover.

Whilst Donald could argue that *The Greatest Show On Earth* (1952) had kick-started his interest in cinema at the formative age of fourteen – after he had slipped into the matinee against the intentions of his parents, who considered the moving image to be the medium of the devil – he couldn't argue at all that *Knife In The Water* (1962) – or to give it the proper title, *Nóż w wodzie* – was certainly the most influential in terms of the autobiography which you immediately burnt.

So now the question: was he ready to burn that memory into print?

A younger Donald journeyed to Poole Harbour on his thumb and a smile. As London fell away in the lorry driver's extended view mirror, Donald imagined the smoke collapsing as if in a controlled explosion, the force propelling him towards the Dorset coast in a surge of apocalyptic fervour. He had chosen his destination through a play on words that intrigued him, coupled by a delayed adolescence which thrived on coincidence and certainties. He had already placed a few articles in *Films and Filming* magazine, and whereas similar magazines publicised films and their stars with little critical appraisal, *Films and Filming* was very much a serious production. His critical eye could gaze from its pages with unfettered restraint, and he knew he was at the start of a glittering *fame by association* career.

Twenty-four years old and a solid piece of muscle. Donald's thumb was good for another two lorries, a motorbike, and three cars on the journey south. The weather uniformly clement: carrying such stillness which matched the pocket knife in his jacket seam. It wasn't until the final stage of the trip, when he had disengaged from the motorbike and almost been hit by a car that had pulled sharply into the lay-by, that Donald experienced a tug of fate which intimated his whim might be tethered to something greater than his ego.

The girl flashed an apologetic smile, but it was her husband who was driving. Whilst the man walked to the roadside to relieve himself, Donald leant on the trim and engaged in conversation. By the time the man had returned, the remainder of Donald's journey into Poole had been sealed.

He took some time to thumb through his archive. For ease of access, his DVDs were filed under date of purchase. Donald's first wife had expressed a preference for alphabetical order, but purchasing *Audition*

(1999) or *Avalon* (2001) created more headaches than *Zardoz* (1974), and – allowing for some artistic licence when it came to his earlier acquisitions – Donald had maintained his chronological archive for over forty years.

To satisfy his inner geek, Donald's system rendered foreign films under their original titles; a process which occasionally pressed on the capabilities of memory. With *Nóż w wodzie*, however, there was no confusion. In a room shelved with thousands of movies, Donald could have placed a successful bet that he would be able to locate it blindfolded.

Only to do so would have been cheating, would have sublimated the pleasure he found in perusing the archive. Similar to searching for a particular definition in a dictionary, Donald enjoyed the process of being sidetracked by entries other than those intended. Whilst a particular DVD might be his destination, he preferred to journey there – as per three lorries, a motorbike, and four cars – through a process of psycho-geography: that exploration of urban environments that emphasizes playfulness and drifting, rather than a direct approach. In this manner he might refamiliarise himself with items in his collection which he might otherwise have forgotten, even if some of the titles – *An Education* (2009), *The Tarnished Angels* (1957) – were better off that way.

The room in which he housed his collection had shrunk since it began: plastic covers an effective soundproof. The visual/sonic dimension changes appealed to Donald's sense of the finite. As his collection grew, so space for it diminished, until – just like himself – as the accumulative knowledge increased, the capacity to contain it would become no more than the size of a withered fist.

Having made his choice that *Nóż w wodzie* would be his seminal movie Donald resolved to watch it three times in succession. The first in pleasure, the second for notes, and the third in remembrance.

His withdrawal of the DVD from the wall which contained it was as slick as conception in reverse.

Donald's invitation onto the boat had been as unlikely as it was inevitable. The older man had something to prove: this was as clear as the sky which ran so bright as to be white. There had been an argument – something blistered and tense. Since his acceptance of the ride the dynamics had shifted. Donald understood he had become the focus of the man's anger, whilst his wife undertook a bystander role. Donald held a dislike of being manipulated. He determined to bring the wife back into the game.

Her name was Shirley. She worked as a hairdresser on Wardour Street. Victor was big in the city. Shirley uttered the word *financier* in a tone which belied her pleasure of the boat. The craft itself could only be described as beyond Donald's nautical understanding. It was sufficient to realise that the challenge – if he should accept it – was to learn the mechanics of its movements in order to facilitate them, whilst Shirley could marvel at the innate prowess of her husband whose commands would enforce his position as overseer.

This was one outcome. Yet there were three of them on the ocean, and each would have their story.

Donald's first viewing adhered to his expectations. The story unfolded as a triptych, the older man – Andrzej – with his younger wife – Krystyna – each carried an agenda in inviting the unnamed male onto the boat. The triptych was mirrored by Donald's participation as viewer, critic, and in reality, with the film playing on three levels: that dramatised on screen, that recalled through memory, and finally the echo of his life experience. The film had been released in March 1962, and his encounter with Shirley and Victor had taken place in the summer of the same year. Whilst Donald hadn't seen *Nóż w wodzie* – and wouldn't do so until June 1965 when it played a Polanski double bill with *Repulsion* – he had never been able to ascertain whether the others had done so.

He expected not – their lifestyles married with the characters rather than those whom Donald might expect to be foreign film goers – but the tug of possibility that the scenario had been as orchestrated as the movie script had resonated on a repeated cycle for the following fifty-six years.

After ninety-four minutes Donald rose and made himself some lunch. A knife was in his hand before he knew it, the serrated edge cutting the sub roll cleanly, its attention turned to the cheese which was easily pared in slivers. Baby plum tomatoes spit seeds when bisected. Donald constructed his lunch methodically, as his thoughts shuffled to deconstruct the movie. Finally he slathered the sub with ill-advised mayo and returned to his armchair together with a glass of ginger beer.

The second viewing proceeded much as the first: the players resuming their roles, going through their motions. This time Donald made notes. He had the notion of the film, his memory of watching it, and his memory of experiencing it, to be separate layers of differently coloured clear plastic. If he took the film itself to be the definitive version, then superimposing his memory added a second dimension, and the final coloured layer depicting the day spent with Shirley and Victor marked a third. Donald considered this structure would form the basis of his essay: how reality becomes supplanted by memory coupled with the irony that the reality of film is already a fiction.

The essay took shape from pen to paper, ambiguity obfuscating each side of the triptych.

The expanse of sail swung from left to right as Victor manipulated the boat, Donald ducking just in time to avoid serious injury. He glared at the older man, aware that Shirley sat on the peripheries of his vision, her legs stretched towards the horizon, her toes the size of buildings held in perspective.

There was a calm to the water that he fought against.

Victor made a comment, apparently benign. Donald pulled a packet of cigarettes out of his pocket and without speaking flicked one to Shirley who caught it as deftly as if they had practiced the movement in a carnival sideshow.

Donald considered the length of the cigarette compared to the length of the boom. A small victory.

The impudence of his youth shot glances at Shirley as succinctly as the cigarette. When Victor dropped anchor and stripped down to his shorts, Donald lowered his gaze and refused the challenge. Shirley clapped as Victor dived overboard, water petalling his wake. Donald imagined her unclipping her bikini, the act an invitation. He would move his body over hers as Victor bobbed unconscious at the underside of the boat, the knife sown into the seam of his jacket burring Shirley's skin until it was tarnished.

When Donald returned to his armchair with another glass of ginger beer in readiness for the third viewing of *Nóz w wodzie* he realised he hadn't drunk the first glass.

Leon Niemczyk was thirty-nine when he played the role of Andrzej. According to Donald's research he had died seventeen years previously, in 2002. The information he found on the actress, Jolanta Umecka, was less detailed. In fact, her name was almost all that he had. The young man who played the hitchhiker – Zygmunt Malanowicz – was Donald's age. As far as Donald could ascertain, he was still alive.

As the film began again, Donald considered the immutability of the moving image. Woody Allen had said *I don't want to achieve immortality through my work, I want to achieve it by not dying*, but, failing opportunities for the latter, Donald had always envied the permanence of the former. More *alive* than a photograph, movies were a persistence of memory and would outlast even those who saw the movies during the actors' lifetimes.

Compared to *actual* memory, film could not be blemished or corrupted.

As Donald had this thought, he turned the pages of his notebook back to the beginning and scribbled down a title: *Always Forever Today*.

Reaching for his ginger beer Donald was immune to the ripple which ran from top to bottom along his television screen.

When he drank, it was from the second glass.

Victor surfaced, spitting ocean.

Donald stood on the bow, looking back to land.

Shirley feigned sleep.

The older man pulled himself onto the boat, water sloughing off his body as though an image glitching. He walked over to where Donald stood.

"We trust the ocean, but we cannot trust the ocean. We give it a name, but it has none. They say that a boat is a woman, but that's sleight of mouth. The ocean is a woman. Do you understand? The ocean is a woman."

Donald remembered shrugging. He held the opinion that when his own life reached the stage where it became important to assess it that he might too speak his dialogue as though he were in a movie, but until then he would pay no attention to others unless – of course – they were in a film.

Did I fuck your wife? he wanted to ask, just to get a reaction. But Victor had barely been in the water fifteen minutes, and he didn't want to give the impression that it could be over so soon.

The sun nudged the belly of the ocean as they returned to port. When Donald had entered the galley for the toilet – at the exact point when Shirley had regained Victor's trust – she had followed and quickly brought him off with her fingers before returning to the deck and trailing her hand in the spume behind the boat.

Mid-way through the third viewing Donald rose to close the curtains. He hadn't realised he had been sitting in the dark for almost half an hour, until the light from the streetlamp created an aurora on the television screen too bright to ignore.

Regaining his seat, he realised the DVD had reached the pivotal knife scene. The young man spread a palm on the deck of the boat and holding the hilt of his knife in the other hand stabbed the spaces of his fingers back and forth in a 1-2-1-3-1-4-1-5-1-6-1-5-1-4-1-3-1-2 formation. Andrzej watched from a distance, whilst Krystyna was in the water tussling with an inflatable. The scene was key to power dynamics. When Donald saw *Nóż w wodzie* for the first time, he had wondered what might have happened should he have attempted something similar with Victor and Shirley. Without question, it would have ended badly.

There was undoubted fascination in the rhythm of the knife. When the sequence ended, Donald played it in reverse until it began again. Watching the film reversed created a frisson of expectation, as though the knife game was potentially more dangerous that way. He realised he was getting obsessed once he'd repeatedly watched the section seven times. Rubbing his eyes, he released his fingers from the remote control which slipped to the floor, enabling the players to continue forward in their roles: Andrzej appearing so exasperated with Donald's actions that he seemed to have aged.

Donald bent to retrieve the remote. As he did so, tiredness transformed him. He bore the sensation of being tucked in bed, his mother's hands slipping between the mattress and the frame as she trapped the sheet between them.

He paused the DVD. The young man grinned at Andrzej as he played the knife game with the older man's splayed hand. Caught in a realm of possibilities.

Donald had never been a fiction writer, although some of his critics – even a critic can have critics – considered him otherwise. Nevertheless as he climbed the stairs to bed he remembered a story idea he once had. That instead of movie stars adhering to the immortality of their screen presences, on each viewing they would age incrementally, until finally they would continue beyond the point of their deaths, trapped within the movie's cycle, their remaining flesh performing their roles, until everything rotted away and returned to dust and only disembodied voices could be heard.

The story would continue in Donald's mind with a protagonist who becomes aware of this occurring, who is tied so tight to cinema that his own reminiscences begin to decay. *The Erasure Of Memory* would be the title of the piece. Although he had always known that he was not the man to write it, and periodically he had clean forgotten the idea.

Yet perhaps he could present this piece to Kelso instead of the autobiographical essay. The correlation of Andrzej and Krystyna and Victor and Sylvia was too difficult to follow. Most readers would consider it a contrivance, in any event.

The lorry driver begs him to wait a moment before leaving the cab and walking around to the passenger side. The door swings wide almost taking Donald with it. He extends a leg to descend but the distance seems ridiculously great. The driver hauls himself up a couple of steps and then reaches out a hand. When Donald grabs it he realises it is much younger than his own.

He stumbles the last step, almost falling into the driver's embrace. Embarrassed, he thanks him profusely, stepping back into the path of a car which has just entered the lay-by, causing it to swerve around him with the customary squeal of tyres on gravel. He smiles at the elderly woman in the passenger seat apologetically. The driver is in shadow, caught in a speckled refraction of light through Autumn leaves.

When Donald restarts the DVD the next morning, Zygmunt Malanowicz is eighty years old. Stanisław Niemczyk is a cadaver.

In the ocean, Jolanta Umecka wrestles with a crocodile.

❀

I remember watching an old film and realising everyone acting in it was dead and – quite possibly – even the original audience were dead. There's a commonly held view that film grants immortality for actors, but of course this isn't actually the case. What if – I wondered – actors might age within the film they were immortalised in, until only cadavers went through the roles until they became dust? This was the starting point for the piece, which then mutated into an aging film reviewer's reminiscences about a filmic incident in his own life, and how memory / fiction / reality can intertwine.

The Caged Sea

Isabelle had been living in Japan for three years – and had been in a relationship with Masaki for almost one year – before she asked him to take her to Aokigahara.

"It's not the most romantic place," Masaki joked. They were seated on the floor, eating *sukiyaki* with *shirataki*, the clear noodles like glass ribbons within their ceramic bowls.

Isabelle shrugged. "But I've heard so much about it. And it will be different for you and I. Maybe we can *make* it romantic."

She handled her chopsticks well, considering she had only started using them since she entered into her relationship with Masaki. He taught her how to hold them properly, the top one with her index finger, middle finger and thumb, the other with the bottom of her thumb and the tip of her ring finger. She was careful not to move the upper chopstick unless she was picking up food. She had gained the approval of Masaki's parents and grandparents primarily from her use of those chopsticks. They had been warned his new girlfriend was French, but she wasn't sure if that had added to or lessened her anxiety at first meeting them.

"People die there," Masaki said. "People *go* there to die."

"We won't be going there to die," Isabelle said. "We can take photographs. It must be beautiful in places. It's at the base of Mount Fuji. Just how romantic is that!"

Masaki shrugged. Traditionally, he would have said *no* and that would have been the end of the matter. But he had known he would need to make allowances when deciding to date Isabelle, and this was one of those moments. When she got an idea into her head she was tenacious. He liked that word. Once he called her his tenacious little dog, but it hadn't gone down well in translation.

Between them they stumbled through conversations in Japanese, English and French. Both of them preferred English whenever they could, so that they could share a foreign language.

Masaki dabbed at his mouth with cloth, then pushed the remains of his meal to one side. "When do you want to go?"

"You mean it?" Isabelle almost squealed in pleasure, although truth be told apart from a morbid fascination and the desire to do something a little taboo she didn't have great interest in the forest.

"Yes, I mean it," Masaki said. Then he leant forward and kissed her.

Isabelle was first attracted to Masaki by his thick crop of black hair. His head resembled the top of a *matsutake* mushroom, and she loved it when she found out his name contained similar characters in translation. It was a mop top mushroom; he could have been another member of The Beatles. Not that she liked The Beatles, but she did like Masaki's hair.

Masaki was attracted to Isabelle by her long sinewy legs and her light brunette hair which when loosened from a pony tail reached down to the middle of her lower back. Sometimes, when they were naked, he would instruct her to lie on her front and then meticulously arrange her hair so it fanned over her skin, like a clam. He was also attracted by a small birthmark over her left eye, which somehow gave her the appearance of winking even when her eyes were wide open or tightly closed. Initially when he kissed her there she would push him away. Now, however, it was their secret place.

"No one has ever kissed me there before," she laughed.

Something in Masaki caught in his throat. It was less that no one had kissed her there, more that he wondered if it was the *only* place no one had kissed her. Whatever thoughts came calling, however, Masaki pushed them to one side and focussed on the positive rather than the negative. In this manner, their relationship blossomed.

Secretly, once Masaki had agreed to visiting the forest, Isabelle had made up her mind that she would tell him there that she loved him. She had decided to find a spot where it was deathly quiet, due to the wind-blocking density of the trees, where it might seem that only she and Masaki were the sole survivors in a post-apocalyptic world. Then she would let her feelings be known. Her true feelings. They had spoken of love before, of course, but this would be different. Here, she decided, he would discover just how beautifully she loved him. If it wasn't for her understanding that he would feel ashamed not asking her himself, she would even have considered proposing. But just as Masaki had made some allowances for her free French behaviour, just so she was cautious about offence. It was easy, though, to respect each other's feelings, because their love told it that way.

They decided to make the trip during the autumn break. Both were students at the University of Tokyo, which was where they had met. A few of the other foreign students had paired off at the same time, and Isaballe hadn't wanted to be left out. As it happened, with his mop of mushroom hair, Masaki was already chosen for her. It had just remained for her to discover him.

Aokigahara was known as the *sea of trees*. A forest at the North West base of Mount Fuji, it was a popular place for suicides. On average, thirty bodies were discovered each year, although when Isabelle had first read about it those numbers were increasing. It was second to the Golden Gate Bridge in San Francisco for suicides, and just before she heard about it she had watched the Eric Steel documentary, *The Bridge*, which had documented suicides as they happened. The subject matter made her sad yet simultaneously interested. One of the English students in her class described it as a car crash documentary. She had to agree.

For some reason, Isabelle needed the proximity of somewhere like Aokigahara just once in her life. Despite her relationship with Masaki she had no real idea how long she would remain in Japan. What if she left and never returned? Life was for living in the present, for doing things now and not in the past or in a future which might never arrive.

They packed two rucksacks with provisions. Small metal tins within which they could heat water, packs of noodles, dried foodstuffs of various kinds which neither of them thought they would eat, and a tent stuffed into Masaki's bag which they were secretly hoping to use; even though the idea of staying the night was only tacitly on the agenda.

Just before they left, Isabelle stripped down to her underwear and lay backwards on the bed, her legs open, one hand squeezing her right breast. She called to Masaki who had his back to her and was clipping together the plastic buckles on his rucksack.

"Masaki?"

"Ummm."

"Come here."

He turned and watched her slide a hand underneath her panties. Stopping to clip together the last two straps he stood over and then knelt between her.

"Fuck me," Isabelle said.
And Masaki did.

It was a clear day when they reached the forest. Masaki wanted them to stick to the designated trails which led to the attractions of the Ice Cave and the Wind Cave. Isabelle was unsure what she wanted. In some respects, she wanted to be completely lost. Only then might she tell Masaki that she loved him. But then, to be *completely* lost? Maybe that was another matter entirely.

They passed the newly erected signs urging those who had come to Aokigahara to commit suicide to turn back and seek help. They walked through the first kilometre of forest littered by plastic tape left by the local volunteers who arranged the yearly 'body hunt'.

"Maybe we should leave something behind, like this tape," said Isabelle. "You know, like Hansel and Gretel."

She then had to explain the fairy tale to Masaki who had never heard of it. Sometimes she forgot the differences between them, so closely had they come to resemble each other.

He was breathing heavily as they walked, his pack being the larger. "But, from what you say, those children were left in the forest. We are entering by choice."

She shrugged. "So maybe we are Hansel and Gretel in reverse. Maybe we are entering the forest with the intention of getting lost."

Masaki only shook his head, pushed forwards into the trees. He wanted to leave those ideas behind.

After a while, though, the basis of the story tugged at his memories, and he told her about *ubasute*.

"Our legend says that this forest might have been a location for *ubasute*. The story goes that in feudal times infirm or elderly relatives were carried to remote places and left there to die by their family members, either by dehydration, starvation or exposure. Whether it is true or not – and nowadays I would think not – the legend has resulted in many poems and literature. In one story, a son carries his mother up the mountain on his back. During the journey she stretches out her arms, catching twigs and leaves and scattering them on the ground behind her so that her son will be able to find his way home."

Isabelle stopped; looked at the trees around them which seemed to press closer. Whereas at the start of the trail there were other couples and walkers she realised that as they had proceeded they had lost sight of those around them.

"That's a sad story," she said.

Masaki nodded. He wanted to add, *you decided to come here*, but he kept his head down and walked further into the forest. In his mind's eye he kept a record of the trail, so that they might find their way home, although he had a feeling that wouldn't be necessary.

After a couple of hours they located a grassy area just off the main trail and opened their backpacks to eat. Masaki had a small gas canister which he fired up and heated some water within which they placed their noodles. Even with some *mentsuyu* sauce the meal tasted bland, as though the oppressiveness of the forest had squeezed the flavour from the meal.

Oppressiveness. Both of them, in their own way, considered their thoughts. It was true that now they were motionless the forest no longer moved with them. There was something in this static situation that unnerved them. To make conversation, Masaki told Isabelle another story.

"Do you know Issei Sagawa?"

Isabelle shook her head, the tip of her chopsticks just at the edge of her lips as she had placed some noodles in her mouth.

"Issei Sagawa was a Japanese student living in France. In the early 80s he murdered and cannibalised a Dutch student. First, he shot her in the back of her head. Then he consumed parts of her after he had sex with her corpse. It was mentioned in a song by the Rolling Stones. *Too Much Blood*. Do you know it?"

Isabelle could only answer *mmmmm* because of the noodles in her mouth. She felt like spitting them out, they were chewy and she couldn't digest them, but she kept them there and finally swallowed because she didn't want Masaki to think he had spooked her.

She had remembered the story. "I don't know *Too Much Blood*, but English punks The Stranglers also wrote about him in song. It was sung in French. *La Folie*. Do you know it?"

Masaki didn't.

"Strangely it was popular in gay bars." Isabelle crossed her arms under her breasts.

There was movement. They both watched as an older Japanese male, dressed in a business suit complete with briefcase, walked along the main trail. He hadn't seen them, slightly off from the path as they were. He walked with his head down, small even paces. When he passed Isabelle stood but Masaki put his hand on her arm. "It's not our business," he said.

For a moment Isabelle thought he was serious, but when a smile spread across his face she realised he was making a poor joke. Neither of them really expected the man to kill himself. The forest was putting thoughts in their heads.

They walked for another hour. After a while, the forest views became so similar as to be boring. They were walking for nothing. Whether they walked for ten more minutes or ten more hours it would make no difference. The view was constant. The trees close together. Isabelle felt if they were to play hide and seek they would never find each other again. It would only take one of them to hide behind one tree to discover they were hiding behind every tree and that the other would have to look behind every tree first in order to get even close to them.

As for the Cave of Ice and the Cave of Wind, they must have passed them by now. In fact, although they had followed the trail, they might as well have wandered off the path for all the sights they had seen.

Masaki strode ahead. Isabelle knew he wanted to leave this place, regretted coming. And one way to leave was to forge ahead as quickly as possible, so that they might reach a point where she would suggest they return. It seemed odd that in order to go back they had to go forwards. She decided they should turn back sooner rather than later, but first of all she wanted to find that special place where she might tell Masaki she loved him.

She decided that when they returned home she would read the novel *Nami No Tō* by Seichō Matsumoto. She had researched it prior to leaving. Translated as *Wave of Trees* it told the story of two lovers who committed suicide in the forest. She hadn't wanted to read it before the trip. For obvious reasons.

"Hey, Masaki," she called ahead. Masaki kept walking forwards. She ran up behind him, her breath catching in her throat. For one terrible instant she had the feeling that if she touched his shoulder and he turned around that he wouldn't be the Masaki that she loved, but someone else. But the worst thing about it would be that she would never know the difference.

Then she touched him all the same.

Shortly afterwards, she pointed to another spot where they might rest. She made an excuse that her legs were aching, which was truth in part; but really she didn't want to go on any farther. There seemed no point. She had *proved* her point, in fact. She had led Masaki into the forest, knowingly against his will, and she knew that he would do anything for her.

There was a small clearing. They sat down on the volcanic rock surface surrounded by a circle of trees. Isabelle pulled off her walking boots and massaged her feet through her socks.

"You shouldn't do that," Matsuki said, "your feet will swell and you won't be able to get your boots on again."

Isabelle shrugged. She knew he was right. "Listen," she said.

They both stopped talking and let the nothingness of the forest envelop them.

For a moment they were statues. To break the silence seemed sacrilege. The forest was a shrine, of sorts. Isabelle found her eyes scanning the trees looking for the suspended legs of the Japanese businessman with the suitcase. Why had they laughed at him? Surely the *only* reason for him being here was to commit suicide?

She felt her heart swell. Contained within that mini-tsunami was the thought that she must tell Masaki exactly how she loved him before she lost him. That feeling was so intense that she opened her mouth to say the words, but in that instance a larger tsunami swept them away. She was overcome with an even more incredible sense of...

Masaki sat silent, looking at the trees surrounding them. He could see how Aokigahara had been named. A sea of trees. It was exactly that. Just as you submerged yourself in water you could submerge yourself in trees. He had a sensation that if he plunged between them, off the path, that he would be drowned and lost forever. Then his mind wandered as to why he had told Isabelle the stories of *ubarte* and Issei Sagawa. He knew an element of him had not told those stories, they had in fact told themselves, through him.

Just as he had this revelation he had the sudden urge to ask Isabelle to marry him. It came upon him with such intensity that when he turned his face to look at her, Isabelle's considerable beauty hit him full force. The feeling was so intense that he decided to open his mouth to say those words, but simultaneously a force surpassed that desire with even more determination. He was overcome with an incredible sense of...

Holding hands they made their way over the dead twigs which broke into pieces under the heaviness of their walking boots. As they approached the entrance to the forest and the wide expanse of the main road they both let out breaths which it seemed they had been holding for the previous two hours.

On their way out of the forest they were questioned by strangers. They had been asked about the man with the briefcase. CCTV had caught him entering the forest and a search was underway. It was unusual, they were told, for a solitary salaryman to enter the forest alone. And if not unusual, then ominous. Between them they wondered if they could have prevented a suicide.

Yet this was at the back of their minds. In the clearing, just as each of them was due to speak, one of them had experienced déjà vu and the other jamais vu.

Déjà vu: the sensation of feeling sure that one has already experienced a situation even though the exact circumstances of that supposed encounter are uncertain and probably imagined.

Jamais vu: an impression of having been in a situation for the very first time despite rationally knowing that one has been there before.

Unlike Hansel and Gretel, one of them had already been in the forest and one of them only thought they had.

Away from the forest, perhaps down on one of the beaches on the Tango Peninsular, a wave broke on the shore. Maybe on a beach which many years ago had contained trees. Or maybe it was Aokigahara which had many years ago been under water. Neither Isabelle nor Masaki would have known.

Upon leaving the forest they could only remember that one of them had déjà vu and the other jamais vu but neither could remember which experience they'd had.

Such a simple thing prised them apart. It was a while before they would love again. And that love would be forever shadowed by death.

❁

I've said before how a story title is essential for me to begin writing, and in many instances the title is the spark itself. In this case the title came to me whilst at the coast (unsurprisingly I guess), while I stood by some steps on the sea defences. The platform at the top of the steps implied a cage over the sea. I made a note of the title and filed it in my memory for later.

In addition to the title, a couple of other ideas then converged to work together: jamais vu and the Aokigahara forest.

Everyone knows of the concept of déjà vu, but I had only recently become aware of jamais vu. Wiki summarises it nicely: *Often described as the opposite of déjà vu, jamais vu involves a sense of eeriness and the observer's impression of seeing the situation for the first time, despite rationally knowing that he or she has been in the situation before.*

Always obsessed with ideas of the perception of reality, I knew this discovery would provide fodder for a story. I just hadn't been sure how to use it.

I had also been intrigued by stories of Aokigahara, a forest in Japan which is a popular place for those wishing to commit suicide. Doing some research on the topic I found that Aokigahara is also known as the Sea of Trees. Often in moments like this I wonder if there is an overseeing force teasing stories out of me, because "The Caged Sea" was obviously the perfect title for this story. It wasn't long before the concept of jamais vu adhered itself and I realised I could work everything together.

Interference

My parents told me the first word I read was *ambulance*.

I was three years old. We were driving through Peckham Rye, South London, when the interior of our vehicle was lit by flashing lights and a familiar siren wove its way in and out of our ears. In those days no one wore seatbelts. I used to recline on the back seat of the Ford Cortina and sleep, my head resting on my older sister's legs whilst she stroked my hair. I don't remember the sirens and I don't remember the lights, but my parents said I rose to a kneeling position and looked out of the rear window.

My dad told me to sit down.

Ambulance, I said; and pointed to the vehicle bearing down on us as my dad waited for a few loose pedestrians to move so that he could pull up on the pavement and let it pass.

"That's clever, Rhys," my mother had said.

My sister said, "Duh! He's reading it backwards." She oscillated from believing me very stupid or very clever.

"It's just that he knows it's an ambulance," my dad said, steering the car back to the road as the vehicle passed.

Apparently my mother had nodded. The incident would have been forgotten if I hadn't then said: "E C N A L U B M A. Ambulance."

I never leave the house without a mirror. I've learnt to palm it, a conjuror's trick where I am both magician and spectator. This way I can see both worlds at once. The world that *you* know, where everything is as it should be, and the world that I know where everything is reversed. I tried to explain this to a girlfriend once, who caught me looking at her via a mirror as she lay on her front, naked on my bed.

"It's about perception," I said. "It's about seeing things simultaneously."

Michelle was open to understanding. Her Lydia Lunch record was playing, the cover of *Some Velvet Morning* where Lunch duets with Rowland S. Howard and their voices overlap in a disconnected yet weirdly compelling sequence. Even so, I felt she leant towards my mirror as some kind of perversion. "Tell me about it," she said.

"Next time you're on a train you should stand in the middle of the aisle. Look straight down the centre of the compartment. Everyone is static. Yet in the peripheries of your vision you'll see the outside world on both sides rush past as though sucking you into a vortex. That's how I see the world most of the time."

She buried her face in the pillow, opened her legs wide so that my gaze was directed between those two narrow limbs and channelled towards the tunnel at their apex. "Is it like this?" she asked.

We fell into each other. Those were the good times.

I palm the mirror in my right hand because I am naturally left-handed and that way I can still operate within the world without it being awkward. The fingers of my right hand are almost permanently cupped. When I remove the mirror at the end of a journey there is a squared indentation of flesh that remains in my palm. Before she left me Michelle had warned that I'd have arthritis one day. If I live long enough maybe she'll be proved right.

Leonardo Da Vinci was left-handed. Many of his notes are in mirror-image cursive. Some believe this was due to secrecy, although as a code it seems suspect to me. Others believe it was through expediency, mirror writing enabled his fingers to keep up with his brain and it would have been easier to write from right to left without smudging. All I know is that Da Vinci was a genius, and sometimes I glimpse a fraction of what he must have known and seen; but I can't focus on it, like *presque vu* those images, those *words*, remain just out of perception and reach.

The sensation of not being in syncopation with the world has dogged me through every relationship, has harnessed me to the whims of others. I imagine this is why each interaction has failed. And whilst that failure buys me freedom, so with freedom comes loneliness.

My parents were punked-up ex-hippies with one toe in the sixties and the other in the seventies.

"Try him with Rhys," my mother said.

I remember these memories. It would have been a month on from the ambulance episode and Sunday afternoons were spent with pen and paper, my pre-school days learning about myself instead of others.

S Y H R, my father wrote on the paper.

"Rhys," I said.

"Damn," said my mother, "he heard me."

"Of course he heard you; you should learn to shut up."

Annoyance simmered on my mother's face. By now I was used to their arguments. They didn't know how to deal with me.

R E H T O M, my father wrote on the paper.

"Mother," I said, and then my father wrote *L O O F*. And so it went on; word after word after word.

My sister leant against the door jamb. Outside it was raining hard, each drop hit the windowpane like a question mark. I remember watching her watching us, realising she had become an outsider because she was normal. There was dislocation there too, between both of us. My learning disability had come between us, caused interference.

I use the term *learning disability* lightly. I have not been diagnosed with such. Throughout my childhood years the system was patient with me. My teachers were provided mirrors so they could mark my essays. Unlike many others who naturally write their way out of the conundrum and reverse their behaviour, or who are forced into learning to write the *proper* way, I was not coerced into being someone I wasn't. It is those progressive teachers I blame for my capacity now.

They should have fixed me.

I duck into the crawlspace which serves as a storage area that runs behind my bedroom in the flat that I rent. It's an anomaly of the house, an aberration of the builders that was then converted into something useful. You can't stand in it. The door itself is Alice In Wonderland-ish. Whilst I don't have to eat something to become small enough to enter, there's a certainty that if I ate too much then I wouldn't be able to leave.

Dark presses around me. The crawlspace is not dissimilar to a coffin. I lie on my back and still my breathing. In here there are no indications of the real world, pulsing on the outside like the chambers of a heart. There are no words, no jumbles of misunderstanding. Its position almost makes it soundproof: a cocoon from which I emerge reborn, if only for a few moments.

It's those few moments that I crave.

Nowadays I'm known as Matt. Rhys is consigned to the past. Although Matt itself isn't specific enough. It has to be MATT. MATT is the only way that I can be.

Two dimensional objects, such as alphabetical letters, are not chiral due to the existence of a horizontal symmetry plane, but many of them do become chiral when written on a piece of paper. So the mirror images of the uppercase letters A H I M O T U V W X Y are virtually identical; except for some line thickness and minor artistic details associated with particular choices of fonts. The lowercase letters are all asymmetric except i m o v w x.

One afternoon I spent some time with those letters, rearranging, attempting to find meaning. But I only found my new name. It didn't matter that it still needed to be written back to front, as TTAM; what was important was that its integrity remained in the mirror.

The expression that the camera never lies has always been a falsehood. We can never see ourselves as others see us. This is also true in respect to mirrors. The face reflected back at you is reversed. Either everyone else sees the real you, or none of them do. You choose.

I have drilled a hole in the back of the crawlspace that emerges within a spiral pattern on the wallpaper on the other side. Into the hole I press a fisheye lens, so that when I put my eye to the hole I can see the curved entirety of my bedroom. Yet this is actually just a reflection. What I'm really looking at is the mirror which dominates the opposite wall.

Later when I look through this hole I wonder if I'll see myself enter the room and lie on the bed.

Michelle left when she realised my weirdness was innate and not affected. She was comfortable in it being an act, but not as reality.

"It's not you," she lied. Then paused. "Well, it *is* you."

I had been cutting a red pepper into tiny slivered strips, ready to be thrown into the wok alongside the carrot, spring onion, and bean sprouts which would make up the rest of the chow mein once I'd added the noodles. The slivers resembled arteries.

Focussing on meals helped me concentrate on the world. There was a clear delineation between cause and effect. I hated interruptions when cooking.

"Does this mean we're eating together or not?"

My teeth were pressed tight. Seeds shot out from the side of the pepper as I sliced into the second half.

"It means I don't know about us, is all."

Michelle was back-peddling. Maybe she'd always thought that way, had been desperate to express it, but then once she had the reality of what she was saying undermined her ability to believe it. All I know is that I turned right then, the tip of the blade pointing towards her stomach, in what I hadn't realised was an aggressive gesture. And because she got scared, she didn't come back. I had given her the excuse that she needed.

On the bus I read the headline of the newspaper of the man sitting opposite. I have to be careful with the mirror. Sometimes it catches the light, reflects it into the eyes of the person I'm observing. There have been a few embarrassing moments. Girls think I'm trying to look up their skirts, but I would never do this. I already know the truth that they think is hidden there.

I get off at my stop. Walk forwards whilst looking backwards into the mirror. The future recedes as the past abates. Or is it the other way around? I read words on advertisement hoardings, house numbers, the names of shops, all correctly represented in the mirror.

Interestingly, from some of the letters A H I M O T U V W X Y you can spell *MOUTH*.

At the retirement home my mother's mouth gapes open. I nudge the base of her chin with my forefinger and close it for her. Moments later it hangs again, like a faulty trapdoor.

After her stroke a few years back she developed acquired mirror writing. The neurologists were particularly interested, knowing my background. It appeared the stroke affected various peripheral and deep locations in her left hemisphere, but it was transient, lasted for just a few weeks, and was confined to a few letters, words and sentences. My mother was ambidextrous, but the mirror writing only affected her left hand. With her right hand she continued to write normally.

For me, the interesting factor was that she didn't realise she was doing this. She rode those two pathways simultaneously.

Just as on the train, with the interior static and calm and the outside world forcing itself either side; coming at you in a rush.

The neurologist spoke in detail of the corpus callosum, about transcallosal deactivation of contralateral crossed pathways. All of this went over my head. It was when he brought up Da Vinci that my attention clicked back in.

"Of course, centuries ago some academics viewed mirror writing as the natural script of the left-hander. It's a compelling view. One that retains some credence today."

He repeatedly moved his hand back and forth across his head as he spoke. A nervous tic manifested and heightened by my presence. He continued:

"The evidence that mirror writing is the natural script of the left hander arises from everyday observations that abductive movements are generally more natural, and also more accurate, than adductive movements. Writing with a pen held in the left hand will therefore be more readily undertaken leftwards; the script, too, would then be reversed compared with the conventional rightward directed script – that is, mirrored.

"So, mirror writing with the left hand is not a bizarre form of writing at all, but predictable, and presumably a form of writing that is normally suppressed or superseded by conventional writing in order to be read."

I saw then how conventional writing *interfered* with my natural ability. How the real world tried to impose – to superimpose – itself over the world that I saw.

Or, to put it my way, how the world tried to superimpose itself over the *real* world that I saw.

I jiggle my mother's jaw up and down. The second stroke slackened everything in her body and mind. Forwards or backwards, she wouldn't be writing again.

My sister enters as I leave. Dad doesn't come, of course; that relationship is long gone. Neither of us see much of him, but then we probably wouldn't have done anyway. I don't even see much of my sister, but I always remember lying on the back seat of the car with the sun burning the rectangle of the back window, and one of her hands in my hair with the other holding a book that occasionally would slip and drop onto my face.

"How's it going?" she always says.

I always reply *fine.*

Then she continues into my mother's room and I re-emerge from the crawlspace that is her confinement and have to find my place within the world again.

Integrity remains in the mirror.

There's a fascination with mirrors in everyone. Mirrors are a cliché of horror movies: the glimpse of something standing behind you which wasn't there a moment ago. The specialists who examined me when I was a child used to impress on me that my writing could only be read when viewed in a mirror. What they failed to perceive was that my writing could only be understood by *them* that way. For me, it was perfect already.

I don't need the mirrors to see the world as I see it, but to see the world as you see it.

And I need to do that to exist in that world, because that world predominates over mine.

But there are things I can do: the modification of the crawlspace, the use of mirrors to confuse and contain, to subtly subvert the expectations of those who don't see things the way I do. To reclaim the world as it should be seen.

After Michelle there was Justina. We were once eating in Soho in a tiny Thai restaurant which had just enough space for diners with the kitchen at the rear and a toilet at the bottom of a perilous set of stairs. Justina descended those steps and turned straight into the full-length mirror which reflected the doorway on the opposite side.

In bed I kissed the raised skin on her forehead. The restaurant had waived the price of our meal, and from the money saved we bought a large box of individually wrapped Belgian chocolates, which sat on our nightstand. I took out a chocolate, divested it of the coloured paper, and held it close to the bulb within the bedside lamp until the tips of my fingers hurt and the chocolate began to drip. I wrote the word E R O H W across her stomach and she laughed and hit me and I bent my head to lick off the words and we fucked like there was no tomorrow.

Once she was asleep, I slipped out of bed and into the crawlspace. I watched her in the dim glow from the streetlight outside the window, through the fisheye, with her body reflected in the mirror.

Sometimes I'm just as normal as everyone else.

If it had been *my* head that had hit the mirror this is what would have happened:

I would have awoken the following day in hospital. Bleary-eyed, I would have looked from left to right, then right to left. There would be no mirror in my hand. A surge of panic would fly through my limbs and into my throat, but then I would pause, allow my breathing to regulate, would remember.

And I would see, quite clearly, the world as everyone else saw it, without reflection.

That would be how it would be if I had hit my head in the mirror.

It's no coincidence that when I went for an eye-test the ophthalmologist asked me to look at a chart which read:

A

H I

M O T

U V W X Y

My existence flits between acceptance and anger, shards of my life oscillate roughly against each other with a grinding noise; or – when I feel particularly displaced – the interference manifests itself through the sound of ripping paper. A continual tear.

A few years before Da Vinci died he was commissioned by the King of France to make a mechanical lion which could walk forward, then open its chest to reveal a cluster of lilies.

That was almost five hundred years ago.

Historical records aren't clear on the circumstances of his death. My belief is that as he rushed towards the void he would have seen everything and nothing simultaneously: an extension of the life that he led.

The pressure of knowledge, of the unseen world being a reflection of the seen world, is a heavy burden to bear. Lesser folk might be driven mad.

Imagine an old-fashioned printing press. The device applies pressure to a print medium such as paper that rests on an inked surface made of moveable type, and in the process transfers the ink. The letters on the press are individually set by the printer. But they're not set in the conventional way that you could read them, because their shapes have to be mirrored onto the paper. For centuries, therefore, knowledge has been transferred from the format I can already understand to a format that you can understand. Which of us has the learning disability now?

One of these days that pressure will become too great. I'll stand at the junction and watch each car, I'll remain static while they pass in a blur of confusions and misunderstandings. The world will press in on me, imprinting all its words that insist on being in the wrong order on my mirror-written brain. That pressure, that insistent inescapable force, will cumulate and persist until I discern a larger than average white vehicle out of the oncoming traffic, until the delineation between pavement and highway, between vehicle and myself, becomes equally blurred.

Maybe there'll be lights – maybe there'll be sirens – but I know the last word I will read will be ecnalubma. My left hand will be embedded with glass.

❀

This story was written for an anthology based around the concept of chiralty. One of the ideas which came into my head revolved around an aspect of chiralty concerning writing backwards and certain letters which are chiral (those whose properties remain identical when looked at in a mirror, such as my main character's name, MATT). I decided my character would become obsessed by chiralty to the extent that he preferred to view the world through mirrors: something which would impact on his entire life and relationships.

Whilst researching the story it was interesting to see who else practised mirror writing, a list which included Leonardo Da Vinci, who wrote most of his personal notes that way. Da Vinci was left-handed and there is an argument that mirror writing is actually the most logical way for left handers to write as it is less awkward for the hand on the page. I also read articles which mentioned that sometimes those who are brain damaged or suffer from neurological diseases might start mirror writing despite never having done so before. Some research also included instances where children who mirror wrote were 'persuaded' to write 'naturally'. My character has his mirror writing untampered with since childhood and he views everyone else as being out of sync with the world, not himself.

Softwood

Apricot brushed a strand of brunette hair away from her right eye. It was a self-conscious movement, yet utterly natural; like a leaf falling from a tree. She stared forwards at the vacant chair behind the large oak desk, resisting the urge to look around the empty, windowless, office. She had been ushered into the room and told to wait until Mr Grantham was available. One of her legs was crossed over the other and she sat straight. She had a feeling there might be a recording device present and so she considered her posture as if Mr Grantham were already in the room. She wanted to keep it professional.

If there were a device, it might be concealed within any of the books which flanked the opposite wall, or within the back of the anglepoise lamp, or be monitoring her through one of the whorls of wallpaper that covered the left hand side of the room. The wallpaper was incongruous with the rest of the office. Yet the office itself seemed incongruous with the rest of Softwood.

She had been employed for over six months. It was a large, rambling estate, filled with intellectuals and scientists, set amongst several acres of woodland populated by both roe and muntjac deer. One of her roles was to decipher any meanings which might be found within the extracts of Linear A, yet she had made little progress. She was expert in Latin and Greek, had studied Linear B and considered Alice Kober to have been a role model, but the data that was available was simply insufficient to discern patterns. It was frustrating, but it was also interesting and the pay was good. Not only that, but the company was better. Softwood was a residential establishment and each evening was filled chatting with dynamic individuals. She never wondered why she was there.

The door opened and Grantham entered. She smiled and he acknowledged her with a nod before taking his seat opposite.

"Apricot."

"Mr Grantham."

She had seen him before, of course, but similar to the deer not up close. She imagined he was in his seventies, he had a good head of only slightly receding white hair, thick black-rimmed spectacles, a brown tie over a cream shirt, and his customary jacket which wasn't part of a suit. Unlike her, his clothes were mismatched. But this leant him a certain charm. In fact, Apricot was a little overawed. If this registered with Grantham then it didn't show.

"I've been looking at your findings with Linear A," he began.

Apricot held back from voicing that *findings* might be a generous word.

"To be honest," he continued, "I'm rather disappointed."

She struggled to maintain her posture. So this was it, she was being discharged from her duties.

"I appreciate the source material is minimal, but we were rather hoping that someone with your previous experience might have been able to pull a rabbit out of the hat, as it were." He leant forwards, picked up a stray paperclip which he then unbent within his fingers and used to pick holes in the doodled green blotting paper which covered part of the desk. "Still, the disappointment isn't with you as such. You've proven to be a valuable member of the team. Roche speaks highly of you, as does Miss Cardamon. So highly, in fact, we've decided to use you for something else."

Apricot wondered if her relief showed. She would have been happy cleaning the ladies' rooms if it meant remaining in Softwood.

Grantham sat back in his chair, regarded the paperclip with curiosity, as if he hadn't seen it before. He placed it in his pocket. "The work we're considering is highly confidential. You will be isolated in a wing of Softwood and your movements will be limited. You won't come into contact with many – if any – of the acquaintances you have already made. Of course, if this isn't acceptable to you then we might have to let you go. Budgets are tight at the moment, and in six months..." he let his hands speak as they opened and their movement triggered his shoulders to shrug.

"I understand," said Apricot, her mind a whirl. "What is it you want me to do?"

A few days later she found herself hugging Miss Cardamon and giving Roche a playful wink.

"The secrets of Linear A will mean nothing without you," he said.

Thankfully she wasn't a girl for blushing. "If you decipher it," she said, "I hope to be the first to know."

Their smiles were warm. Roche came and put his arm around her shoulders, gave her a squeeze. "Of course," he said, then left the room quicker than she expected.

Miss Cardamon looked at her. "He has a crush on you."

"Maybe." Apricot detected the wistfulness in her voice.

Miss Cardamon looked as if she might say more, but then the door opened and Grantham's personal secretary nodded.

"If you're ready follow me. Your luggage has already been taken care of."

She smiled as Miss Cardamon raised an eyebrow. "I'm being relocated both personally and professionally," Apricot said.

The last words she heard as she left the room were: "Don't be a stranger."

Apricot followed the secretary through the winding corridors of Softwood. Grantham's office had no windows as it was deep in the heart of the building, a nest within a nest of boxes. But on these floors the massive leaded windows of the former stately home shone copious amounts of light onto the highly polished floors and added to the grandeur of the building which was filled with artefacts and the unknown.

Apricot was no less swept away than she was when she first arrived. A surge of adventure coursed through her, and she reminded herself how glad she was not to have travelled the beauty therapist, housewife, or even librarian route of some of her contemporaries.

The secretary didn't speak as she followed. He avoided direct eye contact and kept himself to himself.

At the opposite end of the house, passing fewer and fewer people along the way, the secretary unlocked a door which led to a stairwell.

"Your rooms are down there," he said. "Everything you need."

She nodded and waited for him to continue, but he simply held the door open. Eventually she realised he meant her to go down alone.

"Thank you," she said. Then she squeezed passed him and her heels clicked out a rhythm on the stone stairway as she descended. It was a spiral. The constant turning was disconcerting. It was just when she realised that she must be underground that she was sure she heard the door lock above her.

She paused and listened. There were no sounds. Knowing it would be churlish to return upstairs, she continued downwards. Without windows, electric light illuminated the way until eventually she reached the bottom.

If the stairway had seemed sterile, the corridor that greeted her was welcoming. Thickly carpeted; with several rooms leading off to each side. At the end, an earthenware pot fired with a deep blue glaze, stood on a small table beneath a mirror.

She walked towards it, expecting the corridor to branch either left or right at an angle which she couldn't yet see, but quickly realised the corridor was the extent of the space. She stood in front of the mirror, saw herself looking querulously back. Her curiosity was piqued. She returned down the corridor, trying each of the four doors as she went. They all opened. It seemed there were no secrets here.

She casually examined them. The room nearest the foot of the stairway was her bedroom. The appearance was functional; she might have been at a budget hotel. Her bags had been laid on the bed and she spent time restoring normality by hanging her clothes in the wardrobe and placing her underwear and personal items in the bedside cabinet. The room across the corridor was the bathroom and toilet. She quickly realised she would be the only occupant in this part of the building, and the thought both excited and scared her. Whatever she had been chosen for was indeed secret, yet she was a gregarious creature and didn't like to spend much time alone.

The third room contained a computer and little else. The fourth room she was familiar with having done some radio assignments at college. All the right equipment was there for broadcasting.

On the middle of the desk in that room was a note.

She picked it up. It wasn't addressed to her. It bore the name *Vespertine*.

From now on, Vespertine *is your code name. Your only name.*

If we appear to be overly cautious please believe me there is a justifiable reason for this. The work you are to do is highly confidential. You have been chosen because of your background, your past experiences. Should you decide against this task, you can leave at any time. For the moment, however, please take a day or two to familiarise yourself with your surroundings. Your first broadcast won't be until midnight tomorrow evening.

Apricot read the note several times over. Without it bearing her name it had been a while before she had opened it. Over the course of two hours she had frequently walked up and down the stairwell, listening to nothing sounds on the other side of the locked door. Her reflection also revealed no answers. She felt like a lioness in a cage.

The letter had eventually drawn her because she considered it must be meant for her. It was the only object in her quarters that she could interact with. The computer in the other room appeared to have no on/off switch and she realised its power was maintained independently elsewhere. The letter confirmed this. From tomorrow and each day onwards she would be sent an email for that evening's broadcast. The letter made it clear there should be no deviation. It concluded: *Above all else we admire your professionalism*. It was signed, *William Grantham*.

Afterwards she found herself fiddling with the broadcasting equipment under the guise of familiarisation. There was no music saved on the hard drive which powered the mixing desk. The only file available was saved as *jingle*. When she opened it she heard the opening two bars of the folk song, *The Lincolnshire Poacher*, played electronically. There was no soul in the song, but she knew why as soon as she heard it.

Apricot was to be the voice of a numbers station.

The door at the head of the stairs remained locked all night.

She had fully investigated all the rooms which led off the corridor by the time she went to sleep. In the room which housed the computer she realised there was a sliding panel which led to a dumb waiter. Whilst not feeling particularly hungry she took the tray to her bed and ate the ploughman's lunch heartily. Having opened the letter the dread she had initially felt began to dissipate. Even so, to be alone didn't sit well with her, and she found her thoughts continually turning to Roche.

Whilst she had no romantic liaisons during her six months at Softwood, Roche had played an increasing role in her fantasies. His broad shoulders, ready wit, natural intelligence and ease in her presence triggered everything that was female within her. Now, distant from him, she realised she should have eschewed her simmering shyness and played a wider role.

Come morning, she found the computer as awake as herself. A solitary email, under the name of *Grantham*, sat in her inbox. She opened it and saw a brief instruction together with the list of numbers she had been expecting. In every instance, the email stated, she should voice the final digit in each five number sequence with a lilt to her voice.

Apricot couldn't help but be intrigued. Numbers stations were known to her. She knew she would be broadcasting on various shortwave frequencies presumably controlled from outside of the environment she was in. Her voice would be artificially altered; synthesised. What she didn't know – what anyone didn't apparently know – was the purpose of these broadcasts. Although the speculation that she might be working for the British Secret Service sent a thrill up her spine that was hard to ignore.

She deliberated whether to respond to the email, then decided it wasn't necessary. She was sure all her movements must be under surveillance, although she hoped this didn't extend to the bedroom or bathroom.

Much of the day was spent looking into the mirror, practising her tone of voice for the broadcast, and repeatedly making the journey up and down the stairs to check that the door remained locked.

At eleven-thirty pm she initiated checks of the equipment, donned her headphones, and ensured the loudness of her voice was within the boundaries specified in the email.

At midnight she played the jingle.

At fifteen seconds past midnight, she began her broadcast.

0-2-5-8-8
6-9-7-2-1
3-0-1-1-2
9-0-2-3-6
4-4-5-7-3
2-0-0-0-7

The broadcast concluded at one am.

Apricot signed off as directed, a few seconds after the final number, with the solitary word: *vespertine.*

She smiled and switched off the equipment. Assuming they believed she had done her job satisfactorily, she imagined she would repeat the same task tomorrow.

In case you are wondering, the word vespertine *relates to a genus of flowers which only bloom in the evening.*

Apricot re-read the note which had been placed on her breakfast tray. It had been typed on an old fashioned typewriter. She could feel the indentations on the reverse of the paper, and the *e*'s were blocked with excess ink.

She wondered who had sent it. Imagined it couldn't be Grantham, yet found it hard to believe it might be his secretary. Nonsensically, she found herself hoping it had been Roche. And the sensation that he could have chosen her codename appealed to her.

After breakfast she drifted into a dreamless sleep. The day yawned before her. She began to think how long the task might last. Considered it could be indefinite. Searching the rooms she realised she had no way to communicate with the rest of Softwood. There were no writing implements, the computer would print the contents of the email but wouldn't open programmes for anything else, and it had been clear on her first arrival that there was no signal for her mobile.

Again, a sense of panic coupled with excitement gripped her. Whilst she was – in some respects – solely in control of her destiny, she realised this was completely within imposed parameters. *So this is what religion feels like*, she thought. The sense of predetermination was as comforting as it was compelling.

Days began to slide into one. A succession of numbers. No other notes accompanied her breakfast or any other meal, and the emails from constantly changing accounts contained less and less comment and more and more numbers. Her broadcasts became equally uniform:

5-5-3-2-7

6-8-4-3-2

3-3-2-2-3

0-9-0-2-1

1-2-1-1-2

0-0-0-0-0

The one certainty – she had to remind herself – was that the task held purpose and that her contribution was valued.

She had to remind herself over and again.

Apricot became a creature of habit. She set herself routines to deal with the day and allowed transformation to occur during the evening. She reasoned that if she were Apricot whilst the sun was up, so she should be Vespertine as it set. She began to dress accordingly, choosing items from her wardrobe which could delineate between the two personalities. Apricot: the diligent, demure employee. Vespertine: the spy and potential femme fatale. In perpetuating this format, she effectively halved her days.

Mornings she cleansed her face with a salt facial scrub in the bathroom mirror, washed her skin clean until it was as smooth as stone. She wore the professional skirt suit she had attended Grantham's interview with, and imagined the one-way exchange she had with the computer as if she were dealing with clients in a tax office. Come evening, she glammed up from the contents of her make-up bag, overly rouging her lips, choosing clothes she reserved for the occasional decadent party, using the corridor as a catwalk as she sauntered back and forth towards the earthenware pot and the mirror above it. Wondered if Roche could witness her transformation, or whether it was only Grantham who wondered what he had done.

9-2-4-3-2
4-4-6-7-2
0-9-7-2-7
2-8-2-7-4
7-4-8-6-3

Apricot began to find her relationship with Vespertine was a destructive one. Compared to her mundane lifestyle waiting around for something to happen, Vespertine's was one of glamour and public presence. Vespertine was the one who had a life beyond the corridor and its four rooms. Vespertine had a life which extended to all corners of the globe, her voice reaching anyone who tuned in, and possibly affecting some of those listeners deeply, personally; whereas Apricot's circle of influence was all one way, either electronically through email or via the dumb waiter returning empty plates.

One morning, after a shower, after wondering how many showers she had taken downstairs during how many mornings, Apricot remembered that Roche wasn't simply an object of fantasy for Vespertine's occasionally tremulous outbursts, but that he had been a linguist working with her to solve the Linear A code.

The *language* was written on fragments of stone tablets, a Cretan writing system found at Knossos alongside a later language eventually decoded and known as Linear B.

It was then that Apricot gathered together the printed lists of numbers she had retained in what she had designated to be an out-tray beside the broadcasting equipment and gave herself the task of deciphering the meaning.

Within the confines of the rooms which now constituted her existence, she began to unravel the purpose of her life.

A smile returned to Apricot's face which was borrowed from Vespertine's.

She poured herself into the numbers. Made lists of those which occurred more frequently than others. Equated the frequent numbers with some of the more popular vowels. Broke each set of numbers into smaller sets and merged some of the sequences together. She had to do this literally, tearing up the paper and reforming it in a collage. Before she left Softwood she was determined to know its secrets. Her days began to recapture the intrigue she had first found at being there. Apricot began to consider herself a match for Vespertine.

After a number of indeterminate days fraught with frustration, she returned her breakfast toast to the dumb waiter with the crusts shaped to spell *pen*.

The implement arrived with her evening meal.

5-5-6-4-3

7-8-3-6-3

1-1-2-3-2

1-8-7-6-3

0-3-5-0-0

Vespertine signed off, removed her headphones, and gazed into her image dulled by the blackness of the monitor. She listened intently. As usual, apart from a low hum associated with the equipment, her rooms were silent. She focussed on the image of a spy she had created, the one who was eagerly listening to and transcribing her broadcasts. He was broad shouldered, carried humour with his intelligence, not unlike Roche. She wondered what Roche would think of her now, if she ascended the stairs and found the door open. Surely he couldn't equate her with the mousy Apricot? Surely there would be no holding back.

She rose from the desk and went to stand in the corridor before the mirror. She wore an ankle length black dress, low cut at the front and also at the back. Her lips were rouged and mascara almost dripped from her eyelashes. She wanted to dye her brunette hair black, to complete the ensemble. Instead she leant forwards and imprinted a kiss on the mirror, left it for Apricot to clean, before making her way languorously to bed, wishing Roche were watching her every step.

Start with the number you first thought of.

Apricot woke to find her head laying on a sheaf of papers. The printed numbers were underscored in blue ink. Arrows pointed from one to another, like a map of international airways. She rubbed sleep out of the corners of her eyes and stumbled across to the bathroom to splash water on her face, stepping over a black dress she couldn't remember discarding.

Emerging from the bathroom in vest top and pants she returned to the numbers. They swam independently of her gaze. She squeezed her eyes tight, opened them again. The numbers refused to remain static. She shook her head, but the jumbling remained. *I'm going crazy*, she thought. *There's something I'm not seeing.*

The realisation made her sit bolt upright.

Might it not be the numbers which were the key to the code, but the spaces between?

She ran down the corridor to the radio room. Vespertine had recorded each and every broadcast. Apricot donned her headphones and played them back, as many as she could to confirm her suspicions. She could hear tones in the background which hadn't been evident when the broadcasts were made. Could it be that the voice was simply an aid to tuning into the correct frequency, with the actual coded message being sent by modulating the tones, such as with burst transmission?

She shook her head. There was more to it than that. She focused on the spaces between the sets of numbers, on the hiss of white noise, the gradation in tones. She suddenly tore off the headset. She had heard *voices*, she had heard words being transmitted between the numbers.

Still in her vest and pants she ran up the spiral staircase and banged her fists on the door until the skin came off her knuckles.

She slid to the ground, leant tight into the corner. Vespertine found her that way when evening came.

She picked her up. Carried her down the staircase. Into the domain of ghosts.

3-4-5-6-7
3-2-5-6-7
7-8-6-2-2

When Apricot woke she found herself on the floor of the broadcasting suite. Adjacent to her, Vespertine was reading numbers off a sheet of paper, her voice inflecting at the end of each series of five.

2-3-2-3-1
7-6-5-4-3
2-4-5-7-8

Apricot moved into a sitting position, her back against the wall. She rubbed her eyes, bit the inside of her mouth. Vespertine kept reading numbers, until eventually she signed off with that single word.

She turned to face her. "We're working on different things," she said, her voice echoed, as if in a dream. "Your job is to understand the numbers, mine is to detect ghosts through electronic voice perception. Whilst I read the numbers, the machine records. The machine records everything. The voice tunes the channel. Don't you see how that works?"

"I need out," said Apricot, softly.

"We both need out darling."

Vespertine's voice was low and throaty. Apricot goosebumped.

"You're not on the floor," Vespertine said.

Apricot's hair was tied tight at the back of her head. She sat in the chair in Grantham's office. Roche stood behind her, with one hand on her shoulder as if he were holding her down. In reality, she appreciated the comfort.

"Because of you," Grantham was saying, "a lot of lives have been saved. I'm sorry we had to keep details from you. Roche and I considered that if you had simply been given the task of decoding the numbers from the outset, then the chances of success would be lessened. Your talents are not inconsiderable, but Roche was right when he insinuated a frisson of absolute determination should be injected into the work. I hope – in retrospect – that makes sense."

Apricot nodded. It had been two days since she had been released from the cellar, over five weeks since her conversation with Vespertine. She considered charges of unlawful detention, but with the brains of the country against her and issues of national security at risk, she knew nothing would come of it.

She had never been broadcasting the numbers. She had been given numbers already broadcast, and then coerced into a situation where she felt compelled to decode them. But this didn't explain the voices. Grantham and Roche knew nothing about them. She kept them as quiet as Vespertine.

"A vacation is needed," smiled Grantham; the look sat odd on his face. "Your choice."

Away, thought Apricot. *Away*, thought Vespertine. They needed to be away from Softwood and all the covert activities it contained, some of which only they knew.

But *away* wasn't where the discoveries would be made, where the satisfaction would come. They had tapped into knowledge that couldn't be hidden, which they needed to nurture to reap its full potential. That was where the acclaim lay: not with Linear A, nor decoding the numbers. But in the terrible secrets of Softwood revealed by the ghosts. Those harboured by Grantham and Roche.

"I'll stay," Apricot said. She saw Vespertine nod. They would remain to destroy that which they loved.

❀

"Softwood" was a title I had for a while but didn't know where to take it. Was it a character's name, a place, a state of mind, or a metaphor? Subsequent to getting the title I then became aware of numbers stations. These are radio stations characterised by unusual broadcasts, usually the reading out of numbers by female voices, whose origins and purpose are unclear and with which governments deny any involvement. Immediately I sensed some kind of spy story, with a femme fatale at the centre of it, but the character I began to write didn't tick the fatale boxes – although gradually it appeared her alter ego did...

The story went on to merge these broadcasts with the trace of the supernatural through electronic voice phenomenon, whereby the secrets of Softwood aren't so much the broadcasts themselves but what can be picked up within the broadcasts. Or is this true at all? Had the enforced co-operation of my female character in a pseudo-government session unhinged her to the extent that she couldn't interpret the truth in anything? That's for the reader to decide.

My Naked Man

The house was a brownstone on Orange Blossom Drive, the sidewalk a crumpled patchwork of cracks that would take a superstitious person an hour to cross. I paid the cab driver and stood with my hands in my pockets, my head tipping back to scan windows one through to five. She lived on the top floor with an impressive view of the park. From her vantage point the greenery might stretch for miles, the shimmer glimmer of the distant river the only boundary. From my perspective, the park was strewn with discarded corn dog wrappers, rusting metal cans, dirty rain-filled bottles, and excrement.

I didn't envy her position. She had called for me. I hadn't called for anyone. I didn't need to call for anyone.

She buzzed me into the building, her voice a honey glow; buttery. Yet I knew from the society magazines that her appearance didn't resonate with her vocal chords. Short, fat, with a nose that hadn't realigned after a childhood accident and hair which couldn't look after itself. Yet she had money: another reason for my visit. And she had a problem that she thought I could resolve.

I took the stairs two at a time, a habit of mine. Exercise can be found in everyday places. My heels didn't touch the ground until I was standing outside her apartment. Knocking twice, I imagined my features as they might appear through the fisheye: nose prominent, cheeks jovial and rounded, eyes bugging, hair scalped back from my forehead.

When she opened the door I hoped she saw something more agreeable.

"You better come in."

I had removed my hat before I knocked and now I ran the brim in a circular motion through my fingers. She noticed and gesticulated to a chair by the door. I dropped the hat onto it. Then removed my overcoat and draped it over the arm. The white handkerchief in the breast pocket of my jacket had been pulled askew whilst divesting my overcoat, so I removed, re-folded, and replaced it perfectly.

Esme Baker nodded approvingly.

"I like a man who knows how to dress well." Her voice was hoarse through years of nicotine addiction, the words underlined like static on a well-worn vinyl record.

I shrugged. "It's a basic human condition."

She smiled. Smiling didn't improve her looks. "It's *become* human," she said. "It's a cultivation."

I nodded. She turned and led me into the living room. As I walked I cast my eye over the goods and antiques that gave the apartment its identity: original paintings, vases with elaborate designs, old wood furniture polished over the centuries to half its original size. This kind of opulence – despite my attention to my dress – was a million miles from what I knew. In this environment, I had the lifespan of a match-head.

Esme Baker was a socialite, in the old fashioned sense of the word. Although *had* been a socialite might be a more fitting turn of phrase. Her husband had made money in the financial district, and in theory was at his office right now. From our telephone conversation earlier that day, however, I knew this was not the case. Not being the case literally being my case.

Esme sat in an armchair covered with a soft purple furnishing. She directed me to one of the harder chairs that surrounded a table. I took it, turned it, and sat facing her; desperate for a cigarette.

She knew it. "You can't smoke in here. The entire building is cigarette-free."

I took one out from my pack, tapped the end against the box it came from, then returned it. "How do you manage?"

"We have to be adaptable nowadays, don't we, Mr Thackray? What do they say about sharks? They have to keep swimming or they die. That's us, Mr Thackray. Sharks."

I nodded. I had heard the saying; wasn't sure how much was myth but there was no use contradicting. Instead I said: "Tell me about your husband."

She lowered her eyelashes. In a beautiful woman it would have been affecting, but for her it accentuated a manly forehead.

"The matter is delicate, Mr Thackray. It has yet to be announced to the press."

"How long has it been?"

She sighed. "Two weeks, two days."

"And you haven't heard from him?"

"No." She shook her head. "His office believes he is on a business trip. His secretary said she was surprised he hadn't told me."

"Are you surprised?"

She sat back. "No, I'm not surprised. But I am surprised that he wouldn't contact me *during* such a trip. You see, we are close, Mr Thackray. Very close. You have to understand that love makes the ugly beautiful. The business trip might have slipped his mind, but not contacting me shortly after arriving at his destination would have been unthinkable."

"And his destination was?"

"Fabricated. I've checked everything. The trip, the hotel, the flight details: none of it is real."

"So he's travelled to a place that doesn't exist, by a method that doesn't exist, to stay somewhere that doesn't exist."

"You could phrase it that way."

"So instead of somewhere, he's elsewhere."

Esme crossed her legs. The fake tan was blemished by liver spots. "People disappear don't they, Mr Thackray?"

I shook my head. "People don't disappear. Not in the literal sense of the word. People hide and wait to be found."

"They wait?"

"Yes, they wait. They wait to be looked for. Being looked for is why they hide."

Esme stood. Walked over to the window which fronted the park. I wondered how far she looked into the distance. Sun back-lit her skirt and I could see the shape of her legs through it. Because of evolution, I found it hard to turn away.

For a while, dust motes settling on the carpet made more noise than either of us.

Then, as if she had seen something in the park which helped her make up her mind, she turned and gave me the information that I needed.

My husband was always a proper man, Mr Thackray, with the emphasis on the *proper* and not on the *man*. Everything in moderation, including affection, consumption of alcohol, propriety. You may look at this apartment and find it opulent, but that is only because you have not been in more opulent apartments. Believe you me, Mr Thackray, I had some embarrassment entertaining here.

Two months ago something changed. George became more open – about *certain* matters. In short, he became obsessed with his nakedness.

He had always worn nothing in bed. Moderation, as I said. Yet should he need the bathroom he would put on his pyjamas. At the very least, the bottoms. One evening we were discussing literature. I can't remember the exact details, but George left the bed and walked totally naked into the room that functions as our library. He was looking for something. When he returned he told me what he had found, but the meaning was irrelevant. I could only stare at him.

You're naked.

I closed the curtains.

Unless you did so from the doorway with a seven foot pole someone in the opposite apartment could have seen you.

I sneaked in from the side.

You may smirk, Mr Thackray, but this was unheard of. And this was the start. He began to speak of how nakedness was only acceptable or unacceptable dependent on space and time. Of how this fact applied to all aspects of decorum. He expounded quite lengthily on how he could be seen on the toilet in his office if it wasn't for the partitioning wall. The idea fascinated him. The fact that a closed door, or a specific position in time and space, defined the difference between embarrassment and respectability. He mentioned the Spanish film director, the surrealist, Luis Buñuel, and his movie *The Phantom of Liberty*. The scene where people sit around a table to go to the toilet as though it were a social function, and then excuse themselves to eat in a tiny room.

Unhinged, Mr Thackray. He was becoming unhinged. It is one thing to admire the surrealists for breaking social boundaries, but it is another thing to be one within polite society.

There is a saying, isn't there, that clothes maketh the man. My husband took to removing his clothes as soon as he came home. He removed his clothes when in the toilet cubicle at the office. He removed his clothes *in* his office, or so he told me, when the door was closed. He removed his clothes at any opportunity. But only when he was alone or when he was with me.

Maybe you're thinking it isn't unusual. Maybe you've heard of such cases before. But in unmaking himself through his clothes he began to lose his identity. Maybe he thought he was becoming more of himself, but in fact he was becoming less. He divested himself of what characterised him as my husband. He became no more than a naked man. My naked man, albeit that was true, and there was no loss of intimacy or love between us; but simply a naked man. No more, no less.

"And now he's gone."

Esme Baker dabbed at the corners of her eyes. "It appears so, yes."

"And what are you thinking?"

"I believe he's disappeared, Mr Thackray. In the literal sense, which you seem to disbelieve. You see, we don't just clothe ourselves in materials, we clothe ourselves in our beliefs, in our opinions, in our other selves. We present other selves to each and every person we meet. To our true love, we present our true self. Yet even that can be a transitory costume. I'm afraid, Mr Thackray – I'm afraid that George has stripped himself of something that cannot be replaced. I feel he's taken this *experiment* too far. And I believe it to have been an experiment, hence the false business trip should nothing have gone wrong." I watched her fists tighten. "I'm afraid that he's somehow slipped within the interstices of space and time."

I rose to join her by the window. "But you can't really believe that. It's fanciful. Fantasy."

"All life is fantasy, Mr Thackray. I thought you of all people would understand that."

I allowed my teeth to clench. Outside, the park was populated by joggers, dog walkers, children, women with prams. If I closed my eyes they ceased to exist. When I opened my eyes I could use them as characters. I was not a private detective, I was an author. This was why Mrs Baker had contacted me. Because I could create people out of nothing and return them to nothing. She no doubt believed I had an understanding of such things.

"I always thought it would be the opposite, but after a lifetime of reading I know it's not," she said. "Young authors write best about death and old authors write best about youth. It all comes down to perspective."

"I'm forty-seven," I said.

"Then you can write about both."

"Well?"

"As well as anyone," she said. Then she pulled on the drawer of a small bureau to the side of the window. Inside were assorted papers, used tickets, photographs, mementoes. "This is everything that was us," she said. "I want you to write his biography. Leave nothing unsaid – other than what I have told you this afternoon. When it is finished you can return him to me."

I opened my mouth. Thought better of it and closed it again. Esme left the room and returned with a battered leather suitcase that had the initials *G.B.* in gold lettering on the lock. She filled the suitcase with the documents and closed it with a click.

When I left the apartment I felt like an undertaker departing with a coffin. Everything that was George Baker lay within the suitcase. Everything except his skin.

On the street I looked across the park, my eyes darting sideways at any movement, anticipating a taxi. Did it matter that George Baker from my perspective might be different from the version that Esme Baker had created? I could only write the truth as I saw it, yet even truth contains embellishment.

The taxi arrived and I ducked inside. Whilst I didn't turn around I became convinced that Esme was watching me from the apartment window. Her eyes like lasers on the back of my neck.

You will know the rest as history. George Baker did not return. A body was never found. After a year had passed, Esme Baker also disappeared. The truth is no one knows what happened, but I believe that each is alive – in some small part. Even if it is no more than dancing dust motes containing miniscule particles of skin lit by the sun coming through the window of a run-down apartment.

We are all born naked, yet to be naked is an affront. I remember an article where a famous actor described waking at night and seeing a naked man wearing his leather jacket at the foot of the bed. He was eating a Fudgesicle. Yes, he described him as *naked* even as he wore a jacket. For me, this summarises how society has come to consider nakedness. That we can be naked even as we are clothed. That being naked is the fantasy and to embrace clothing is the reality.

Standing now in my apartment with the window open, each follicle is affected by the breeze. In the mirror, shadows play on my skin, my penis a comedic opening act on the theatre of my body. My eyes: my eyes seem the only route to my interior. To the soul.

On a chair by the window sits the closed suitcase Esme gave me that I have yet to open. Since I took it I have written nothing. Not a word of her husband's biography, nor – until today – any of my own work. I'm recording this now for one reason only. Later this evening I plan to open the suitcase and garb myself in the skin of George Baker that I am convinced his documents, mementoes, used tickets and photographs have been transformed into.

And when I make my reappearance on the financial sector, when I regain my position in his apartment, when I find my Esme and see within her the beauty that only he saw, then I will know that the transformation is complete, and this written record will be the only indication that I was once something other than what I am.

Words clothe the page just as clothes clothe the man.

We are as we are written: mysterious, unfathomable, confusing and blind. Each of us contains our own park.

I walk down to the street, one step at a time. Naked underneath my clothes.

❀

This is another story where the title came first – out of nowhere, as they often do – and a tale subsequently formed around it. This one is quite simple, and concerns the front that we present to the world and the true nature of ourselves which is often hidden.

Tokyo In Rain

Asahara's mouth moved rhythmically as the body emerged from the waters of the false city. His tongue flicked the half-moon fingernail back and forth: a tiny boat on a raging current. When the edges pricked his skin, he spat it out into the river. His men were preoccupied. He raised his right hand to his chin, held it there in quiet contemplation.

The body was wrapped in a white sheet. Being underwater had given it the semblance of an octopus, the tight hooded head allowing the remainder of the material to billow. As the boat hook pulled it ashore the sheet gathered contours, moulded around the flesh. Asahara noticed the crudely-drawn eyes which – unlike his – could not reflect the skyscraper lights of Tokyo which were mirrored in the Sumida. The sensation was akin to removing an alien entity from a simulacrum. Once the body was fully free of the water, the lights danced back and forth like tiny coloured balls on a music amplifier, until their pattern returned a copy of the city in which Asahara lived.

His officers struggled with the knot of rope around the victim's neck. Asahara wasn't expecting life. Released, the body fell out of the sheet like the viscera of a gutted shark. One of his officers retched. The hands were tied behind the back. The body was male. The face had bloated smooth, the tightness of the rope had prevented animal life deterioration, but the skin had a dull grey shine, the eyes were white and sightless, the mouth gaped as though desperate for breath.

The searchlight reanimated the corpse, the beam enhancing each detail. Asahara stepped aside for the photographer to capture the find. In doing so, the skies reopened; a culmination of a ritual gone wrong. The respite had been brief. Asahara was handed a yellow mac which he slipped over his torso. The rain beat a discordant rhythm. He stood a while longer before returning to his car.

Morning light revealed more rain. Asahara slipped under the bedcovers alongside his sleeping wife. He ran a hand across her curve, drawing her in. She smelt of marshmallow. He stopped short of waking her, and lay on his back, the thin sheet held to his chest. Suddenly he sneezed – a fine layer of moisture propelled upwards before settling like mist on his face. His wife stirred. Asahara grimaced, prevented a further sneeze. Gently, he used the edge of the sheet to wipe himself dry.

He drifted between sleep and wakefulness. Sometime within the first hour he felt his wife's body pull away from him, as though they were separated by a flood. Outside the windows the rain hardened, the sky darkening in false nightfall. On the bedside table, Asahara's mobile repeatedly lit like a beacon, silently shouting. When he woke he found he couldn't remember his dreams, was unaware if he had dreamt. The knowledge he might have another life he couldn't recollect disturbed him. The pathologist had confirmed the body showed no signs of trauma. Asahara wondered if the man had struggled when captured – or at any time during the ordeal before his death.

His wife beckoned him into the kitchen. He rose slowly, pulled on a robe. Picking up his mobile he flicked through the missed calls. On a tatami mat his wife had placed a bowl of white rice, *natto*, two raw eggs, and some tea. Asahara picked up the eggs and broke them on the side of the bowl, using chopsticks to mix them into the rice. Breaking the seal on the *natto*, he added the fermented soy beans to the dish. Staring into nothing he began to shovel the mixture into his mouth. His wife leant backwards against the kitchen counter. He considered her thoughts. She came to stand behind him, gently massaged his shoulders.

He grunted contentedly as her thumbs dug into his skin. Both her touch and the meal enlivened him. Through the window, the rain continued to hammer. He remembered the other bodies – four – and then placed the chopsticks to one side, reached his right hand upwards until it connected with his wife's and their fingers interlocked.

She tugged gently. He stood and she led him back to the bed. Reaching into the folds of his robe her fingers connected with his penis. He lay backwards onto the mattress as the edge of her thumb connected with the base of his glans. His wife was a mute. He reciprocated her silence as she masturbated him to climax.

Mid-afternoon Asahara drove across rain-soaked streets, his windscreen wipers elbowing a view. The man had not been identified. Clothing remnants indicated he was a farmer. His stomach contents suggested miso soup. Despite the week he had spent in the river, there was still the detectable odour of sake.

Asahara paused at a traffic light. Pedestrians crossed in an X.

He needed motion. On impulse he drove to Iwabuchi, to the source of the Sumida, where it branched from the Arakawa. The distinction was against nature. During the Meiji era the path of the Arakawa had been split to prevent flooding. It was there that the Sumida was born.

Asahara parked the vehicle. The rain remained intense. He scanned the ground, exited into the wet. Picking up a stick, bent at the middle – almost a V, for recognition – he approached the water's edge and hurled it into the current.

Puddles splashed dirty water against his trousers as he returned to the vehicle. He lost no time starting the engine. He zig-zagged Tokyo in two hours. Twenty-six bridges – the Senju, the Kototoi, the Azuma – twenty-seven kilometres. Rush hour traffic impeded progress. Finally, at Tokyo Bay, rain pummelled into the water; soft punches. Asahara watched it happen, allowing the stick a theoretical possibility.

His radio crackled. He returned to the vehicle. Water ran down his face, but his hands were hot. Asahara listened to the static, to the *shush* of empty space. He listened to the sound of the disintegrating city.

Crossing the school courtyard, girls in *sailor fuku* uniforms deferred to his authority.

The principal led him to a classroom where *teru teru bōzu* dolls hung from a window. Asahara was familiar with the dolls, but had also forgotten them. There were eight in the window space. They hung from cords tied around the neck. The principal explained – enthusiastically and unnecessarily – that they were fashioned from white cloth.

Asahara looked at the dolls, with their rounded golf ball-sized heads and attendant capes.

The principal reminded him of the *warabe uta*, the traditional song, wherein the *teru teru bōzu* represented a monk who promised farmers he could bring clear weather during a prolonged period of rain which was ruining crops. When the monk failed to bring sunshine, he was executed.

Asahara plucked one of the dolls from the window and placed it within his jacket pocket.

He drank *happoshu* in a small bar. The beer felt no less watery than the rain. He sank four of these before clouding his way to the exit.

Fine-weather priest, please let the weather be good tomorrow.

Light pollution hid the stars. Asahara tipped his head back, regarded the sky. Pinpricks of rain materialised a few meters before his eyes. He closed them.

His wife was out when he got home. He remembered her signing her sister's name. After a brief shower where he recreated the scene on the street, Asahara eased himself under the bedcover and pulled it over his head.

His right arm outside the cover, he gripped his throat.

His mouth sucked at the material before he relaxed his strength.

He imagined a rain never ending. A deluge. His ceiling cracked and spilt, rain fell in a torrent soaking the sheet which adhered to his face and absorbed his breath. At some point during the night his wife returned and after she fell asleep he woke and walked across to the window, hanging the *teru teru bōzu* doll up by its thread.

He dreamt of gunfire, a repetitive noise.

The rain had not ceased. He stood at the window whilst his wife prepared breakfast.

Asahara considered the possibility of returning to work.

He rubbed a hand through his thick hair. Leaning forwards, his breath condensed on glass. The *teru teru bōzu* doll bobbed by his head. His wife entered the room and signed her confusion. He flicked a finger at the doll, which silently swung back and forth. He was gripped by inaction.

In the morgue a fifth body lay in rest. Asahara stood with his hands clasped behind his back as the attendant revealed the face. Another male. With a white-gloved hand the pathologist pointed to the contusions around the neck, but emphasised post-death, caused by rope rubbing against the fabric as the body had rocked in the river. Asahara opened his mouth but found he had nothing to say. The corpse held no ID and did not match any missing person report. Dental records revealed nothing. It was as though none of the bodies had existed prior to being bound and hooded.

He was halfway out of the building when he turned and returned.

The pathologist was in the dining area, spooning *somen* noodles into his mouth served cold with carrot and mung beans. He listened attentively without any sign of cooperation. Only when he had wiped his mouth with a piece of tissue paper did he stand and return to the morgue. They stood side by side as the attendant wheeled each of the five gurneys into the room.

The faces had ballooned beyond identification. The only comparison was with each other.

Asahara looked at the pathologist. He was without articulation.

Teru-teru-bōzu, teru bōzu
Ashita tenki ni shite o-kure
Sore de mo kumotte naitetara
Sonata no kubi wo chon to kiru zo

The annual Tokyo rainfall averages nearly 1,530 millimetres with a wetter summer and a drier winter.

Asahara considered filing a report.

He stood with his back to the desk, looking through his office window at the streaks of water which distorted the city view. Shortly, the entirety of Tokyo would be underwater. He wondered what would happen to the reflection he had witnessed within the Sumida. Whether that would drain as reality filled. As if one could replace the other, like the sands in an hourglass. Knowing this was impossible, he extenuated the fantasy. Perhaps within this new city his wife would be vocal and he would be unable to speak for fear of drowning. Would this reversal be acceptable?

He sighed and sat at the desk. His hands were fluid on the keyboard.

After work, Asahara visited a hostess bar and paid for conversation. Talk gravitated towards the weather. He had more beers than he intended.

On his way home he crossed Ryōgoku Bridge. The original structure had been built in 1659 and immortalised many times by the artist Hiroshige. During the crossing he imagined a white shape bobbing in the water. The intensity of the downpour slowed cars to a crawl, visibility no more than five meters ahead.

It was late by the time he entered his apartment. His wife had left out *kushikatsu,* pieces of deep-fried skewered pork. Asahara savoured the taste. He remembered the girl in the hostess bar: the colour of her laugh. Quietly, he entered the bedroom.

Undressing, Asahara noticed the *teru teru bōzu* doll was gone from the window. Careful not to wake his wife, he checked if it had fallen. After a more detailed search he found it resting in his wife's bedside cabinet.

Holding it in his palm, it lolled to one side; the eyes directed towards the window. Under moonlight it was not dissimilar to the caricature of a ghost.

Asahara became curious as to the formation of the bulb of the head. His thumb connected with the base where the string was tied, and he exerted a little pressure. Clearly it was just fabric. He stopped short of untying the string around the neck and revealing the contents.

His wife shifted her position under the covers. He believed her to be dreaming.

Asahara returned the *teru teru bōzu* doll to the drawer and climbed into bed. His wife's body was cool to his skin and softer than his.

It wouldn't take much for the mystery to evaporate. Just a word. Just a glimmer of sunshine.

❖

I wanted to write an unconventional crime story laced with a possible speculative element, but underplayed so that no conclusions other than conjecture might be drawn. For me, defining moments in life as being concrete in interpretation is a fallacy. We like to think we have a grasp on reality, but actually don't understand that any given *reality* is simply a construct of society. Likewise, we enjoy adding mystery where there is none.

The Day My Heart Stood Still

I ran inside from outside, abandoning Charlotte in the paddling pool that smelt of everlasting summer.

My mother lay on the kitchen floor. The sudden change from light to dark tripped me over, my hands shooting star-like to break my fall. If she felt my unintended kick then she didn't make a sound.

I lay quiet for a moment, my palms stinging with impact, my body lying over my mother's cross-like, the sound of Charlotte's splashing carrying on the humid air.

She must be asleep. I pulled myself up roughly, as if clambering over rocks. Then I inspected my hands. Both palms were reddened, yet that faded as I looked. I opened the fridge door and poured out the glass of lemonade I had been after. Popping a couple of ice cubes from the freezer compartment into the drink I then swallowed a long draft. The cool liquid felt like burning. Through the kitchen window I could see Charlotte lying on her tummy, face pressed into the side of the deflating pool, whilst her legs kicked behind her; rhythmically.

Stepping over my mother I ran back outside, my cold interior emphasised through the heat of the sun. Charlotte lifted her head.

"You could have got *me* a drink."

I shrugged. I was ten. I hadn't even thought of it.

Charlotte grimaced. "Shout Mum for me."

"She won't get it, she's asleep. Anyway," I ran and kicked the side of the pool, jettisoning water over the edge, "go get it yourself. *I* did."

She pulled a pout and pushed herself up. Two years older, with the attitude of a teenager. Water droplets ran over her one-piece swimsuit and it shone. I got into the pool after her.

"Don't wee in it," she called over her shoulder.

I already had.

I turned onto my back. Through the thin material of the pool I could feel grass blades knead my skin. I squinted at the sun, condensed the rays. Surrounded by the glow, I imagined myself teleported skywards in a beam of UFO light. I closed my eyes. Imbued by warmth, the world felt so much with me. Then a shadow darkened my view and I squealed as Charlotte poured a glass of cold water over my exposed belly.

Standing quickly, I slipped on the polyvinyl chloride and went down again, banging my right elbow. It was a day for knocks and bruises. I stood again, chased Charlotte around the garden, until finally, panting, we held onto each other and laughed. On the other side of the fence, Mrs Jackson joined in.

"You young'un's," she said.

We nodded respectfully. The rich smell of baked cakes wafted over the fence as she raised the plate she was carrying.

"Now, take one for each of you, and take one through to your mother."

"Mum's asleep," Charlotte said.

"Well save her one for later. And don't eat it, mind." Mrs Jackson winked conspiratorially, as if she expected us to fight over it.

We reached out our hands and made the selection. My cake was *stuck together* with a second and Mrs Jackson pretended not to notice. We said thanks and wandered back to the pool, sitting on towels spread on the grass. The cakes were delicious, still warm. I imagined they melted the ice in our bellies formed by the lemonade.

Despite mine being bigger I finished first. Charlotte gestured to the remaining cake on the floor. "Go on, take it to Mum. I've got to watch my figure."

That was the first I'd heard of it, but I picked up the cake and carried it indoors.

My mother remained on the floor. I called her a couple of times, nudged one arm with my foot, and then placed the cake near where her head faced the tumble dryer. Perhaps the smell would wake her up.

Charlotte was back in the pool when I returned.

"What time is it?"

Charlotte shielded her eyes against the sun, as if her extended arm could make a sundial of her face.

"I don't know. Late I think. Dad should be getting home soon."

I scratched my leg where I must have caught it against something that afternoon. It doubly hurt because of the mild sunburn received through not replenishing suncream when I'd left the pool.

"Mum's usually out by now."

I nodded. After she had completed her chores she usually spent the afternoon reading under the tree. Sometimes we helped her so that she could read sooner, but the pool had absorbed our attention.

Charlotte lay on the grass, reached sideways and plucked a daisy. I watched as she turned it around and around in her fingertips. "Should we wake her?"

"Maybe." Truth be told, I didn't care. My father could wake her when he came home, if necessary.

"Getting hungry though." A couple of hours had passed since the cakes. Charlotte stood, pushing the stem of the daisy under her long blonde hair and tucked it against her ear. "I'm going to see how she is."

I watched her walk towards the house. The backs of her legs were whiter than the front, especially white in the area of her knee pits. Soon she would get like the older girls in the neighbourhood and want nothing to do with me, just as they scorned *their* brothers. It would hurt but it was natural, my father said. That's just a part of growing up.

I scratched the blemish on my leg again. It seemed a little redder than previous.

Charlotte came over. "She's still sleeping."

I exaggerated a frown. "Really?"

"Yup. Hasn't moved."

Charlotte sat back down on the grass. She was carrying an ice lolly. "You could have got me one."

"Snap."

"Anyway, you shouldn't have that so close to tea." I began walking to the house. If Charlotte had a lolly, I wanted one too.

The kitchen faced east and didn't get much sun in the afternoon. I turned on the light as I entered, and then stepped over my mother and opened the refrigerator, searched for the packet of lollies. Then I saw it lay empty on the work surface. Charlotte had taken the last one.

"Hey!" It was a half-hearted shout. Charlotte was too far away for effect.

I threw the box to the floor and stamped it flat, before placing it in the recyclable cardboard container. Then I stepped back over my mother and was halfway to the door before stopping.

My mother's position that afternoon hadn't changed. The cake was the same distance from her face where I had placed it. That wasn't right. My dad always complained that she tossed and turned when asleep, and certainly when I was younger and shared their bed I knew that from experience.

I walked across to her and knelt on the lino, shook her shoulder. "Mum?"

She didn't answer. Her eyes were closed, not a flicker beneath. I decided to roll her onto her back, not sure for what purpose. It took three attempts, and then she lolled lazily. She still hadn't woken.

I sat beside her for a few minutes before glancing at the clock. Dad would be home soon and would know what to do. On a whim I reached out and peeled her left eyelid over the cornea. The returned stare was vacant but again she didn't wake. I was getting bored. I stood and wandered to the doorway. I was also getting hungry. The eye regarded me impassively. I turned off the light but the eye was still visible, so I nipped back and pulled the lid down again before returning to Charlotte and the pool.

"How long's she been like this?"

My father crouched over my mother. He had eaten half of the cake and I noticed crumbs drop onto her blouse.

"Since early afternoon," Charlotte said. "Not sure of the time."

My father looked to me, a puzzle in his eye.

I shrugged. "Early afternoon, like she said."

My father ran a hand over my mother's cheek. "Strange," he said, but it was to himself, not to us.

He stood. "Let me just get out of this suit and take a shower. You kids stay outdoors, ok."

We nodded. Outside, the light was dimmer. Mrs Jackson was in her garden collecting washing. Her white sheets resembled a painter's canvasses. She saw us and beckoned us over.

"Did you enjoy the cakes?"

We nodded, in unison.

"How about your mother? Did she get the chance of one?"

"She's been sleeping all afternoon," Charlotte said. "Dad had it."

Mrs Jackson nodded. She continued unpegging, folding, and sorting her laundry. After a few minutes, my father came out of the house and walked over to us, standing between us with his hands on our shoulders. Mrs Jackson smiled at him.

"Ellie. If you've got a moment, can you come in and look at something?"

Mrs Jackson nodded. "Let me just put the washing away."

My father smiled. Then he turned to us. "Empty the pool you two, or it will be full of leaves before the day is out."

We bent to the task. Charlotte picked up one end quickly and my side of the pool V'ed and pooled water around my feet.

After she'd upended it I chased her a bit, then saw Mrs Jackson open our side gate and we accompanied her indoors where my father was bent over my mother.

"You ever seen this?"

We sat on the kitchen chairs whilst my father slapped my mother once, twice, three times across the side of her face. It wasn't a light slap and something inside me twisted. I'd never seen him do that before. Perhaps that was what he had meant.

Mrs Jackson frowned. "Never," she said.

She also bent over my mother, picked up one arm, dropped it. She might as well have picked up a strip of cooked spaghetti. That reminded me of how hungry I was.

"That's strange," she muttered.

"That's what I said."

She shrugged. "Don't see as how there's anything we can do."

"I don't like it," my father said.

Mrs Jackson shrugged again.

We all sat in silence for a moment. Then my father said, "I heard you baked that cake. It was delicious."

Ellie Jackson smiled. "Thank you. I do my best."

Again there was silence. None of us knew what to do.

After what seemed like an age my father said, "I think I'll call my parents."

I watched my grandparents park their car next to my father's in the drive. It was close to twilight, night air had begun to wipe the heat from the day. They walked arm in arm, both dressed in beige. My mother described them as *conventional,* and I supposed they were.

The kitchen was getting crowded. Mrs Jackson stood.

"Perhaps I should leave?"

"Oh don't leave on our account," said my grandmother.

My grandfather looked down at my mother. "So, what's happened here?" he said.

My father stood. "It's like I told you on the phone. She's sleeping and won't wake."

We all stood around her for a while, and then my grandfather crouched by my mother. He shifted her around, a little roughly I thought. Then, as I had done, he moved back an eyelid. As far as I could tell, the eye hadn't moved position from when I had last seen it.

"Curious," he said. My father nodded.

"Any ideas?"

My grandfather scratched his head, then turned to my grandmother. "Mother, what do you think to this?"

She opened her mouth but I could see she had nothing to say. Eventually, she said: "Maybe she's just tired. Perhaps we should let her rest. I mean," she continued, "it's only been a few hours hasn't it? If she slept this length of time at night none of us would bat an eyelid."

All of us exchanged looks. Suddenly, in the room with my sister, father, grandparents and Mrs Jackson, I felt elevated above my years. In those looks we were one. A thrill raced through me as though I'd attained adulthood.

My father made a decision. "Move her into the living room. We need space to cook dinner and she can rest in there for a bit."

The lasagne wasn't as good as my mother made. My grandmother added something I could only pinpoint as *age*.

Mrs Jackson hadn't stayed for the meal, but afterwards she popped her head around the door with the remainder of the afternoon's plate of cakes. "Share these out amongst yourselves," she said. "My Ollie says he doesn't want anymore."

"Is he there?" my father asked, and as though bidden Mr Jackson appeared behind his wife.

It was becoming a ritual. I watched Mr Jackson examine my mother to no avail and then leave with a puzzled look on his face, his arm around Mrs Jackson.

I glanced at the clock. It was close to nine.

As though my father sensed it, he turned to myself and Charlotte. "You get to bed, kids."

"Oh, Dad. I'm almost thirteen."

"Just go to bed. I'll see you both in the morning."

We kissed our grandparents and Father, and then bent to kiss Mother where she lay so relaxed on the sofa.

At the top of the stairs Charlotte pulled my arm and whispered: *you go to sleep and you'll end up like Mum.*

I felt sick.

Then, downstairs, I heard my grandfather say: "I'm going to call *my* parents. Maybe they'll know what to do."

Lying on my bed, I watched the last vestiges of the day become obliterated by night. My bedroom was situated immediately above the living room and it was impossible to ignore the voices that I heard just as much as it was impossible to understand them. Muffled by the floorboards they became a sonorous noise which might easily have put me to sleep. Yet I couldn't sleep. I was wide awake, mulling over what Charlotte could have meant.

Of course, I knew it was banter. Charlotte understood no more than I did and was developing the mean streak my father had mentioned; but even so, if I were to sleep would it be true that I wouldn't be roused, just like my mother?

I strained my ears to catch the sound of her voice rising from downstairs. *What are you all looking at?* she would say. *What's got into you?*

After a while, lights pushed shadows out the corner of my room and I stood and watched my great-grandparents park amongst the other cars in our drive.

There wouldn't be enough cakes to go around.

I sat on the bed, heard them enter the room below me. Then I pulled out some of my comics and flicked through them, absentmindedly scratching the blemish on my leg. Under my touch it had a rough texture, a raised burr. I angled my bedside lamp and looked at it impassively. A lump had formed. I rubbed it again, this time with the flat of my palm. Itching but not itching. Then I put the comics on the floor, tucked myself into bed, and closed my eyes to sleep.

Just as I drifted off I wondered if my mother was dreaming. If this was why she slept so long: that she was caught in a wonderful dream and didn't want to wake from it. That because it was so good she had abandoned her family and remained in the dream world. That must be it. She didn't *want* to wake.

Time passed. I drifted in and out of reverie, the illuminated clock face on the bedside cabinet beside me marking out the hours. Eleven. Twelve. One.

At two o'clock I heard Charlotte's door open and knew she was listening at the top of the stairs. The voices were still muffled, but in greater abundance. I stilled my breathing until I heard Charlotte descend halfway. She would be in the crook of the stairs where they bent at the corner. She wouldn't be seen by my father and I wouldn't be heard by her. Lifting my legs out of bed, I swung them to the floor. Standing, I looked out of the window.

My father's car, my grandparents car, and my great-grandparents car had been joined by my great-great-grandparents' car, my great-great-great-grandparents' car, my great-great-great-great-grandparents' car, my great-great-great-great-great-grandparents' car, and even my great-great-great-great-great-great- grandparents' car. It was a proper family reunion.

I clutched the doorknob softly, turned it almost imperceptibly, as if going to the toilet in the middle of the night.

Charlotte's shadow was cast against the stairway. She turned and placed a finger to her lips.

I nodded. My movements were stiff from sleeping, and the thing on my leg itched as furiously as I wanted to scratch it.

"What's happening?" I whispered, once I was close enough to be sure they wouldn't hear.

She waved her finger erratically over her lips. I sat on the step next to her. She pulled my ear until it touched her lips. "Great-great-great-great-great-great grandfather's telling a story. About something called *death*."

The way she said the word made it sound distasteful, but I found some poetry in it. *Death*. There was finality to it. Just like the end of a summer's day.

Yet knowing my great-great-great-great-great-great grandfather I knew it would simply be some boring anecdote that everyone but me had probably heard. He'd probably heard it himself from his grandfather. I'd never met members of our family further back than that, but no doubt it was an old *old* story.

Curiosity being what it is, we craned our heads around the corner of the stairs. The living room was crowded. A succession of grandmothers sat on chairs, sipping tea and dunking biscuits, whilst the grandfathers stood around my mother. With a shock I realised she was naked. Her clothes were folded neatly on the floor. I saw my great-great-great-great-great-great grandfather, the one talking about *death*, point to something I couldn't quite see on the inside of my mother's thigh.

And then he moved. And for a moment I did see it. And then, in the sallow half-light of the stairwell, I regarded the lump on my own leg with more than the idle inquisitiveness it had hitherto deserved.

❀

As with much of my work, this story started with the title which just popped into my head. It's an amalgamation of "The Day The World Stood Still" and "The Beat That My Heart Skipped". I like titles which come like this, because they create an existing evocation in the reader's mind but also contain something new. (I've done this before with "One Day All This Will Be Fields", which mixes the phrases one day all this will be yours and I remember when this was all fields).

Once you have a title like that, it's very hard for the story not to automatically follow and this piece almost wrote itself. The basic premise is simple – massive spoiler here – what if death had been eradicated for so long that no one in living memory was aware of it. Then what would happen if someone died? It's a bittersweet, almost Bradbury-esque kind of tale, I think, seen through the summer-honeyed gaze of a young boy.

Drowning In Air

It was the photograph of a gas mask wedding that first brought Aiko Van Der Berg to the volcanic island of Miyake-jima.

The ghostly skull-like circles of the masks adorning the hidden faces of the wedding party in their sepia drenched formal clothing added mystery to what might otherwise be a familiar family shot: the white-dressed bride clinging to the arm of her brown-suited husband; guests in rain macs with hoods over their heads; the repetition of figures scuffed at the edges of the picture as though they had been partially erased.

Perhaps most significantly, the masks imparted anonymity to the bride and groom on what otherwise would have been *their* day. The occasion was lost to them. The masks held sway.

Aiko had been fascinated. Additionally, he had respiratory problems. Maybe this was also why the picture appealed.

He had boarded the overnight ferry at ten-thirty the previous evening, leaving from the Takeshiba Sanbashi Pier near Hamamatsuchō, Tokyo. It had been a clear day: pale blue skies opalescent, as though signalling new beginnings. As night descended, a blanket of cloud had shrouded the city, raising the temperature. He felt stifled in his tiny cabin on the ferry, declined the offer of a meal with a fellow traveller, and spent an uncomfortable night rolling from side to side with the swell of the sea. Instead of rocking him asleep, it reminded him he was alive and didn't afford much of a slip into unconsciousness.

Aiko was in Japan on holiday. His Dutch company had willingly granted him extended leave following the exacerbation of his health problems. He wanted to see the land of his mother's birth. She had married his Dutch father shortly after the war. Aiko meant *love child* in Japanese. A Dutch boy's name as well as a Japanese girl's name. Aiko had sometimes been uncomfortable about the indistinction in gender, but mostly he had been proud of his foreign origins. Other than some high school teasing he had avoided bullying, unlike another boy he had known who had been beaten to death.

Perhaps it was the sea air, or the movement of the waves, but on the journey Aiko's memories pitched and rolled, fantasy and reality jumbled like two dice in a shaker. When he was awoken after a desultory two hours' sleep shortly after five a.m. he dressed semi-comatose, going through the motions of being awake without actually *being* awake. Come the time to stand on deck and view the island appearing out of the night, the dream canopy still had yet to lift. He saw himself as others might see him whilst watching a film: a figure on deck with suitcase in hand, fifty-two years old, thinning white hair, a paunch which moved ahead of him wherever he went. Indistinctive features. Just another man amongst the many men who lived in the world. Not a bad man. But a man all the same.

The remainder of the passengers were Japanese. It wasn't quite yet the tourist season. On the shore he could see families waiting, hugging themselves for warmth in the cold morning light. None of them wore gas masks, but each of them carried one. He could see them dangling from straps in their hands, or slung over shoulders, or peeking out of day sacks, like disembodied alien heads or cyberpunk Halloween masks.

It was because of the high sulphuric gas volume that the residents of the island were required to carry gas masks with them at all times. The volcanic Mount Oyama being the culprit. Aiko stood on deck and breathed deeply. There was little trace of anything untoward in the air, only the familiar sulphur smell of bad eggs drifting onwards over the waves.

Seeing the early morning crowds, he was reminded of a second photograph he had found whilst researching the island. A party of boy scouts, their numbers stretching back into the horizon, each traditionally dressed but wearing those masks which appeared white in the contrast of the monochrome image, tubing snaking from their mouthpieces like corrugated snakes or the trunks of deformed elephants. Upon observing the photo, Aiko realised it was the human face which defined humanity. Without it – without expression – the race was reduced to nothingness.

One of the Japanese on shore held a cardboard sign. The name *Aiko Van Der Berg* had been written on it in black ink. As he disembarked from the ferry he made his way over to the sign holder: a man in his late-thirties. The man waited until Aiko reached him and identified himself, even though he must have been aware that Aiko was the person he was waiting for because he had been the only European to make the trip.

Aiko's Japanese was rudimentary, the man's Dutch and English non-existent. They acknowledged each other and exchanged simple pleasantries, before Aiko was beckoned into a waiting vehicle and driven to the hotel where he intended to spend the following week.

Even from the short journey Aiko could see that the volcanic island was a mixture of hard rock punctuated by areas of extremely vibrant and varied flora. The juxtaposition of life and death intrigued him. Without the volcano, the richness of the soil would not be so great. Yet with the volcano the possibility of evacuation and death would always be present. Whilst only a handful of people had died through eruptions and lava flow since the 1940s, the island had been evacuated completely during 2000, with residents only allowed to return permanently five years later.

Aiko's room at the hotel proved perfunctory and clean. Although the sun was now sapping the final vestiges of night from the sky, he lay flat on the bed in his clothes and sank into a sleep which was as alien as his surroundings.

A tightening in his chest woke him. The dream dissipated as smoke, leaving no more than a vague sensation rather than a memory. Sulphur smells lingered like olfactory residues of cooked breakfasts. He felt around in his jacket pocket for his inhaler and took a blast, easing his air passage. Sitting up, he realised he could see the volcano through the hotel window. Naturally, it was immobile, but even so he had the intimation that it might move closer towards him, belching fumes directly into his lungs.

His respiratory problems had lain beneath the surface until cycling to work in high wind one cold February morning had forced what seemed to be a never-ending stream of damp air into his mouth. He had pulled up at the side of the cycleway and waited as other cyclists flew past, their battle with the wind less tempestuous than his. Struggling through a morning's work with a wheeze louder than the antiquated heating system, he had excused himself early and visited the medical centre. It was here they prescribed the inhaler, and the palpable association of breathing with life had begun for him.

In the hotel room he undressed, showered, and put on clean clothes. Then he made his way into the dining area for a simple breakfast.

The daughter of the owner sat one table away; school books spread out in front of her like fallen leaves.

She looked sixteen. Wore a sailor suit and had a red ribbon in her jet black hair. Plain shoes and white knee length socks adorned her feet and legs. She glanced up, smiled the smile of someone who has made an effort to smile, and then put her head back down amongst the books. Not to study, but as if to sleep, with one eye half-opened in his direction.

Hanging over the back of her chair was a gas mask.

The man who had driven Aiko to the hotel presented him with a menu. Then he nodded over to the girl, who feigned reluctance and came to stand by Aiko's table. They exchanged a few words in Japanese which Aiko didn't understand. It was then that the girl spoke.

"My father says I am to show you around the island. That is, if you want me to."

Her English was falteringly perfect, accented with distorted vowels, but refreshingly uncomplicated.

"The question is," said Aiko, "do you want to?"

She nodded slowly. He wasn't sure she had understood the slyness in his question, or whether the presence of her father meant that she couldn't refuse. Whatever might be, he would allow her to accompany him today and then she could do whatever she pleased. It was a Saturday and there was no school and he imagined she had over a hundred things better to do than show an aging Dutchman around an island which he could easily discover himself.

She held out a hand, her nails bitten to the quick. "My name is also Aiko," she said. And for a moment Aiko felt himself part of a circle which was now complete.

She let him eat in peace, gathered up her school books, and shovelled them into a backpack covered with anime stickers and smiley faces. Then she exited the dining area with a quick promise to return. Aiko noticed she had left the gas mask on the corner of her chair.

He swiftly finished his meal, drank some coffee. Then stood and walked over to where she had sat and lifted up the mask. It was rudimentary in design, mass-produced. The large glass eye-holes reflected his face. The breathing apparatus looked simple. He presumed there was a filter within the extended mouthpiece. It struck him that he didn't know exactly how a gas mask worked. It was too small for him, although the temptation to place it over his head was intense. He almost wanted there to be some kind of volcanic eruption, so he could put it to the test. Yet strangely he wasn't sure if he wanted the mask to succeed or fail.

Returning it to the chair, he realised he had been holding his breath. He exhaled. Inhaled. Exhaled again.

Behind him there was a cough, and he turned to find the hotel owner standing stiffly. In his hand he held a mask suitable for Aiko to wear. He nodded at it. Smiled disconcertingly, like an air hostess demonstrating safety procedures with the wan hope that they would never need to use them. Aiko bowed and thanked him, took the mask in his hands, realised how heavy it was in comparison to the girl's, and then he returned to his room, cleaned his teeth, and packed his camera and a few other items into his day pack.

In the lobby of the hotel, Aiko was waiting.

"There isn't much to see," she said.

Aiko shrugged. "Show me what you can."

She nodded. "Do you have your mask?"

"It's in the bag."

"You won't need it." She almost laughed. "But they make us carry them. It's such a pain."

He smiled at her youth. Imagined what she might be like twenty, thirty, forty years hence. Imagined how she might die. For her, death was an eternity away, a slight smudge on a distant horizon. For Aiko himself it was leering into his face, gripping him by the shoulders, forcing him to look directly into its maw.

It was a cloudier day than the previous one in Tokyo. The sun backlit clouds, gave them fabled silver linings.

Miyake-jima was no more than a large village. Aiko wandered with her hands behind her back. He wondered if she were avoiding the gazes of her friends. They occasionally passed small groups of girls who exchanged a few words with her then giggled. But Aiko realised that she must frequently show guests around the island and was reluctantly used to her position. Yet despite that presumed experience not even an uneasy camaraderie drifted between them, which he was sure he was as much to blame for as she was.

In actuality, it was disconcerting to be in the presence of someone so young. Aiko hadn't married. He had no children. The budding sexuality of Aiko which was tethered to the surface of her skin unnerved him. Once, he found himself reaching for his inhaler before realising he didn't need it.

Around midday he offered to buy her lunch at a small noodle bar. They ate *kitsune soba* quietly, the taste reminded Aiko of his Japanese mother. He had grown up with Japanese food, and it comforted him with the knowledge that she was once around.

Maybe it was then – in that first mouthful – that suddenly he took stock of who and where he was. The week he had spent in Tokyo had been disorientating yet familiar: a large city, lights, the harbour, shopfronts, skyscrapers, these were indigenous now to modern life, regardless of location. But here, in a relatively small village on a small island, Aiko felt himself placed in the universe as succinctly as if a large hand had manoeuvred him in some otherworldly game of chess.

By mid-afternoon, the female Aiko was kicking her heels against the pavement and Aiko had to conclude there was nothing more for her to show him.

"You can go if you want," he said, when he saw her looking fondly towards a group of her friends who were chatting silently behind their hands. Then, so as not to be offensive: "Please. I would like it if you joined them. I found our time together to be most useful."

She nodded. The girl and the woman fought inside her. "There is a *taiko* performance this evening. My father asked me to invite you."

Aiko knew of *taiko*. The island was famous for its traditional performances, known as *kamitsuki kiyari taiko*. They were drum performances. Myth had it that the sun goddess hid herself in a cave until she was tempted out by an erotic dance performed by a shaman-like deity, Ame no Uzume, who stamped her feet on a wooden tub. After hearing the dance the sun goddess was persuaded out of the cave and light returned to the world.

Aiko had some taiko performances on CD, and once his mother had taken him to a show in Amsterdam when an ensemble led by the famous Daihachi Oguchi had visited the Netherlands.

He thanked Aiko again, and watched her join her friends. A butterfly returned to the wild.

Truth be told, Aiko realised there was little on Miyake-jima to interest him. He decided to curtail his week to just one or two more days. He would tell the hotel owner the following day, not wanting him to think that Aiko had been slack with her enthusiasm for the island.

Instead, back in his hotel room he showered again, then pulled the gas mask over his head and lay face upwards on the bed, looking at thin black cracks in the white ceiling plaster through the tinted glass of the mask.

When he had visited the medical centre following the windy bicycle incident, he had described the sensation of being unable to breathe as drowning in air. His doctor had nodded, explained that he meant suffocation rather than drowning, because drowning referred only to water whilst suffocation implied a lack of air.

Aiko had nodded and kept his opinions to himself. He knew what he meant. It wasn't insufficient air, but too much.

His breathing was laboured. Although he hadn't considered it prior to wearing the mask, he now reached his hand down his torso and held his penis. It refused to stiffen. He tried to think of something to enliven it, and refused to think of Aiko; repeatedly. Eventually he gave up. The inside of the mask was hot and he couldn't have fitted it correctly because the lens became dappled with condensation. Even so, he kept it on, and whilst in one moment he was awake the next he was asleep.

Again, he woke with a tightening sensation in his chest. Aiko opened his eyes and jolted. Someone wearing a gas mask was holding him down. He jerked his body against the bed but couldn't move. The figure was naked and he recognised the body. Searching behind the eye sockets in the mask he glimpsed himself. He immediately relaxed. He had experienced sleep paralysis before and knew what he should do. He had to regulate his breathing; by controlling his breathing he could control his fear.

Then he remembered he was wearing the gas mask and the pain in his chest intensified. He couldn't concentrate on regulated breathing. The knowledge he was awake and unable to do anything exacerbated his fear. The figure in the mask kept him pressed to the bed. He could feel a layer of sweat between his back and the sheet. He tried to breathe – realised he had been breathing. Clenching and unclenching his fists began to dissipate the sensation. Finally, the figure over him faded away in a burst of volcanic ash and he wrenched the mask off his head. Sitting up, he breathed deeply, stutteringly. He reached for his inhaler and took two blasts. Perched on the side of the bed, he held his head in his hands. The small bedside clock showed it was six in the early evening. The sun was being consumed by the night.

He stood and looked back at the wet stains on the bed. They were outlined by a thin layer of dust.

If Aiko's father noticed Aiko had slipped her hand into Aiko's then he made no acknowledgement.

They sat in the auditorium as the lights were dimmed and the curtains opened revealing the stage set with drums; their skins as taut as that on Aiko's chest.

Aiko started breathing again.

Aiko leant across and whispered into his ear: "During the Miyake festival in July they play the taiko from eleven in the morning until eight at night, leading the mikoshi shrines around the town."

Aiko nodded. A peculiar sensation gripped his stomach at Aiko's proximity. He released her hand from his grip.

The drums began. They pounded a beat which bore into Aiko's chest.

Aiko realised he had left his inhaler back at the hotel.

Earlier that evening, he had wiped sweat from the inside of the gas mask. He wondered what other guests had worn it. Who they might have been. How important or unimportant. He realised that there was a line of importance which stretched from youth until old age. That the youth believed unequivocally in their importance and the old realised with increasing fear the nature of their unimportance.

He wondered how important he was right at that moment.

With the death of his parents. With no wife or children. With business colleagues who respected him but with whom he didn't socialise. With these certainties he realised his importance was minimal.

Importance for him equated to impotence.

In the auditorium he glanced at Aiko, but even she had lost interest. He decided not to dwell about her hand in his. Wondered if – in fact – it had actually happened.

It was of no importance.

The drums continued.

Not only did their beat repeat throughout the performance, but they followed an historical journey that had begun over two and a half thousand years previous. Aiko felt enraptured by time. He could imagine the shaman teasing the sun goddess out of the cave. He wondered if an erupting volcano and the resulting lava would mimic the flow of light from the sun; yet knew in reality what would descend could only be blackness.

Should the volcano erupt, and sulphuric fumes enter the auditorium through the air vents, his inhaler would no longer be sufficient.

Aiko had left the gas mask back at the hotel.

Aiko was wearing the mask.

Each beat of the drum danced ash from its surface back into the air.

Aiko turned his head. Aiko turned hers. The eye-holes of her mask regarded him blankly.

Aiko stood. The entirety of the audience were masked. He gripped the back of the seat in front, and a head turned to watch him. Aiko could hear breath passing in and out of the tube, in and out of lungs.

He clutched his chest. He could hear his own breath.

He saw Aiko leaning over him, her mouth parted in a stifling kiss.

Aiko stood on the deck of the ferry, watched the shoreline of Miyake-jima recede as the boat headed towards Tokyo. Mount Oyama dominated the background, pumping gas into the atmosphere. It was only a slight eruption, but no doubt had contributed to Aiko's attack.

Thankfully, Aiko had been schooled in cardiopulmonary resuscitation.

Aiko waved goodbye from the shoreline. Standing next to Aiko's father. Aiko waved back until they were no more than heads on sticks. Night enclosing them in a fist, obliterating their traces as might volcanic ash, before distance took them completely.

Overnight, amid desultory sleep, Aiko's memories rolled and pitched; reality and fantasy jumbled like two dice in a shaker.

The journey had begun. No mask required. Aiko wondered if Amsterdam would be exactly like her mother had told her.

❀

This story is set on the Japanese island of Miyake-Jima where – due to the risk of volcanic activity – residents are required to carry gas masks with them at all times and raid alarms sound should there be a dramatic increase in the levels of sulphur in the air. I discovered this island through eerie sepia-tainted photographs of the residents which I saw online.

Of course, the photographs suggest an element of horror which in fact isn't actually there. I'm always intrigued by the contrast between what we see and what we want to see, and how we interpret life in order to rationalise it, so I knew that the idea of masks themselves wouldn't be sinister and that they would simply provide a background to the effectiveness of the tale.

I had the story title in mind before I knew of Miyake-Jima. Cycling to work one morning with a strong wind blowing in my face felt suffocating, and the line 'drowning in air' came from that. When I saw the gas mask images I knew the title – the sense of suffocation – would fit.

Finally, upon searching for the names of my Japanese protagonists I came upon a name – Aiko – which not only is a Japanese girl's name but also a Dutch male name and which means *love child*. Suddenly I had two characters who would be somehow linked due to that name, who might almost be interchangeable. From the photos to the story title to the name I now had all the elements I needed to write. The examination of the relationship between these two quite different characters forms the crux of the piece.

White Matter

Towards the end of her life Marshall's wife fell in love with another man. Marshall had been expecting it. Anna had told him she hoped it would happen. The man wasn't new on the scene, you could make an argument that Anna was on the rebound. Once the process started, Marshall made a lot of arguments, but they were of no consequence by then. It was too late for any rational discussion.

Marshall kept his eyes on the white lines in the centre of the road. Fancifully he had once considered they might be Morse code: dash dash dash. But the repetition seemed unlikely, and after he had spent a little time on the internet it was clear the *message* was no more than *T T T*. There were some days, such as this one, when he wanted to see signs everywhere. He needed validation for existence. But perhaps the first sign he should have seen was his meeting Anna. He had been a pallbearer at her husband's funeral.

"Lovely day for it."

He hadn't known the woman he was standing next to was the deceased's wife.

She looked up. A little cross, but not enough to mention it. "It is that too."

She was trim in black, a wide-brimmed hat with the obligatory veil criss-crossing her face as though her features had been scribbled out. She wasn't old: late twenties. He would never have guessed they would spend another forty years together. Her heels stabbed the soft ground, as though puncturing it for air.

"I'm Greg Marshall," he said. "One of the pallbearers."

"I hope you've got a strong shoulder," she said. "My husband wasn't light."

Marshall felt himself redden. "I'm sorry, I didn't..."

She waved a hand, as though brushing away an insect. "It doesn't matter. You weren't to know."

"But I could have guessed. I haven't been doing the job long."

"It's commendable," she said. "He didn't have a lot of friends. Sometimes it's important to be a friend, even if it's just for one day. Don't you think?"

Marshall nodded. In truth, he no longer knew what to say. The funeral director caught his eye and within a few moments they were tied up in the proceedings. When it came to standing graveside, Marshall kept his head down. The ropes squeaked against the side of the coffin. If Marshall were inside, he would be desperate to get out.

The car ate tarmac under his wheels. Marshall considered the phrase. Didn't like it. He watched trees blur in the peripheries of his vision: a perpetual rushing. Once, along this journey which he had now undertaken almost forty times, he had fallen asleep at the wheel and veered onto the verge, the jolt waking him as abruptly as a fall in a dream, before he wrestled the car back onto the road. After a moment, after the slowing of his heartbeat, the aberration became absorbed into the repetition of the journey, until, after another few miles, it was almost erased. Now it was akin to a false memory.

Memory was always at the forefront of Marshall's mind. Not in a physical, brain-map kind of way, but with his advancing years memory became something more than recollection. He considered it also a hope. Or a security blanket.

Anna had her opinion too. Marshall remembered a conversation in the early stages of their relationship. A half-drunk bottle of wine on the coffee table, their arms around each other as they leant with their backs against the sofa, their bare feet finding purchase within the soft weave of the carpet. They had spent some time kissing. Marshall was amazed at the quality of light captured by Anna's eyes. Anna said she liked him too.

Their conversation meandered through the detonated minefield of the newly drunk, pithy fragments that the listener was more likely to remember than the speaker. Marshall skirted around the subject of memory without focussing on the death of Anna's husband – throughout their relationship, it was always in the background – whereas Anna seemed to circle it, as though it were prey.

After another sip of wine, she caressed the back of his neck with one hand, and said: "Imagine that the world exists purely on the memories of all of us who are alive. But that reality is a shifting

216

sandstorm. We're kind of holding up a collective consciousness above our heads through memory, as though it were a crowd surfer. Or maybe reality is a relay race for memories where we hand on the baton to those who come after. Without memory, there can be no civilisation."

"Deep."

"Is that it?"

"Have you read that somewhere? It has to be a philosophy, doesn't it?"

For a moment he thought she was angry with him. Then she said: "I thought of it just now. Maybe something *like* that idea has been thought of before, but it doesn't negate *my* thought."

"Perhaps your thought is part of that collective consciousness."

"Perhaps."

Anna's husband had developed a brain tumour at a young age. His medical reports stated he had no history of headache, hypertension, or medications, but he had begun to exhibit some strange behaviour and Anna had persuaded him to visit his GP who escalated it to the hospital. Using MRI, brain imaging showed abnormalities in the white matter of the occipital lobes. He was placed on a follow-up appointment without treatment. A few months later he suddenly became apneic followed by hyperventilation. The hyperventilation did not disappear when he was asked to breathe in and out of a paper bag, following a dose of diazepam, or during sleep.

A further brain MRI showed multiple lesions, but the abnormalities in the occipital lobe had disappeared spontaneously. The mechanism of the spontaneous regression was unclear. Anna told Marshall this on their second date. A few days following the funeral he had been on other burial duties when he saw her placing flowers at her husband's grave. He went over, plucking up the courage to make a further apology. Anna had only smiled at him and asked if he wanted a drink.

"A drink?"

He must have appeared surprised, because Anna said: "It's one of the most toxic substances known to man. They call it alcohol. Care to share some with me?"

She leant on her fingertips with her elbows on the table. The wine glass gave the impression it should be suspended within that arch, but its base clung firmly to the wooden table top with an almost lipstick-stick.

"They called it a spontaneously vanishing primary cerebral lymphoma *ghost tumour*," she said. "And then within two years it was back – or certainly something like it – but this time it was there for good. Memory couldn't erase it again."

"Memory?"

"I'm talking in superlatives," she said.

Marshall wasn't sure that was the right word, but he didn't challenge it.

"I had so much more to say to him," Anna said.

Marshall considered the few elderly relatives he had known who had passed. No doubt he might have said more to each of them, but he barely spoke a word to them whilst they were alive.

"I can't quite imagine it," he said.

She blinked: once, twice. "Imagine I'm gone: just like that. The next sentence you have on your lips is never spoken. Nor the next, nor the next. Can you imagine how that would echo throughout the rest of your life?"

Marshall nodded. But in truth he couldn't imagine it. He didn't imagine it until many years later when the reality of an absence hit harder than a theoretical one.

He changed gear.

Another driver had pulled out a hundred yards ahead. In truth, it was perfectly acceptable. Other cars had to join the flow when they could. But Marshall had braked harshly and the vehicle behind his had flashed its lights, as though they couldn't see more than one vehicle in front of them.

A few years previously, Marshall had read an SF novel. *The Destructives* by Matthew De Abaitua. There was one phrase which had struck him, which he had taken the time to write down. As he pressed his foot on the accelerator and regained his position behind the new lead car, he remembered it now:

The clouds have lifted and I realise the road I am travelling runs parallel to death. A coast road with death as the sea; every time I glance out of the window, death is there.

218

Anna had been protective of him. Marshall sometimes used the word *suffocating*, but never voiced it. He knew it was because her first husband had been taken so quickly, and in some respects Anna's behaviour reassured him. He was on a par with her first husband. He was not a substitute, but a man in his own right. Anna's acknowledgement of this was a cocoon. Marshall had never been in a long relationship before Anna, and he never would be again. Anna was the sole guide through which he might traverse a relationship. Whereas for Anna, her existence had been stuttered, much like a vehicle that has to slow because another vehicle – an unexpected happening – has pulled out in front of it.

Marshall thrummed his hands on the wheel. He was full of metaphor that morning.

The road was so familiar he could have driven it blindfold. He considered the phrase. Didn't like it. Too many stock phrases were meaningless the more you came to examine them. *Cheap at half the price. I knew her like the back of my hand.* There were many more. Marshall wasn't sure he would be able to pick out the back of his hand in an identity parade. There was nothing distinctive about him – about *any* of them – in the end, was there? People were mutated by time.

He came across the short row of detached houses which must once have been farm cottages but had now fallen into disrepair. They zipped by him, empty windows and doors like so many mouths. One day, he always decided, he would stop by the side of the road, wind down his window, and stare straight into those gaping maws. Might even take a photograph. It was scenic enough for one, in an abandoned building kind of way.

But not today. They disappeared in his wake – or rather, he disappeared in theirs. They were no more a pattern of his existence as was each blade of grass in the field beyond, which he could only view as a mass of green and yet which existed solely through the presence of each of those individual blades.

On his last visit, Anna had rummaged in her sewing bag. She handed him a key.

"Take this, Matt," she said.

"What's it for?"

"Everything."

Marshall had been unable to get more from her. He wanted to get more from her today.

If they had been cautious with money. If they had not decided to see the world, to spend most of their time outside their regular vista, then they might have had sufficient savings to deal with retirement. More importantly, Marshall might have been able to fund the preferred nursing home he had found which was closer to where they lived. Yet the rates were far above those funded by social services, and there was no money in the pot – nor even a pot – for a top-up. Seventy miles wasn't too far when you thought about it. Marshall remembered driving through great tracts of Australia with Anna by his side in the blue Nissan long-wheel base campervan they had bought, where two hundred miles could pass without sight of another driver. Seventy miles, given that perspective, was nothing.

It was on that trip, standing on a salt lake just off the Stuart Highway on the way from Adelaide to Coober Pedy, where Anna had said: "It looks like it stretches forever, but it doesn't, does it?"

"Of course it doesn't. But it is beautiful."

"It appears permanent too. But once it wasn't here and once it won't be here again."

Marshall put his arm around her. He had become used to these moments of rueful introspection. If he headed them off quickly they never came to much.

"How can you get maudlin in a place like this?"

Anna turned her mouth to his, tipped onto tip-toes, kissed.

"There are days when I miss Matt. It's nothing to do with you. But there are says when I wonder what it would feel like standing here with Matt rather than Greg."

Marshall's jaw tensed. He held back the words.

"Don't be sad. I don't mean anything by that. It's inevitable because he's part of my past. And my past isn't on my wish-list."

Marshall had nodded. Raced her to a hunk of metal they couldn't identify which was embedded in the surface of the lake.

It hadn't been a wish-list, he could see that now. But it had become part of her bucket-list.

Swinging into the drive of the nursing home, Marshall's view became bombarded by vegetation. Bougainvillea, hydrangeas, the spires of conifers, all conspired to create a *softening* of the atmosphere as the highway was left behind. Marshall knew it was a placebo to the realities of the lives of those who resided there, but even as a visitor he became pacified. His anger at the driver who had cut him up – twenty miles since – dissipated; although as he pulled up the gravel drive this initial silencing became transformed into the anxiety of seeing Anna again.

He could understand how some of the residents never received visitors. Out of sight, out of mind, after all; and for the residents, out of mind also meant out of sight. Did it matter if you sat and held the hand of someone who wouldn't remember you *had* been there, wouldn't remember that you were *still* there, within moments of their functions looking the other way? But of course it did matter. It mattered to Marshall. Even if he didn't matter to Anna.

Everyone talks about grey matter, he remembered the doctor saying, as though grey matter is the be all and end all. *Our little grey cells*, he had said, tapping the side of his head, channelling Hercule Poirot, that's what everyone thinks about. But the cells and other components of the brain can be classified as either grey or white matter, and these perform different functions. Grey matter consists mostly of neurons and some supporting brain cells. White matter allows messages to be sent between brain cells much faster, protecting the parts which make those connections. So when white matter is damaged, it can affect brain function.

Marshall's eyes wandered between his left hand, which rested on Anna's right shoulder as she sat on a chair in front of him, and the doctor's mouth. Afterwards he could remember nothing of the doctor other than that mouth, topped by a white-flecked moustache, as though the moustache itself was an extension of the white matter damaged by the leakage from his wife's blood vessels.

Marshall began to view the white matter as the highway of communication within Anna's brain. Almost a *ghost highway* due to the whiteness of the raw material, the analogy further complicated by the description of the ghost tumour which Anna had discussed in relation to her dead husband. These two – disparate – images forged themselves in Marshall's mind. The doctor continued by saying that with Alzheimer's disease, damage to white matter is frequently seen. It wasn't all about the importance of the little grey cells after all. They couldn't operate without the highway to connect them. The corruption of that highway, the *ghosting* of the white matter, would take his wife and she would be lost to him.

They hadn't even a child who might carry their memories for them.

The key was cool to Marshall's touch. He turned it within his fingers inside his left trouser pocket as he signed into the nursing home with his right hand.

"How is she?" he asked.

One of the nurses – one who he wouldn't give a second glance to in the street but within the context of the nursing home was an imperative contact – smiled a well-meaning smile and said, *She's as good as she can be.*

She told him he could find her in the day room. Anna was always in the day room. When visitors were expected the residents were wheeled out into that room as though they were performers in a show. Marshall couldn't harbour bitterness towards the staff – that was an empty channel for anger. He couldn't harbour bitterness towards Anna either. Her face lit up as she saw him, as though she held a buttercup under her chin.

"Matt," she said.

He didn't correct her. He sat and held her hand, looked into her milky eyes. She had aged faster than he had. He supposed most women did. Sometimes he felt that their existences had been extrapolated, that if she were on that parallel highway then her vehicle was travelling much faster than his. He kissed the top of her head.

"Now, now," she said. "We'll have none of that here."

She wasn't always lucid. Sometimes when she was, Marshall wasn't around. The staff would provide him with accounts of her stories without realising that those anecdotes were not about him. Maybe they thought Matt was a pet name, that he didn't like Greg. He often thought of signing the visitor's book as Matt, but felt somehow he would not only be deceiving the staff, but also Anna. Although Anna never saw him as Greg anyway.

A few years previously a mutual friend, someone Anna had once worked with, had also developed Alzheimer's.

"It's terrible," Anna said. "It's stripped everything away from her."

"Does she know you?"

Anna nodded, slowly. "Yes, she does. But it's not the *me* I am now, it's the me she first met, over twenty years ago."

"You've remained young in her memory," Marshall said.

"Yes," Anna said. "I suppose I have."

"Does it worry you?"

"Worry me?"

"That she doesn't see you as you see you?"

Anna ran a tongue hard against her bottom lip. "No, it doesn't worry me," she said. "Because it doesn't worry her."

Marshall wheeled Anna out through the patio doors and into the garden.

"Does *this* worry you," he said, unaware of the cessation of the memory in his head and the actuality of his words.

"Does what worry me, Matt?"

"All this," Marshall swept his hand to take in the view of the South Downs. "All this otherness."

Anna laughed. "You are funny. You remind of someone I used to..."

She fell silent. Marshall knew Anna couldn't recollect someone who had yet to enter her life. Even when they were standing right beside her.

"Take me away, Matt. I don't like being here."

Marshall bent down so he was level with the wheelchair. It wasn't that Anna couldn't stand, but her mobility had dropped even before the onset of Alzheimer's, and he no longer had the strength to hold her.

"I'm working on it," he said. "I've got a place for us. Remember this?"

Marshall pulled out the key.

"Of course I remember it," Anna laughed. "It's where we live."

The journey home was always quicker, as though by travelling in one direction Marshall had flattened existence to make the return less resistant. It wasn't simply this trip: he had noticed it on returning from holidays, on the flight back from Australia, on the short walk from work. Maybe it was much easier to go back rather than forwards. Although that analogy completely depended on understanding the point of departure.

The point of departure for Anna began with the loss of her glasses.

"I was sure I put them down somewhere."

Marshall was reminded of a short movie he had once seen on television. *La pince à ongles*, directed by Jean-Claude Carrière. In the movie – little more than a vignette – a pair of nail clippers goes missing when a couple rent a hotel room. Eventually other items go missing too. Until the only thing that remains are the nail clippers, collected by a member of the hotel staff who – bemused by the couple's absence – begins to use them.

"They're in your hand," he said.

"My hand?"

Marshall realised it wasn't that Anna hadn't understood that she was holding her glasses, but more than she hadn't understood the meaning of *hand*.

It hadn't taken many more instances of such behaviour for Marshall to have booked an initial meeting with their GP, and then a specialist, eventually leading to the conversation with the doctor about the white matter.

Some time between the diagnosis and the almost total loss of short term memory, Anna had said:

"I've always felt this would happen."

"What would happen?"

"That Matt would call me back."

"Oh don't be silly."

Tempers were fraught, at times.

"I'm not being silly. I always thought he was just there, just at my shoulder, waiting for me to acknowledge him again."

Marshall shivered. It was winter but there was no lack of logs on the fire. "You know that's nonsense," he said.

"Maybe, but a long time ago I decided that if I got Alzheimer's or dementia or whatever it might be called that I'd use it as a blessing, not as a debility. I'll be able to talk to Matt again."

"You'll only *believe* that you're talking to Matt again, if you regress."

"But I *will* believe it, won't I, mightn't I? And if I believe it, then it will be true." She paused. "For me, anyway."

Marshall parked his car in their drive, avoided a conversation with a neighbour by hearing the imaginary ringing of a telephone from within the house.

Must get that!

He slipped upstairs without removing his shoes. Anna would disapprove. There was a box at the back of Anna's side of the wardrobe where she kept their legal papers. Marshall hadn't been so good at the financial side of the relationship. It had been Anna who had kept them in holidays, in part-time jobs rather than full-time work. He had gone along with it, ignoring the white matter in his own brain which drew the connection between the death of Anna's husband and the insurance payout which kept them in good stead. He had never been a freeloader, after all. On more than one occasion Anna had violently defended that very accusation.

Some of the papers had yellowed with age, mirroring Marshall's skin. He flicked through them: what had been the most recent bills – dated two years ago, just as the Alzheimer's had taken hold – and the documentation regarding the purchase of the house within which he now sat. Further down he passed their marriage certificate, and shortly afterwards a letter of condolence about Anna's miscarriage that both of them had sought to bury. Finally the addresses on the letters changed to those unfamiliar to him. His name didn't figure on the envelopes. He found documentation in relation of a house purchase to Mr and Mrs Matt Huxley but nothing regarding the subsequent sale. He took a breath, worked through the paperwork again. He hadn't missed anything. Anna was methodical. The documentation was filed chronologically. He reached into his pocket and pulled out the key.

It's where we live.

The garden was so tidy Marshall thought he must have the wrong house.

Rosebushes recently pruned hung back from the gravel pathway. He wasn't a prince battling through brambles to reach a sleeping beauty. He imagined Anna must have employed a gardener, and that the funds hadn't run out. He wondered how regularly she visited. They were inseparable, rarely went out alone from each other. If she came here it would be in snatched moments, extended shopping trips. He wondered if any of her friends knew. If her friend with Alzheimer's knew, and that because both of them knew then that past had to be erased alongside the paths of memory, just as Matt had been erased by the warning ghost of his eventual tumour.

There were no neighbours to shout a *Must get that!* to. Marshall stood at the front door. There was a glass panel at face height. The glass itself was textured, distorting the interior view. He wondered if he should knock. Whether something indistinguishable would emerge from the back of the property and press its features against the glass. The thought horrified him. Instead he placed the key inside the lock and turned it.

To no surprise the door opened.

"There's so much I still had to say to him," Anna said, shortly after she placed flowers on Matt's grave and had then asked Marshall for a drink. "So much that went unsaid."

Marshall entered the house and closed the door behind him. Anna had never taken him here. He remembered discussions that she would find it disrespectful. It had taken a few months for Matt's tumour to take him, it wasn't that she had leapt into bed with Marshall, but even so, she said, she wanted some distance between them. A distance which was no longer in existence.

Marshall walked into the living room. Anna's funds must have stretched to a cleaner. The top of the 1970s sideboard was Mr Sheen fresh. Marshall wondered what the cleaner thought, whether she considered it a process of restoration. He wondered if Anna came and mixed things up, gave the impression of someone living there, or whether the cleaner knew the situation right from the start. He suspected the latter. Anna was always honest, always direct.

He couldn't even shrug at that statement being negated by his very presence in the house.

Their wedding photograph stood on the mantelpiece. Not his. *Theirs.* Marshall picked it up. She had been so young, just out of her teens. Matt bore one of those haircuts that in hindsight seemed impossible anyone would choose. Marshall entered the kitchen. The refrigerator was connected. He opened the door but nothing was inside. He wondered if Anna used to lay out sandwiches for the gardener, a bottle of milk for the cleaner. He wondered if they knew why they hadn't seen her in two years. He wondered if they cared.

He turned the cold tap in the kitchen, found a glass, and took a long drink of water. All amenities intact. He presumed the mortgage was paid by the insurance policy. But even so, forty years of utility bills for an empty house was staggering. For the first time he wondered about the security of his own future. Anna had always provided for him. He had never considered the extent of her assets. Even during the Alzheimer years he had assumed it would all just pan out. He wondered if he would have to sell this house. If he would have the right.

Upstairs a spare room contained antiquated sporting equipment, a nod to the eighties. Anna had probably worn leg warmers. For the first time in a while, Marshall allowed himself a smile.

"I will welcome Alzheimer's," Anna said, defiantly. "I will believe he is alive again."

"It doesn't always affect people like that."

"I *will* believe it."

"Oh Anna, what about me?"

She snorted. "We've had our years. Damn good ones. Forty or thereabouts. Don't be greedy, Greg. If I am to lose my marbles, at least let me enjoy it. Would you rather I didn't remember anyone?"

But Marshall couldn't answer. Jealousy was a curious rage. Even against the dead.

Marshall flicked through the wardrobes. The clothes were vintage. He wouldn't sell them, but he did wonder how much they might fetch.

He sat on the bed. He realised over the course of their marriage Anna had made trips back to this house, to compound her memories, so its existence didn't become absorbed by time, so that *their* life didn't completely supersede it.

It was the biggest lie he could imagine.

Yet it was impossible for him to cry.

There was still no Morse code on the highway. Marshall couldn't even think what *T* might stand for.

He didn't know what to do.

It had been three weeks since he had visited the house. Since he had left it as it was. He had thought of staking it out, like a PI in a crummy detective movie, waiting for the gardener or cleaner to arrive so he might question them. But then he'd had a vision of Anna and Matt pulling up in a pale blue 1970s Ford Cortina and any desire to remain anywhere near the house left him.

Marshall didn't like the analogy, but he and Anna were grey cells and the highway was the white matter which connected them. Without the highway, without him as the *message* travelling the highway, then the connection between them would be lost. It didn't matter if for Anna that connection was already lost. Or that she spoke to *Matt* whether Marshall was there or not. She anticipated his presence, she obtained pleasure from it. She was in love. Didn't he owe her that much, for forty years of genuine happiness? It wasn't her fault Matt had died. For Marshall, it had been a godsend. He had benefited.

That pang of jealousy again.

That nursing home up ahead, looming out of the late morning mist. Ten miles to go but it was there whether he could see it or not.

He didn't know what to say to her. He didn't know who to be.

He had to remind himself she wasn't with him. Or – more importantly – that *he* wasn't with her.

Marshall wished he might believe in an afterlife which existed outside of wishful thinking.

Trees rushed by, impatient to get somewhere.

In outer space, light rays passing massive objects such as stars are seen to travel in curves.

What are memories but ghosts of ourselves?

He could drive this stretch of road with his eyes closed.

❁

This story originally appeared in "Ghost Highways" edited by Trevor Denyer. The remit was simple, the story had to have something to do with the anthology title and be at least 5,000 words in length. Interpretation would be down to the author.

Although I had no immediate ideas I knew from the start that my story would be unlikely to feature a ghost and probably unlikely to feature a highway. At least, not in the traditional sense. I began to think around the concepts of ghosts and what could be construed as highways. I was increasingly drawn to the idea of neural pathways, and searching online around these topics I discovered 'ghost tumours' – which appear to be normal cerebral tumours but can subsequently disappear – and also the role of white matter within the brain which – to put it very simply – forms the highways for information to be passed by grey matter. In Alzheimer's, white matter is frequently damaged. The deterioration of white matter into a ghosted highway would form the crux of my tale.

Around the same time I had been thinking about dementia and the circumstances where sufferers appear to live in the past – where short-term memory disappears and long-term memory comes to the fore. I decided to write a character whose first husband died early and who then married again, but who always hankered after the first husband despite being perfectly satisfied with the second. What if she looked forward to the possibility of Alzheimer's as a way of connecting to the past, what if she had made preparations? How would her new husband feel about this? What are memories anyway, other than ghosts? Suddenly I had my story.

About the Author

Andrew Hook is a much-published writer in a variety of genres from literary to SF/F/H to crime. Recent short story collections include *Human Maps* (Eibonvale Press) and *The Forest of Dead Children* (Black Shuck Books), and he is currently seeking a publisher for a collection of 'Hollywood death' stories titled *Candescent Blooms*. Also available in 2020 is *O For Obscurity, Or, The Story Of N*, a biography of The Mysterious N Senada written in collaboration with the San Francisco avant-garde band, The Residents, published by Psychofon Records. He can be found at www.andrew-hook.com

Also from NewCon Press

London Centric – Edited by Ian Whates

Militant A.I.s, virtual realities, augmented realities and alternative realities; a city where murderers stalk the streets, where drug lords rule from the shadows, and where large sections of the population are locked in time stasis, but where tea is still sipped in cafés on the corner and the past still resonates with the future… Stories that look at the possible tomorrows of this multi-faceted city.

Dark Harvest – Cat Sparks

Award-winning author Cat Sparks writes science fiction with a distinct Australian flavour – stories steeped in the desperate anarchy of Mad Max futures, redolent with scorching sun and the harshness of desert sands, but her narratives reach deeper than that. In her tales of ordinary people adapting to post-apocalyptic futures, she casts a light on what it means to be human; the good and the bad, the noble and the shameful.

Lockdown Tales – Neal Asher

Best-selling author Neal Asher kept himslf busy during lockdown: he wrote. Five brand new novellas and novelettes and one reworked and expanded from a story first published in 2019. Together, they form Lockdown Tales, exploring the Polity universe and beyond. What lies in wait for humanity after the Polity has gone? Six stories, 150,000 words of fiction that crackle with energy, invention and excitement.

Ivory's Story – Eugen Bacon

In the streets of Sydney a killer stalks the night, slaughtering and mutilating innocents. The victims seem unconnected, yet Investigating Officer Ivory Tembo is convinced the killings are sar from random. The case soon leads Ivory into places she never imagined. In order to stop the killings and save the life of the man she loves, she must reach deep into her past, uncover secrets of her heritage, break a demon's curse, and somehow unify two worlds.

CPSIA information can be obtained
at www.ICGtesting.com
Printed in the USA
FSHW011257241120
76266FS

SCANDAL
PROOF